RACHEL DYER

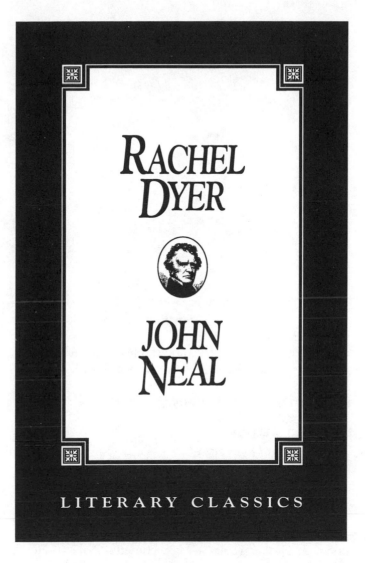

RACHEL DYER

JOHN NEAL

LITERARY CLASSICS

 **Prometheus Books**

59 John Glenn Drive
Amherst, New York 14228-2197

Published 1996 by Prometheus Books

59 John Glenn Drive, Amherst, New York 14228–2197,
716–691–0133. FAX: 716–691–0137.

Library of Congress Cataloging-in-Publication Data

Neal, John, 1793–1876.
    Rachel Dyer / John Neal.
        p.   cm. — (Literary classics)
    Originally published: Portland : Shirley and Hyde, 1828.
    ISBN 1–57392–049–5 (pbk.)
    1. Salem (Mass.)—History—Colonial period, ca. 1600–1775
—Fiction. 2. Trials (Witchcraft)—Massachusetts—Salem—
Fiction. 3. Quaker women—Massachusetts—Salem—Fiction.
I. Title. II. Series: Literary classics (Amherst, N.Y.)
PS2459.N28R29   1996
813'.2—dc20   96–1253
                                                        CIP

Printed in the United States of America on acid-free paper.

JOHN NEAL was born in Portland, Maine, of Quaker parentage, on August 25, 1793. Trained as as lawyer, Neal throughout his life defended such radical causes as female suffrage, abolition of slavery, and capital punishment reform. In 1823, Neal left a promising law practice in Baltimore to travel to England, where he lived for the next four years. There he became acquainted with Jeremy Bentham and the Utilitarians. He also published a series of essays in *Blackwood's Magazine* reviewing American authors, partly as a rebuttal to England's dismissal of American literature.

It was in *Blackwood's* that Neal published a short story that he would revise and expand as the novel *Rachel Dyer*. While a practicing lawyer, Neal had already published six novels and had gained a reputation as an astute literary critic. *Rachel Dyer*, published in 1828 and considered his best work, is loosely based on the events surrounding the trial for witchcraft of the seventeenth-century New England preacher George Burroughs. The Salem witch trials, and the choice of a Quaker heroine, Rachel Dyer, gave Neal the opportunity to expose a shameful period of religious repression as well as to indict English law and procedure in colonial America. Using a fiery preacher and a Quaker woman as his protagonists, Neal highlights the real issues of the trials, which are injustice and bigotry—a theme that would be taken up more than a century later in Arthur Miller's *The Crucible*.

John Neal died in Portland, Maine, on June 20, 1876.

Neal's other works include the novels *Keep Cool* (1817), *Logan* (1822), *Seventy-Six* (1823), *The Down-Easters* (1833) and *True Womanhood* (1859), the play *Our Ephraim* (1835), and several tales and short stories.

Rachel Dyer

PREFACE.

I have long entertained a suspicion, all that has been said by the novel-writers and dramatists and poets of our age to the contrary notwithstanding, that personal beauty and intellectual beauty, or personal beauty and moral beauty, are not inseparably connected with, nor apportioned to each other. In ERRATA, a work of which *as a* work, I am heartily ashamed now, I labored long and earnestly to prove this. I made *my* dwarf a creature of great moral beauty and strength.

Godwin, the powerful energetic and philosophizing Godwin, saw a shadow of this truth ; but he saw nothing more—the substance escaped him. He taught, and he has been followed by others, among whom are Brown, Scott and Byron, (I observe the chronological order) that a towering intellect may inhabit a miserable body ; that heroes are not of necessity six feet high, nor of a godlike shape, and that we may be deceived, if we venture to judge of the inward by the outward man. But they stopped here. They did not perceive, or perceiving, would not acknowledge the whole truth ; for if we consider a moment, we find that all their *great* men are scoundrels. Without one exception I believe, their heroes are hypocrites or misanthropes, banditti or worse ; while their good men are altogether subordinate and pitiable destitute of energy and wholly without character.

Now believing as I do, in spite of such overwhelming authority, that a man may have a club-foot, or a hump-back, or even red hair and yet be a good man—peradventure a great man ; that a dwarf with a distorted shape may be a giant in goodness of heart and greatness of temper ; and that moral beauty *may* exist where it appears not to have been suspected by the chief critics of our age, and of past ages—namely, in a deformed body (like that of Æsop,) I have written this book.

Let me add however that although such was my principal, it was not my only object. I would call the attention of our novel-writers and our novel-readers to what is undoubtedly native and peculiar, in the early history of our Fathers ; I would urge them to believe that though there is much to lament in that history, there is nothing to conceal ; that if they went astray, as they most assuredly did in their judgments, they went astray conscientiously, with what they understood to be the law of God in their right hands. The "*Salem Tragedie*" is in proof—that is the ground-work of my story ; and I pray the reader to have patience with the author, if he should find this tale rather more serious in parts, and rather more argumentative in parts, than stories, novels and romances generally are.

I do not pretend to say that the book I now offer to my countrymen, is altogether such a book as I would write now, if I had more leisure, nor altogether such a book as I hope to write before I die ; but as I cannot afford to throw it entirely away, and as I believe it to be much better, because more evidently prepared for a healthy good purpose, than any other I have written, I have concluded to publish it—hoping it may be regarded by the wise and virtuous of our country as some sort of atonement for the folly and extravagance of my earlier writing.

PREFACE.

The skeleton of this tale was originally prepared for Blackwood, as the first of a series of North-American Stories : He accepted it, paid for it, printed it, and sent me the proofs. A misunderstanding however occurred between us, about other matters, and I withdrew the story and repaid him for it. It was never published therefore ; but was put aside by me, as the frame-work for a novel—which novel is now before the reader.

JOHN NEAL.

Portland, October 1, 1828.

P. S. After some consideration, I have concluded to publish a preface, originally intended for the NORTH AMERICAN STORIES alluded to above. It was never published, nor has it ever been read by any body but myself. Among those who are interested for the encouragement of our native literature, there may be some who will not be sorry to see what my ideas *were* on the subject of novel-writing, as well as what they *are.* Changes have been foretold in my views—and I owe it to our people to acknowledge, that in a good degree, the prediction has been accomplished. I do not feel now as I did, when I wrote Seventy-Six, Randolph, and the rest of the works published in America ; nor even as I did, when I wrote those that were published over sea. The mere novel-reader had better skip the following pages and go directly to the story. The introductory chapter in all human probability will be too much for him.

J. N.

UNPUBLISHED PREFACE

TO THE NORTH-AMERICAN STORIES, ALLUDED TO IN PAGE V.

The author of this work is now under the necessity of bidding the novel-readers of the day, on both sides of the water, farewell, and in all probability, forever. By them it may be considered a trivial affair—a time for pleasantry, or peradventure for a formal expression of what are called good wishes. But by him, who does not feel like other men—or does not understand their language, when they talk in this way, it will ever be regarded as a very serious thing. He would neither conceal nor deny the truth—he would not so affront the feeling within him—and he says therefore without affectation or ceremony, that it goes to his heart even to bid the novel-readers of the age, the few that have read his novels, it were better to say—farewell.

These volumes are the last of a series which even from his youth up, he had been accustomed to meditate upon as a worthy and affectionate offering to his family and to those who have made many a long winter day in a dreary climate, very cheerful and pleasant to him—the daughters of a dear friend—of one who, if his eye should ever fall upon this page, will understand immediately more than a chapter could tell, of the deep wayward strange motives that have influenced the author to say thus much and no more, while recurring for the last time to the bright vision of his youth. And the little that he does say now, is not said for the world;—for what care they about the humble and innocent creatures, whose gentleness and sincerity about their own fire-side, were for a long time all that kept a man, who was weary and sick of the great world, from leaving it in despair? No, it is not said for them; but for any one of that large family who may happen to be alive now, and in the way of remembering "the stranger that was within their gates"—when to the world he may be as if he never had been. Let them not be amazed when they discover the truth ; nor afraid nor ashamed to see that the man whom they knew only as the stranger from a far country, was also an author.

In other days, angels were entertained in the shape of travellers and way-faring men; but ye—had ye known every stranger that knocked at your door to be an angel, or a messenger of the Most High, could not have treated him more like an immortal creature than ye did that unknown man, who now bears witness to your simplicity and great goodness of heart. With you it was enough that a fellow-creature was unhappy—you strove to make him happy ; and having done this, you sent him away, ignorant alike of his people, his country and his name.

*   *   *   *   *

This work is the last of the sort I believe—the very last I shall ever write. Reader—stop!—lay down the book for a moment and answer me. Do you feel no emotion at the sight of that word? You are surprised at the question. Why should you feel any, you ask. Why should you?—let us reason together for a moment. Can it be that you are able to hear of the final consummation of a hope which had been the chief stay of a fellow-creature for many—many years?—Can it be that you feel no sort of emotion at hearing him say, Lo ! I have finished the work—it is the last—no sensation of inquietude? Perhaps you now begin to see differently; perhaps you would now try to exculpate yourself. You are willing to admit now that the affair is one of a graver aspect than you first imagined. You are half ready to deny now that you ever considered it otherwise. But mark me—out of your own mouth you are condemned. Twice have I said already—three times have I said already, that this was the last work of the sort I should ever write, and you have read the declaration as you would, the passing motto of a title-page. You neither cared for it, nor thought of it; and had I not alarmed you by my abruptness, compelled you to stop and think, and awed you by steadfastly rebuking your inhumanity, you would not have known by to-morrow whether I had spoken of it as my last work or not. Consider what I say—is it not the truth?—can you deny it? And yet you—*you* are one of the multitude who dare to sit in judgment upon the doings of your fellow men. It is on what you and such as you say, that authors are to depend for that which is of more value to them than the breath of life—character. How dare you!—You read without reflection, and you hear without understanding. Yet upon the judgment of such as you—so made up, it is that the patient and the profound, the thoughtful and the gifted, are to rely for immortality.

To return to what I was about saying—the work now before you, reader, is the last of a series, meditated as I have already told you, from my youth. It was but a dream at first—a dream of my boyhood, indefinite, vague and shadowy; but as I grew up, it grew stronger and braver and more substantial. For years it did not deserve the name of a plan—it was merely a breathing after I hardly knew what, a hope that I should live to do something in a literary way worthy of my people—accompanied however with an inappeasable yearning for the time and opportunity to arrive. But so it was, that, notwithstanding all my anxiety and resolution, I could not bring myself to make the attempt—even the attempt—until it appeared no longer possible for me to do what for years I had been very anxious to do. The engagement was of too sacred a nature to be trifled with—perhaps the more sacred in my view for being made only with myself, and without a witness; for engagements having no other authority than our moral sense of duty to ourselves, would never be performed, after they grew irksome or heavy. unless we were scrupulous in proportion to the facility with which we might escape if we would.

This indeterminate, haunting desire to do what I had so engaged to do, at last however began to give way before the serious and necessary business of life, and the continually augmenting pressure of duties too solemn to be slighted for any—I had almost said for any earthly consideration. Yea more, to confess the whole truth, I had begun to regard the enterprise itself—so prone are we to self-deception, so ready at finding excuses where we have a duty to perform—as hardly worthy of much power, and as altogether beneath an exalted ambition. But here I was greatly mistaken; for I have an idea now, that

a great novel—such a novel as might be made—if all the powers that could be employed upon it were found in one man,
would be the greatest production of human genius. It is a law
and a history of itself—to every people—and throughout all
time—in literature and morals—in character and passion—
yea—in what may be called the fire-side biography of nations.
It would be, if rightly managed, a picture of the present for futurity—a picture of human nature, not only here but every
where—a portrait of man—a history of the human heart—a
book therefore, written not only in a universal, but in what
may be considered as an everlasting language—the language
of immortal, indistructable spirits. Such are the parables of
Him who spoke that language best.

Again however, the subject was revived. Sleeping and
waking, by night and by day, it was before me ; and at last I
began to perceive that if the attempt were ever to be made, it
must be made by one desperate, convulsive, instantaneous effort. I determined to deliberate no longer—or rather to stand
no longer, shivering like a coward, upon the brink of adventure, under pretence of deliberation ; and therefore, having
first carefully stopped my ears and shut my eyes, I threw myself headlong over the precipice. Behold the result ! If I have
not brought up the pearls, I can say at least that I have been
to the bottom—and i might have added—of the human heart
sometimes—but for the perverse and foolish insincerity of the
world, which if I had so finished the sentence, would have set
their faces forever against my book; although that same world,
had I been wise enough—no, not wise enough but cunning
enough, to hold my peace, might have been ready to acknowledge that I had been sometimes, even where I say—to the very bottom of the human heart.

I plunged. But when I did, it was rather to relieve my own
soul from the intolerable weight of her own reproach, than
with any hope of living to complete the design, except at a sacrifice next in degree to that of self-immolation. Would you
know what more than any other thing—more than all other
things determined me at last ? I was an American. I had
heard the insolent question of a Scotch Reviewer, repeated on

every side of me by native Americans—"*Who reads an American Book?*" I could not bear this—I could neither eat nor sleep till my mind was made up. I reasoned with myself—I strove hard—but the spirit within me would not be rebuked. Shall I go forth said I, in the solitude of my own thought, and make war alone against the foe—for alone it must be made, or there will be no hope of success. There must be but one head, one heart in the plan—the secret must not even be guessed at by another—it must be single and simple, one that like the wedge in mechanics, or in the ancient military art, must have but one point, and that point must be of adamant. Being so it may be turned aside : A thousand more like itself, may be blunted or shivered ; but if at last, any one of the whole should make any impression whatever upon the foe, or effect any entrance whatever into the sanctity and strength of his tremendous phalanx, then, from that moment, the day is our own. Our literature will begin to wake up, and our pride of country will wake up with it. Those who follow will have nothing to do but *keep* what the forlorn hope, who goes o irretrievable martyrdom if he fail, has *gained*.

Moreover—who was there to stand by the native American that should go out, haply with a sling and a stone, against a tower of strength and the everlasting entrenchments of prejudice ? Could he hope to find so much as one of his countrymen, to go with him or even to bear his shield ? Would the Reviewers of America befriend him ? No—they have not courage enough to fight their own battles manfully.(1) No—they would rather flatter than strike. They negociate altogether too much—where blows are wanted, they give words. And the best of our literary champions, would they ? No ; they would only bewail his temerity, if he were the bold headlong creature he should be to accomplish the work ; and pity his folly and presumption, if he were any thing else.

After all however, why should they be reproached for this ? They have gained their little reputation hardly. "It were too much to spend that little"—so grudgingly acquiesced in by their beloved countrymen—"rashly." No wonder they fight shy.

(1) Or had not before this was written. Look to the North-American Review before 1825, for proof.

It is their duty—considering what they have at stake—their little all. There is Washington Irving now; he has obtained the reputation of being—what?—why at the best, of being only the American Addison, in the view of Englishmen. And is this a title to care much for? Would such a name, though Addison stood far higher in the opinion of the English themselves, than he now does, or ever again will, be enough to satisfy the ambition of a lofty-minded, original thinker? Would such a man falter and reef his plumage midway up the altitude of his blinding and brave ascent, to be called the American Addison, or even what in my view were ten thousand times better, the American Goldsmith.(2) No—up to the very key stone of the broad blue firmament! he would say, or back to the vile earth again: ay, lower than the earth first! Understand me however. I do not say this lightly nor disparagingly. I love and admire Washington Irving. I wish him all the reputation he covets, and of the very kind he covets. Our paths never did, never will cross each other. And so with Mr. Cooper; and a multitude more, of whom we may rightfully be proud. They have gained just enough popular favor to make them afraid of hazarding one jot or tittle of it, by stepping aside into a new path. No one of these could avail me in my design. They would have everything to lose, and nothing to gain by embarking in it. While I—what had I to lose—nay what have I to lose? I am not now, I never have been, I never shall be an author by trade. The opinion of the public is not the breath of life to me; for if the truth must be told, I have to this hour very little respect for it—so long as it is indeed the opinion of the public—of the mere multitude, the careless, unthinking judgment of the mob, unregulated by the wise and thoughtful.

To succeed as I hoped, I must put everything at hazard. It would not do for me to imitate anybody. Nor would it do for my country. Who would care for the *American* Addison where he could have the English by asking for it? Who would languish, a twelvemonth after they appeared, for Mr. Cooper's imitations of Sir Walter Scott, or Charles Brockden Brown's

---

(2) I speak here of Goldsmith's prose, not of his poetry. Heaven forbid!

imitations of Godwin ? Those, and those only, who after having seen the transfiguration of Raphael, (or that of Talma,) or Dominichino's St. Jerome, would walk away to a village painting room, or a provincial theatre, to pick their teeth and play the critic over an imitation of the one or a copy of the other. At the best, all such things are but *imitations.* And what are imitations ? Sheer mimicry—more or less exalted to be sure ; but still mimicry—wherever the *copies* of life are copied and not life itself : a sort of high-handed, noon-day plagiarism—nothing more. People are never amazed, nor carried away, nor uplifted by imitations. They are pleased with the ingenuity of the artist—they are delighted with the closeness of the imitation—but that is all. The better the work is done, the worse they think of the workman. He who can paint a great picture, cannot copy—David Teniers to the contrary notwithstanding ; for David never painted a great picture in his life, though he has painted small ones, not more than three feet square, which would sell for twenty-five thousand dollars to day.

Yes—to succeed, I must imitate nobody—I must *resemble* nobody ; for with your critic, resemblance in the unknown to the known, is never anything but adroit imitation. To succeed therefore, I must be unlike all that have gone before me. That were no easy matter ; nor would be it so difficult as men are apt to believe. Nor is it necessary that I should do *better* than all who have gone before me. I should be more likely to prosper, in the long run, by worse original productions—with a poor story told in poor language, (if it were original in spirit and character) than by a much better story told in much better language, if after the transports of the public were over, they should be able to trace a resemblance between it and Walter Scott, or Oliver Goldsmith, or Mr. Addison.

So far so good. There was, beyond a doubt, a fair chance in the great commonwealth of literature, even though I should not achieve a miracle, nor prove myself both wiser and better than all the authors who had gone before me. And moreover, might it not be possible—*possible* I say—for the mob are a jealous guardian of sepulchres and ashes, and high-sounding names, particularly where a name will save them the trouble of judging for themselves, or do their arguments for them in the shape of a perpetual demonstration, whatever may be the nature of the controversy in which they are involved—might it not be possible then, I say, that, as the whole body of mankind have been growing wiser and wiser, and better and better, since the day when these great writers flourished, who are now ruling " our spirits from their urns," that authors may have improved with them?—that they alone of the whole human race, by some possibility, may not have remained altogether stationary age after age—while the least enquiring and the most indolent of human beings—the very multitude—have been steadily advancing both in knowledge and power? And if so, might it not be *possible* for some improvements to be made, some discoveries, even yet in style and composition, by lanching forth into space. True, we might not be certain of finding a new world, like Columbus, nor a new heaven, like Tyho Brahe; but we should probably encounter some phenomena in the great unvisited moral sky and ocean ; we should at least find out, after a while—which would of itself be the next greatest consolation for our trouble and anxiety, after that of discovering a new world or a new system,—that there remained no new world nor system to be discovered ; that they who should adventure after us, would have so much the less to do for all that we had done ; that they must follow in our steps ; that if our health and strength had been wasted in a prodigious dream, it would have the good effect of preventing any future waste of health and strength on the part of others in any similar enterprize.

Islands and planets may still be found, we should say, and they that find them, are welcome to them ; but continents and systems cannot be beyond where we have been : and if there be any within it, why—they are neither continents nor systems.

But then, after all, there was one plain question to be asked, which no honest man would like to evade, however much a mere dreamer might wish to do so. It was this. After all my fine theory—what are my chances of success? And if successful, what have I to gain ? I chose to answer the last ques-

tion first.   Gain!—of a truth, it were no easy matter to say.
Nothing *here*, nothing *now*—certainly nothing in America, till
my bones have been canonized ; for my countrymen are a
thrifty, calculating people—they give nothing for the reputation
of a man, till they are sure of selling it for more than they give.
Were they visited by saints and prophets instead of gifted men,
they would never believe that they were either saints or prophets, till they had been starved to death—or lived by a miracle
—by no visible means ; or until their cast-off clothes, bones,
hair and teeth, or the furniture of the houses wherein they were
starved, or the trees under which they had been chilled to death,
carved into snuff-boxes or walking-sticks, would sell for as
much as that sympathy had cost them, or as much as it would
come to, to build a monument over—I do not say over their un-
sheltered remains, for by that time there would be but little or
no remains of them to be found, unmingled with the sky and
water, earth and air about them, save pernaps in here and there
a museum or college where they might always be bought up,
however, immortality and all—for something more than com-
pound interest added to the original cost—but to build a monument or a shed over the unappropriated stock, with certain
privileges to the manufacturer of the walking-sticks and snuff-
boxes aforesaid, so long as any of the material remained ; taking care to provide with all due solemnity, perhaps by an act
of the legislatue, for securing the monopoly to the sovereign
state itself.

Thus much perhaps I might hope for from my own people.
But what from the British?   They were magnanimous, or at
least they would bear to be told so ; and telling them so in a
simple, off-hand, ingenuous way, with a great appearance of
sincerity, and as if one had been carried away by a sudden im-
pulse, to speak a forbidden truth, or surprised into a prohibit-
ed expression of feeling by some spectacle of generosity, in
spite of his constitutional reserve and timidity and caution,
would be likely to *pay well*.   But I would do no such thing.
I would flatter nobody—no people—no nation.   I would lie to
nobody—neither to my own countrymen, nor to the British—

unless I were better paid for it, than any of my countrymen were ever yet paid either at home or abroad.

No—I choose to see for myself, by putting the proof touch like a hot iron to their foreheads, whether the British are indeed a magnanimous people. But then, if I do all this, what are my chances of reward, even with the British themselves? That was a fearful question to be sure. The British are a nation of writers. Their novel-writers are as a cloud. True—true—but they still want something which they have not. They want a real American writer—one with courage enough to write in his native tongue. *That* they have not, even at this day. *That they never had.* Our best writers are English writers, not American writers. They are English in every thing they do, and in every thing they say, as authors—in the structure and moral of their stories, in their dialogue, speech and pronunciation, yea in the very characters they draw. Not so much as one true Yankee is to be found in any of our native books : hardly so much as one true Yankee phrase. Not so much as one true Indian, though you hardly take up a story on either side of the water now, without finding a red-man stowed away in it ; and what sort of a red-man? Why one that uniformly talks the best English the author is capable of —more than half the time perhaps out-Ossianing Ossian.

I have the modesty to believe that in some things I am unlike all the other writers of my country—both living and dead ; although there are not a few, I dare say who would be glad to hear of my bearing a great resemblance to the latter. For my own part I do not pretend to write English—that is, I do not pretend to write what the English themselves call English —I do not, and I hope to God—I say this reverently, although one of their Reviewers may be again puzzled to determine " whether I am swearing or praying" when I say so—that I never shall write what is now worshipped under the name of *classical* English. It is no natural language—it never was— it never will be spoken alive on this earth: and therefore, ought never to be written. We have dead languages enough now ; but the deadest language I ever met with or heard of, was that in use among the writers of Queen Anne's day.

[handwritten marginalia: "British" with a mark next to "They want a real American writer"]

[handwritten marginalia: "truly American = above Mason-Dixon line"]

At last I came to the conclusion—that the chances were at least a thousand to one against me. A thousand to one said I, to myself, that I perish outright in my headlong enterprise. But then, if I do not perish—if I triumph, what a triumph it will be! If I succeed, I shall be rewarded well—if the British *are* what they are believed to be—in fair proportion to the toil and peril I have encountered. At any rate, whether I fail or not, I shall be, and am willing to be, one of the first hundred to carry the war into the very camp, yea among the very household gods of the enemy. And if I die, I will die with my right arm consuming in the blaze of their altars—like Mutius Scævola.

But enough on this head. The plan took shape, and you have the commencement now before you, reader. I have had several objects in view at the same time, all subordinate however to that which I first mentioned, in the prosecution of my wayward enterprise. One was to show to my countrymen that there are abundant and hidden sources of fertility in their own beautiful brave earth, waiting only to be broken up; and barren places to all outward appearance, in the northern, as well as the southern Americas—yet teeming below with bright sail—where the plough-share that is driven through them with a strong arm, will come out laden with rich mineral and followed by running water: places where—if you but lay your ear to the scented ground, you may hear the perpetual gush of innumerable fountains pouring their subterranean melody night and day among the minerals and rocks, the iron and the gold: places where the way-faring man, the pilgrim or the wanderer through what he may deem the very deserts of literature, the barren-places of knowledge, will find the very roots of the withered and blasted shrubbery, which like the traveller in Peru, he may have accidentally uptorn in his weary and discouraging ascent, and the very bowels of the earth into which he has torn his way, heavy with a brightness that may be coined, like the soil about the favorite hiding places of the sunny-haired Apollo.

Another, was to teach my countrymen, that these very Englishmen, to whom as the barbarians of ancient story did by

their gods when they would conciliate them, we are accustomed to offer up our own offspring, with our own hands, whenever we see the sky darkening over the water—the sky inhabited
of them; ay, that these very Englishmen, to whom we are
so in the habit of immolating all that is beautiful and grand
among us—the first born of our youth—our creatures of immortality—our men of genius, while in the fever and flush of
their vanity, innocence and passion—ere they have had time
to put out their first plumage to the sky and the wind, all
above and about them—that they, these very Englishmen,
would not love us the less, nor revere us the less, if we loved
and revered ourselves, and the issue of our blood and breath,
and vitality and power, a little more. No—the men of England *are* men. They love manhood. They may smile at our
national vanity, but their smile would be one of compassionate
benevolence and encouragement, if we were wise enough to
keep our young at home, till their first molting season were
well over—and then, offer to pair them, even though there
would be a little presumption in it, high up in the skies, and the
strong wind—with their bravest and best: not, as we do now,
upon the altars of the earth—upon the tables of our money-
changers—half fledged and untrained—with their legs tied,
and wings clipped ; or, peradventure, with necks turned, and
heads all skewered under their tails—a heap of carrion and
garbage that the braver birds, even among their enemies,
would disdain to stoop at. Such would be their behavior. if we
dealt as we ought with our own ; there would be no pity nor disdain with them. They would cheer us to the conflict—pour their
red wine down our throats if we were beaten ; and if their
birds were beaten, they would bear it with temper—knowing
that their reputation could well afford an occasional trumph,
to the young of their favorite brood. The men of England are
waiting to do us justice : but there is a certain formality to be
gone through with, before they will do it. We must claim it.
And why should we not ? I do not mean that we should claim
it upon our knees as the condemned of their courts of justice are compelled to claim that *mercy*, which the very law itself, has predetermined to grant to him—but will not, unless

that idle and unworthy formality has been submitted to ; no—
I mean no such thing. We do not want mercy : and I would
have my countrymen, when they are arraigned before any mere
English tribunal—not acting under the *law of nations* in the
world of literature, to go at once, with a calm front and untroubled eye, and plead to their jurisdiction, with a loud clear
voice, and with their right hand upon the great book of English law, and set them at defiance. This, they have the right,
and the power to do; and why should they not, when some of
the inferior courts, of mere *English* criticism, have the audacity at every little interval, to call upon a sovereign people,
to plead before them—without counsel—and be tried for some
infringement of some paltry municipal provision of their statute book—some provincialism of language—or some heresy
in politics—or some plagiarism of manner or style ; and
abide the penalty of forgery—or of ecclesiastical censure—or
the reward of petit-larceny ; re-transportation—or re-banish-
ment to America.

It is high time now, that we should begin to do each other
justice. Let us profit by their good qualities; and let them, by
ours. And in time, we shall assuredly come to feel like
brothers of the same parentage—an elder and a younger—different in temper—but alike in family resemblance—and alike
proud of our great ancestry, the English giants of olden time.
We shall revere *our* brother ; and he will love his. But when
shall this be ?—not, I am sorely afraid—till we have called
home all our children, from the four corners of the earth;
from the east and from the west ; from the north and from the
south—and held a congress of the dead—of their fathers, and
of our fathers—and published to the world, and to posterity—
appealing again to Jehovah for the rectitude of our intentions
—another DECLARATION OF INDEPENDENCE, in the great RE-
PUBLIC OF LETTERS. And, yet this may soon be. The time
is even now at hand. Our representatives are assembling :
the dead Greek, and the Roman ; the ancient English, and
the fathers of literature, from all the buried nations of all the
earth, and holding counsel together, and choosing their dele-
gates. And the generation is already born, that shall yet hear

the heavens ringing with acclamations to their decree—that another state has been added to the everlasting confederacy of literature !

And now the author repeats to the people of America, one and all, farewell ; assuring them that there is very little proba. bility of his ever appearing before them again as a novel-wri- ter His object has been, if not wholly, at least in a great degree accomplished. He has demonstrated that a bold and direct appeal to the manhood of any people will never be made in vain. Others may have been already, or may hereafter be incited to a more intrepid movement; and to a more con- fident reliance upon themselves and their resources, by what he has now accomplished—where it is most difficult to ac- complish any thing—among his own countrymen : and most devoutly does he pray, that if they should, they may be more fortunate, and far more generously rewarded, than he has ever been; and if they should not, he advises them to go where he has been already—and trust to another people for that, which his own have not the heart to give him, however well he may deserve it. Abroad—if he do not get a chaplet of fire and greenness—he will, at least, get a cup of cold water,—and it may be, a tear or two of compassion, if nothing of encourage- ment—whatever he may do. At home—he may wear himself out—like one ashamed of what he is doing, in secrecy and darkness—exhaust his own heart of all its power and vitality, by pouring himself into the hearts of others—with a certain- ty that he will be called a madman, a beggar and a fool, for his pains—unless he persevere, in spite of a broken heart, and a broken constitution, till he shall have made his own country- men ashamed of themselves, and afraid of him.

It is a sad thing to say good bye, even for an author. If you mean what you say—it is a prayer as well as a blessing, an audible breathing of the heart. And if you do not—it is a wick- ed profanation. So far, reader, you have been the familiar companion of the author ; and you may be one of those, who have journied with him before, for many a weary day, through much of his wandering and meditation :—that is, you may be one of those who, having been admitted before, to touch his heart with a naked hand—have felt in one pulsation—in one single hour's fellowship with it, all that he had felt and thought for many a weary year. You have been *with* him to a more holy place than the fire-side ; *to* him, more like the invisible creatures—for he hath never seen your face, and peradventure never may, though you have been looking into his very soul— that hover about the chamber of prayer—the solitude of the poet —or the haunted place under the shadow of great trees, where the wearied man throws himself down, to muse upon the face of his Creator, which he sees in the sky over him, or beneath the vast blue water before him. Is it wonderful therefore that there should be a little seriousness about his brow—although ye *are* invisible to him—when he is about to say farewell to you— farewell forever—without having once heard the tone of your voice—nor one of the many tears, that you may have dropped over him, when you thought yourself altogether alone :—

Nor can he look back, without some emotion, upon the labour that he has undergone, even within that flowery wilderness, where he hath been journeying with you, or lying and ruminating all alone, for so long a time ; and out of which, he is now about to emerge—forever—with a strong tread, to the broad blue sky and the solid earth ; nor without lamenting that he cannot go barefooted—and half-naked among men ;—and that the colour and perfume—the dim enchantment, and the sweet, breathing, solemn loneliness of the wild-wood path, that he is about to abandon, for the broad dusty highway of the world, are so unpropitious to the substantial reputation of a man : nor, without grieving that the blossom-leaves, and the golden flower-dust, which now cover him, from head to foot, *must* be speedily brushed away ;—and that the scent of the wilderness may not go with him—wherever he may go—wandering through the habitation of princes—the courts of the living God—or, the dwelling places of ambition—yea, even into the grave.

* * * * * * *

I have but one other request to make. Let these words be engraven hereafter on my tomb-stone : "Who reads an American Book ?"

RACHEL DYER.

THE early history of New-England, or of Massachusetts Bay, rather; now one of the six New-England
States of North America, and that on which the Plymouth settlers, or "Fathers" went ashore—the shipwrecked men of mighty age, abounds with proof that
witchcraft was a familiar study, and that witches and
wizards were believed in for a great while, among the
most enlightened part of a large and well-educated religious population. The multitude of course had a like
faith ; for such authority governs the multitude every
where, and at all times.

The belief was very general about a hundred years
ago in every part of British America, was very common
fifty years ago, when the revolutionary war broke out,
and prevails now, even to this day in the wilder parts of
the New-England territory, as well as in the new States
which are springing up every where in the retreating
shadow of the great western wilderness—a wood where
half the men of Europe might easily hide from each
other—and every where along the shores of the solitude,
as if the new earth were full of the seed of empire, as
if dominion were like fresh flowers or magnificent herbage, the spontaneous growth of a new soil wherever
it is reached by the warm light or the cheerful rain of a
new sky.

It is not confined however, nor was it a hundred and thirty five years ago, the particular period of our story, to the uneducated and barbarous, or to a portion of the white people of North-America, nor to the native Indians, a part of whose awful faith, a part of whose inherited religion it is to believe in a bad power, in witchcraft spells and sorcery. It may be met with wherever the Bible is much read in the spirit of the New-England Fathers. It was rooted in the very nature of those who were quite remarkable in the history of their age, for learning, for wisdom, for courage and for piety ; of men who fled away from their fire-sides in Europe to the rocks of another world —where they buried themselves alive in search of truth.

We may smile now to hear witchcraft spoken seriously of ; but we forget perhaps that a belief in it is like a belief in the after appearance of the dead among the blue waters, the green graves, the still starry atmosphere and the great shadowy woods of our earth ; or like the beautiful deep instinct of our nature for worship,—older than the skies, it may be, universal as thought, and sure as the steadfast hope of immortality.

We may turn away with a sneer now from the devout believer in witches, wondering at the folly of them that have such faith, and quite persuading ourselves in our great wisdom, that all who have had it heretofore, however they may have been regarded by ages that have gone by, were not of a truth wise and great men; but we forget perhaps that we are told in the Book of Books, the Scriptures of Truth, about witches with power to raise the dead, about wizards and sorcerers that were able to strive with Jehovah's anointed high priest before the misbelieving majesty of Egypt, with all his court and people gathered about his throne for proof, and of others who could look into futurity with power, interpret the vision of sleep, read the stars, bewitch and afflict whom they would, cast out devils and prophesy—false prophets were they called, not because that which they said was untrue, but because that which they said, whether true or untrue, was not from above—because the origin of their preternatural power was bad or untrue. And we forget moreover that laws were made about conjuration, spells and witchcraft by a body of British lawgivers, renowned for their sagacity, deep research, and grave thoughtful regard for truth, but a few years ago—the other day as it were—and that a multitude of superior men have recorded their belief in witchcraft—men of prodigious power—such men as the great and good Sir Mathew Hale, who gave judgment of death upon several witches and wizards, at a period when, if we may believe a tithe of what we hear every day of our lives, from the mouth of many a great lawyer, there was no lack of wit or wisdom, nor of knowledge or faithful enquiry; and such men too as the celebrated author of the Commentaries on the Laws of England, which are, " as every body knows, or should know, and a man must be exceedingly ignorant not to know" the pride of the British empire and a pillar of light for the sages of hereafter; and that within the last one hundred and fifty or two hundred years, a multitude of men and women have been tried and executed by authority of British law, in the heart of England, for having dealt in sorcery and witchcraft.

We may smile—we may sneer—but would such things have occurred in the British Parliament, or in the British courts of law, without some proof—whatever, it was— proof to the understandings of people, who in other matters are looked up to by the chief men of this age with

absolute awe—that creatures endowed with strange, if
not with preternatural power, did inhabit our earth and
were able to work mischief according to the popular
ideas of witchcraft and sorcery?

We know little or nothing of the facts upon which
their belief was founded. All that we know is but hearsay, tradition or conjecture. They who believed were
eye-witnesses and ear witnesses of what they believed;
we who disbelieve are neither. They who believed
knew all that we know of the matter and much more;
we who disbelieve are not only ignorant of the facts, but
we are living afar off, in a remote age. Nevertheless, they
believed in witchcraft, and we regard all who speak of it
seriously, with contempt. How dare we! What right
have we to say that witches and witchcraft are no more,
that sorcery is done with forever, that miracles are never
to be wrought again, or that Prophecy shall never be
heard again by the people of God, uplifting her voice
like a thousand echoes from the everlasting solitudes of
the sea, or like uninterrupted heavy thunder breaking
over the terrible and haughty nations of our earth?

Why should we not think as well of him who believes
too much, as of him who believes too little? Of him
whose faith, whatever it may be, is too large, as of him
whose faith, whatever it may be, is too small? Of the
good with a credulous temper, as of the great with a
suspicious temper? Of the pure in heart, of the youthful,
of the untried in the ways of the world, who put much
faith in whatever they are told, too much it may be, as
of them who being thoroughly tried in the ways of the
world put no faith in what they hear, and little in what
they see? Of the humble in spirit who believe, *though*
they do not perfectly understand, as of the haughty who
will not believe *because* they do not perfectly understand?

Of the poor child who thinks a juggler eats fire when he does not, as of the grown-up sage who thinks a juggler does *not* swallow a sword when he *does*? Of the believer in Crusoe, who sits poring over the story under a hedge, as of the unbeliever in Bruce who would not believe, so long as it was new, in the Tale of Abyssinia? Of those in short who are led astray by self-distrust, or innocence, or humility, as of them who are led astray by self-conceit, or corruption, or pride?

In other days, the Lion of the desert would not believe the horse when he came up out of the bleak north, and told a story of waters and seas that grew solid, quiet and smooth in the dead of winter. His majesty had never heard of such a thing before, and what his majesty had never heard of before could not be possible. The mighty lord of the Numedian desert could not believe—how could he?—in a cock-and-a-bull-story, about ice and snow; for to him they were both as a multitude of such things are to the philosophy of our age, out of the course of nature.

A solid sea and a fluid earth are alike to such as have no belief in what is new or contrary to that course of nature with which they are acquainted—whatever that may be. There is no such thing as proof to the over-wise or over mighty, save where by reason of what they already know, there is not much need of other proof.— They would not believe, though one should rise from the dead—they are too cautious by half; they are not satis-fied with any sort of testimony; they dare not believe their own eyes—they do not indeed ; for spectres when they appear to the eye of the philosopher now, are attri-buted altogether to a diseased organ.(1.) They care not for the cloud of witnesses—they withdraw from the Bible, they scoff at history, and while they themselves

_____

(1) As by the printer of Berlin. See also Beasley's Search after Truth.

reject every kind of proof, whatever it may be, such
proof as they would be satisfied with in a case of murder, were they to hear it as a jury —such proof as they
would give judgment of death upon, without fear, proof
under oath by men of high character and severe probity,
eye-witnesses and ear-witnesses of what they swear to—
they ridicule those who undertake to weigh it with care,
and pursue with scorn or pity those who shiver through
all their arteries at a story of the preternatural.

As if it were a mark of deplorable fatuity for a babe to
believe now as a multitude of wise and great and gifted
men have heretofore believed in every age of the world!
As if to think it possible for such to have been right in
their belief, were too absurd for excuse now—such men
as the holy Greek, the upright immovable Socrates,
who persuaded himself that he was watched over by
a sort of household spirit; such men too as the " bald"
Cæsar, and the rock-hearted Brutus, both of whom
spite of their imperial nature and high place among the
warlike and mighty of their age, believed in that, and
shook before that which whether deceitful or not, substance or shadow, the very cowards of our day are too
brave to be scared with, too full of courage to put their
trust in—afraid as they are of that, which the Roman pair
would have met with a stern smile and a free step; such
men too of a later age, as the profound, wise and pure
Sir Matthew Hale, who put many to death for witchcraft
—so clear was the proof, and so clear the nature of the
crime—while the nature of larceny, the nature of common theft was forever a mystery to him, if we may believe what we hear out of his own mouth; such men too
as the celebrated Judge Blackstone, who after a thorough
sifting of the law, says--" It seems to be most eligible
to conclude that in general there has been such a thing
as witchcraft, though we cannot give credit to any par-

ticular modern instance of it;" such men too as Doctor
Samuel Johnson, L L. D. who saw through all the hy-
pocricy and subterfuge of our day, when he said, speaking of a superstitious belief, that men who deny it by
their words, confess it by their fears—nothing was ever
so true! we who are most afraid, want courage to own
it; such men too as the Lord Protector of England,
while she was a commonwealth ; and such as he, the Des-
olator—

> "..............From whose reluctant hand,
> The thunder-bolt was wrung"—

for they were both believers in what the very rabble of
our earth deride now; such men, too, as the chief among
poets—Byron—for he believed in the words of a poor
old gypsey, and shook with fear, and faltered on the way
to his bridal-chamber, when he thought of the prophecy
she had uttered years and years before, in the morning of
his haughty youth; such men too as the head lawgiver
of our day, the High-Priest of Legislation, the great and
good, the benevolent, the courageous Bentham, who to
this hour is half afraid in the dark, and only able to satisfy himself about the folly of such fear, when his night-
cap is off, by resorting with suitable gravity to his old refuge, the exhaustive mode of reasoning. If a ghost appear at all, argues he, it must appear either clothed or
not clothed. But a ghost never appears not clothed,
or naked ; and if it appear clothed, we shall have not only
the ghost of a human creature—which is bad enough ;
but the ghost of a particular kind of cloth of a particular fashion, the ghost of a pocket-handkerchief, or a
night-cap—which is too bad.

Thus much for authority : and here, but for one little
circumstance we should take up our narrative, and pursue it without turning to the right or the left, until we
came to the sorrowful issue ; but as we may have here

and there a reader, in this unbelieving age, who has no
regard for authority, nor much respect for the wisdom
of our ancestors, what if we try to put the whole argument into a more conclusive shape ?   It may require
but a few pages, and a few pages may go far to allay
the wrath of modern philosophy.   If we throw aside the
privilege of authorship, and speak, not as a multitude but
as one of the true faith, our argument would stand thus:

In a word, whatever the philosophy of our age may
say, I cannot look upon witchcraft and sorcery as the
unbeliever does.   I know enough what the fashion is
now ; but I cannot believe, I do not believe that we
know much more of the matter than our great progeni-
tors did ; or that we are much wiser than a multitude
who have been for ages, and are now, renowned for their
wisdom ; or that we are much more pious than our noble
fathers were, who died in their belief—died *for* their
belief, I should say, and are a proverb to this hour on
account of their piety.   Nor can I persuade myself that
such facts would be met with in grave undoubted history,
if they were untrue, as are to be met with in every page
of that which concerns the period of our story ; facts
which go to prove not only that a fixed belief in witchcraft prevailed throughout Europe as well as America,
and among those with whom there was no lack of probity or good sense, or knowledge, it would appear ; but
that hundreds of poor creatures were tried for witchcraft
under the authority of British law, and put to death,
under the authority of British law, (and several after
confession) for the practice of witchcraft and sorcery.

May it not be worth our while therefore, to speak
seriously and reverently of our mighty forefathers ? to
bear in mind that the proof which they offer is affirmative and positive, while that which we rely upon, is
negative—a matter of theory ? to keep in view, more-

not much has
changed since 1421,
still "in dark"
about witchcraft

over, that if a body of witnesses of equal worth were
equally divided, one half saying that on such a day and
hour, at such a place, when they were all together, such
or such a thing, preternatural or not, mysterious or not,
occurred ; while the other half say positively, man for
man, that so far as they heard or saw, or know or believe, no such thing did occur, at such a time or place,
or at any other time or place, whatsoever—still, even
here, though you may believe both parties, though you
may give entire credit to the words of each, you may be
justified, in a variety of cases, in acting upon the testimony of the former in preference to that of the latter.
And why ? Because the contradictory words of both
may not be so contradictory as they appear—not so contradictory as to neutralize each other on every hypothesis ; but may be reconcilable to the supposition that such
or such a fact, however positively denied by one party,
and however mysterious it may seem, really did occur :
and this while they are not reconcilable to the supposition
that such or such a fact really did *not* occur.—It being
much more easy to overlook that which is, than to see
that which is not ; much more easy to *not* see a shadow
that falls upon our pathway, than to see a shadow where
indeed there is no shadow ; much more easy to *not* hear
a real voice, than to hear *no* voice.

If the multitude of trustworthy and superior men,
therefore, who testify to the facts which are embodied
in the following narrative, and which may appear incredible to the wise of our day, or out of the course of
nature to the philosophy of our day, like ice or snow to
the Lord of the Desert ; if they were positively contradicted step by step, throughout, by another like multitude of trustworthy and superior men—still, though the
two parties were alike numerous and alike worthy of
credit, and although you might believe the story of each,

and every word of it, and give no preference to either :
—Still I say, you might be justified in supposing that
after all, the facts which the former testify to really did
occur.   And why ?   Because *though* both speak true,
that hypothesis may still be supported ; while *if* both
speak true, the contrary hypothesis cannot be supported.
Facts may occur without being heard or seen by the
whole of a party who are together at the time they occur : but how are they to be seen or heard, if they do
not occur at all ?

I have put a much stronger case than that on which
the truth of the following story is made to depend ; for
no such contradiction occurs here, no such positive testimony, no such array of multitude against multitude of
the same worth, or the same age, or the same people.
On the affirmative side are a host here—a host of respec-
table witnesses, not a few of whom sealed their testimony
with their blood ; on the negative, hardly one either of
a good or a bad character.   What appears on the negative side is not by facts, but by theory.   It is not positive
but conjectural,   The negative witnesses are of our age
and of our people ; the affirmative were of another age
and of another people.   The former too, it should be
remarked were not only not present, but they were not
born—they were not alive, when the matters which they
deny the truth of, took place—if they ever took place at
all.   Now, if oaths are to be answered by conjecture,
bloodshed by a sneer, absolute martyrdom by hypothesis,
much grave testimony of the great and the pious, by a
speculative argument, a brief syllogism, or a joke—of
what use are the rules by which our trust in what we
hear is regulated ? our faith whatever it may be, and
whether it concern this world or the next, and whether
it be of the past, the present or the future ?   Are we to
believe only so far as we may touch and see for our-

selves ? What is the groundwork of true knowledge ?
where the spirit of true philosophy? Whither shou'd
we go for proof; and of what avail is the truth which
we are hoarding up, the truth which we are extracting
year after year by laborious investigation, or fearful experiment? If we do not believe those who go up to the
altar and make oath before the Everlasting God, not as
men do now, one after another, but nation by nation,
to that which is very new to us, or wonderful, why
should posterity believe us when we testify to that which
hereafter may be very new to them or very wonderful ?
Is every day to be like every other day, every age like
every other age in the Diary of the Universe? Earthquake, war and revolution—the overthrow of States and
of empires, are they to be repeated forever, lest men
should not believe the stories that are told of them ?

CHAPTER II.

BUT enough. It is quite impossible to doubt the sincerity of the Plymouth settlers, the Pilgrims, or Fathers of New-England, who escaping over sea laid the foundations of a mighty empire on the perpetual rocks of New-Plymouth, and along the desolate shores of a new world, or their belief in witchcraft and sorcery, whatever *we* may happen to believe now; for, at a period of sore and bitter perplexity for them and theirs, while they were yet wrestling for life, about four hundred of their hardy brave industrious population were either in prison for the alleged practice of witchcraft, or under accusation for matters which were looked upon as fatal evidence thereof. By referring to the sober and faithful records of that age, it will be found that in the course of about fifteen months, while the Fathers of New-England were beset on every side by the exasperated savages, or by the more exasperated French, who led the former through every part of the British-American territory, twenty eight persons received sentence of death (of which number nineteen were executed) one died in jail, to whom our narrative relates, and one was deliberately crushed to death—according to British law, because forsooth, being a stout full-hearted man, he would not make a plea, nor open his mouth to the charge of sorcery, before the twelve, who up to that hour had permitted no one who did open his mouth to escape; that a few more succeeded in getting away before they were capitally charged; that one hundred and fifty were set free after the outcry was over ; and that full two hundred more of the accused who were in great peril without knowing it, were never proceeded against, after the death of the individual whose character we have attempted a sketch of, in the following story.

Of these four hundred poor creatures. a large part of whom were people of good repute in the prime of life, above two-score made confession of their guilt —and this although about one half, being privately charged, had no opportunity for confession. The laws of nature, it would seem *were* set aside—if not by Jehovah, at least by the judges acting under the high and holy sanction of British law, in this day of sorrow; for at the trial of a woman who appears to have been celebrated for beauty and held in great fear because of her temper, both by the settlers and the savages, three of her children stood up, and children though they were, in the presence of their mother, avowed themselves to be witches, and gave a particular account of their voyages through the air and over sea, and of the cruel mischief they had perpetrated by her advice and direction; for she was endowed, say the records of the day, with great power and prerogative, and the Father of lies had promised her, at one of their church-yard gatherings that she should be " Queen of Hell."

But before we go further into the particulars of our narrative which relates to a period when the frightful superstition we speak of was raging with irresistible power, a rapid review of so much of the earlier parts of the New-England history, as immediately concerns the breaking out, and the growth of a belief in witchcraft among the settlers of our savage country, may be of use to the reader, who, but for some such preparation, would never be able to credit a fiftieth part of what is undoubtedly true in the following story.

The pilgrims or " Fathers" of New-England, as they
are now called by the writers of America, were but a
ship-load of pious brave men, who while they were in
search of a spot of earth where they might worship their
God without fear, and build up a faith, if so it pleased
him, without reproach, went ashore partly of their own
accord, but more from necessity, in the terrible winter
of 1620-21, upon a rock of Massachusetts-Bay, to which
they gave the name of New-Plymouth, after that of the
port of England from which they embarked.

They left England forever....England their home and
the home of their mighty fathers—turned their backs
forever upon all that was dear to them in their beloved
country, their friends, their houses, their tombs and
their churches, their laws and their literature with all
that other men cared for in that age ; and this merely
to avoid persecution for a religious faith ; fled away as
it were to the ends of the earth, over a sea the very
name of which was doubtful, toward a shore that was
like a shadow to the navigators of Europe, in search of
a place where they might kneel down before their Father, and pray to him without molestation.

But, alas for their faith ! No sooner had these pilgrims
touched the shore of the new world, no sooner were they
established in comparative power and security, than
they fell upon the Quakers, who had followed them over
the same sea, with the same hope ; and scourged and
banished them, and imprisoned them, and put some to
death, for not believing as the new church taught in the
new world. Such is the nature of man ! The persecuted of to-day become the persecutors of to-morrow.
They flourish, not because they are right, but because
they are persecuted ; and they persecute because they
have the power, not because they whom they persecute
are wrong.

The quakers died in their belief, and as the great always die—without a word or a tear ; praying for the misguided people to their last breath, but prophecying heavy sorrow to them and to theirs—a sorrow without a name—a wo without a shape, to their whole race forever; with a mighty series of near and bitter affliction to the judges of the land, who while they were uttering the words of death to an aged woman of the Quakers, (Mary Dyer) were commanded with a loud voice to set their houses in order, to get ready the accounts of their stewardship, and to prepare with the priesthood of all the earth, to go before the Judge of the quick and the dead. It was the voice of Elizabeth Hutchinson, the dear and familiar friend of Mary Dyer. She spoke as one having authority from above, so that all who heard her were afraid—all ! even the judges who were dealing out their judgment of death upon a fellow creature. And lo ! after a few years, the daughter of the chief judge, before whom the prophecy had been uttered with such awful power, was tried for witchcraft and put to death for witchcraft on the very spot (so says the tradition of the people) where she stayed to scoff at Mary Dyer, who was on her way to the scaffold at the time, with her little withered hands locked upon her bosom....her grey head lifted up....not bowed in her unspeakable distress....but lifted up, as if in prayer to something visible above, something whatever it was, the shadow of which fell upon the path and walked by the side of the aged martyr ; something whatever it was, that moved like a spirit over the green smooth turf....now at her elbow, now high up and afar off....now in the blue, bright air ; something whose holy guardianship was betrayed to the multitude by the devout slow motion of the eyes that were about to be extinguished forever.

Not long after the death of the daughter of the chief

judge, another female was executed for witchcraft, and
other stories of a similar nature were spread over the
whole country, to prove that she too had gone out of
her way to scoff at the poor quaker-woman. This occurred in 1655, only thirty-five years after the arrival
of the Fathers in America. From this period, until 1691,
there were but few trials for witchcraft among the Plymouth settlers, though the practice of the art was believed to be common throughout Europe as well as
America, and a persuasion was rooted in the very hearts
of the people, that the prophecy of the quakers and of
Elizabeth Hutchinson would assuredly be accomplished.

It *was* accomplished. A shadow fell upon the earth
at noon-day. The waters grew dark as midnight. Every thing alive was quiet with fear—the trees, the birds,
the cattle, the very hearts of men who were gathered
together in the houses of the Lord, every where,
throughout all the land, for worship and for mutual succor. It was indeed a "Dark Day"—a day never to be
thought of by those who were alive at the time, nor by
their children's children, without fear. The shadow of
the grave was abroad, with a voice like the voice of the
grave. Earthquake, fire, and a furious bright storm
followed; inundation, war and stife in the church.
Stars fell in a shower, heavy cannon were heard in the
deep of the wilderness, low music from the sea—trumpets, horses, armies, mustering for battle in the deep sea.
Apparitions were met in the high way, people whom
nobody knew, men of a most unearthly stature ; evil
spirits going abroad on the sabbath day. The print of
huge feet and hoof-marks were continually discovered
in the snow, in the white sand of the sea-shore—nay, in
the solid rocks and along the steep side of high moun-

tains, where no mortal hoof could go ; and sometimes they could be traced from roof to roof on the house-tops, though the buildings were very far apart ; and the shape of Elizabeth Hutchinson herself, was said to have appeared to a traveller, on the very spot where she and her large family, after being driven forth out of New-England by the power of the new church, were put to death by the savages. He that saw the shape knew it, and was afraid for the people ; for the look of the woman was a look of wrath, and her speech a speech of power.

Elizabeth Hutchinson was one of the most extraordinary women of the age—haughty, ambitious and crafty; and when it was told every where through the Plymouth colony that she had appeared to one of the church that expelled her, they knew that she had come back, to be seen of the judges and elders, according to her oath, and were siezed with a deep fear. They knew that she had been able to draw away from their peculiar mode of worship, a tithe of their whole number when she was alive, and a setter forth, if not of strange gods, at least of strange doctrines : and who should say that her mischievous power had not been fearfully augmented by death ?

Meanwhile the men of New Plymouth, and of Massachusetts Bay, had multiplied so that all the neighborhood was tributary to them, and they were able to send forth large bodies of their young men to war, six hundred, seven hundred, and a thousand at a time, year after year, to fight with Philip of Mount Hope, a royal barbarian, who had wit enough to make war as the great men of Europe would make war now, and to persuade the white people that the prophecy of the Quakers related to him. It is true enough that he made war like

a savage—and who would not, if he were surrounded as
Philip of Mount Hope was, by a foe whose hatred was
a part of his religion, a part of his very blood and being?
if his territory were ploughed up or laid waste by a superior foe ? if the very wilderness about him were fired
while it was the burial-place and sanctuary of his mighty
fathers? if their form of worship were scouted, and
every grave and every secret place of prayer laid open
to the light, with all their treasures and all their myste-
ries ? every temple not made with hands, every church
built by the Builder of the Skies, invaded by such a foe
and polluted with the rites of a new faith, or levelled
without mercy—every church and every temple, whether of rock or wood, whether perpetual from the first, or
planted as the churches and temples of the solitude are,
with leave to perpetuate themselves forever, to renew
their strength and beauty every year and to multiply
themselves on every side forever and ever, in spite of
deluge and fire, storm, strife and earthquake; every
church and every temple whether roofed as the skies
are, and floored as the mountains are, with great clouds
and with huge rocks, or covered in with tree-branches
and paved with fresh turf, lighted with stars and purifi-
ed with high winds ? Would not the man of Europe
make war now like a savage, and without mercy, if he
were beset by a foe—for such was the foe that Philip of
Mount Hope had to contend with in the fierce pale men
of Massachusetts Bay,—a foe that no weapon of his
could reach, a foe coming up out of the sea with irresistible power, and with a new shape ? What if armies
were to spring up out of the solid earth before the man
of Europe—it would not be more wonderful to him than
it was to the man of America to see armies issuing fro m
the deep. What if they were to approach in balloons—
or in great ships of the air, armed all over as the foe of

the poor savage appeared to be, when the ships of the water drew near, charged with thunder and with lightning, and with four-footed creatures, and with sudden death ? Would the man of Europe make war in such a case according to what are now called the usages of war ?

The struggle with this haughty savage was regarded for a time as the wo without a shape, to which the prophecy referred, the sorrow without a name; for it occupied the whole force of the country, long and long after the bow of the red-chief was broken forever, his people scattered from the face of the earth, and his royalty reduced to a shadow—a shadow it is true, but still the shadow of a king ; for up to the last hour of his life, when he died as no king had ever the courage to die, he showed no sign of terror, betrayed no wish to conciliate the foe, and smote all that were near without mercy, whenever they talked of submission ; though he had no hope left, no path for escape, and every shot of the enemy was fatal to some one of the few that stood near him. It was a war, which but for the accidental discovery of a league embracing all the chief tribes of the north, before they were able to muster their strength for the meditated blow, would have swept away the white men, literally to the four winds of heaven, and left that earth free which they had set up their dominion over by falsehood and by treachery. By and by however, just when the issue of that war was near, and the fright of the pale men over, just when the hearts of the church had begun to heave with a new hope and the prophecy of wrath and sorrow was no longer to be heard in the market-place, and by the way-side, or wherever the people were gathered together for business or worship, with a look of awe and a subdued breath—just when it came to be no longer thought of nor cared for by the

judges and the elders, to whom week after week and
year after year, it had been a familiar proverb of death
(it bad news from the war had come over night, or news
of trouble to the church, at home or abroad, in Europe
or in America) they saw it suddenly and wholly accomplished before their faces—every word of it and every
letter.

The shadow of the destroyer went by....the type was
no more. But lo! in the stead thereof, while every
mother was happy, and every father in peace, and every
child asleep in security, because the shadow and the
type *had* gone by—lo! the Destroyer himself appeared!
The shadow of death gave way for the visage of death
—filling every heart with terror, and every house with
lamentation. The people cried out for fear, as with one
voice. They prayed as with one prayer. They had no
hope; for they saw the children of those who had offered outrage to the poor quaker-woman gathered up, on
every side, from the rest of the people, and after a few
days and a brief inquiry, afflicted in their turn with reproach and outcry, with misery, torture and cruel death;
—and when they saw this, they thought of the speech of
Elizabeth Hutchinson before the priesthood of the land,
the judges and the people, when they drove her out from
among them, because of her new faith, and left her to
perish for it in the depth of a howling wilderness; her,
and her babes, and her beautiful daughter, and her two
or three brave disciples, away from hope and afar from
succor;—and as they thought of this, they were filled
anew with unspeakable dread: for Mary Dyer and Elizabeth Hutchinson, were they not familiar, and very dear
friends? were they not sisters in life, and sisters in
death? gifted alike with a spirit of sure prophecy, though
of a different faith? and martyrs alike to the church?

CHAPTER III.

" A strange infatuation had already begun to produce misery in private families, and disorder throughout the community," says an old American writer, in allusion to the period of our story, 1691—2. " The imputation of witchcraft was accompanied with a prevalent belief of its reality ; and the lives of a considerable number of innocent people were sacrificed to blind zeal and superstitious credulity. The mischief began at Naumkeag, (Salem) but it soon extended into various parts of the colony. The contagion however, was principally within the county of Essex. The æra of English learning, had scarcely commenced. Laws then existed in England against witches ; and the authority of Sir Matthew Hale, who was revered in New England, not only for his knowledge in the law, but for his gravity and piety, had doubtless, great influence. The trial of the witches in Suffolk, in England, was published in 1684 ; and there was so exact a resemblance between the Old England dæmons and the New, that, it can hardly be doubted the arts of the designing were borrowed, and the credulity of the populace augmented from the parent country. * * * * *

" The gloomy state of New England probably facilitated the delusion, for ' superstition flourishes in times of danger and dismay.' The distress of the colonist, at this time, was great. The sea-coast was infested with privateers. The inland frontiers, east and west, were continually harassed by the French and Indians. The abortive expedition to Canada, had exposed the country to the resentment of France, the effects of which were perpetually dreaded. The old charter was gone, and what evils would be introduced by the new, which was very reluctantly received by many, time only could determine, but fear might forbode.   *   *   How far these causes operating in a wilderness that was scarcely cleared up, might have contributed toward the infatuation, it is difficult to determine. It were injurious however, to consider New England as peculiar in this culpable credulity, with its sanguinary effects ; for more persons have been put to death for witchcraft, in a single county in England, in a short space of time, than have suffered for the same cause, in all New-England, since its first settlement."

Another American writer who was an eye witness of the facts which are embodied in the following narrative, says, "As to the method which the Salem justices do take in their examinations, it is truly this : A warrant being issued out to apprehend the persons that are charged and complained of by the afflicted children, (Abigail Paris and Bridget Pope) said persons are brought before the justices, the afflicted being present. The justices ask the apprehended why they afflict these poor children ; to which the apprehended answer they do not afflict them. The justices order the apprehended to look upon the said children, which accordingly they do ; and at the time of that look (I dare not say *by* that look as, the Salem gentlemen do) the afflicted are cast into a fit. The apprehended are then blinded and ordered to touch the afflicted ; and at that touch, though not *by* the touch (as above) the afflicted do ordinarily come out of their fits. The afflicted persons then declare and affirm that the apprehended have af-

flicted them ; upon which the apprehended persons
though of never so good repute are forthwith committed
to prison on suspicion of witchcraft."

At this period, the chief magistrate of the New-Plymouth colony, a shrewd, artful, uneducated man, was not
only at the head of those who believed in witchcraft as
a familiar thing, but he was a head-ruler in the church.
He was a native New-Englander of *low birth*—so say
the records of our country,—where birth is now, and
ever will be a matter of inquiry and solicitude, of shame
perhaps to the few and of pride to the few, but of inquiry
with all, in spite of our ostentatious republicanism.   He
was the head man over a body of men who may be regarded as the natural growth of a rugged soil in a time
of religious warfare ; with hearts and with heads like
the resolute unforgiving Swiss-protestant of their age,
or the Scotch-covenanter of an age that has hardly yet
gone by.   They were the Maccabees of the seventeenth
century, and he was their political chief.   They were
the fathers of a new church in a new world, where no
church had ever been heard of before ; and he was ready
to buckle a sword upon his thigh and go out against all
the earth, at the command of that new church.   They
were ministers of the gospel, who ministered with fire
and sword unto the savages whom they strove to convert;
believers, who being persecuted in Europe, hunted out
of Europe, and cast away upon the shores of America,
set up a new war of persecution here—even here—in the
untrodden—almost unapproachable domain of the Great
Spirit of the Universe ; pursued their brethren to death,
scourged, fined, imprisoned, banished, mutilated, and
where nothing else would do, hung up their bodies between heaven and earth for the good of their souls ;
drove mother after mother, and babe after babe, into the
woods for not believing as their church taught ; made

war upon the lords of the soil, the savages who had been
their stay and support while they were strangers, and
sick and poor, and ready to perish, and whom it was
therefore a duty for them—after they had recovered
their strength—to make happy with the edge of the
sword ; such war as the savages would make upon the
wild beast—way-laying them by night, and shooting them
to death, as they lie asleep with their young, without so
much as a declaration of war; destroying whithersoever
they went, whatsoever they saw, in the shape of a dark
man, as if they had authority from above to unpeople
the woods of America ; firing village after village, in the
dead of the night—in the dead of winter too—and going
to prayer in the deep snow, while their hands were
smoking with slaughter, and their garments stiffening
with blood—the blood, not of warriors overthrown by
warriors in battle, but of the decrepit, or sick, or help-
less ; of the aged man, or the woman or the babe—set
fire to in their sleep.—Such were the men of Massachusetts-Bay, at the period of our story, and he was
their political chief.

He had acquired a large property and the title of *Sir*;
a title which would go a great way at any time among
the people of New-England, who whatever else they
may be, and whatever they may pretend, are not now,
and were not during the governship of Sir William
Phips, at the period we refer to, and we dare say, never
will be, without a regard for titles and birth, and ribbons,
and stars, and garters, and much more too, than would
ever be credited by those who only judge of them by
what they are pleased to say of themselves in their
fourth-of-July orations.   His rank and wealth were acquired in rather a strange way—not by a course of rude
mercantile adventure, such as the native Yankee is familiar with from his birth, through every unheard-of

sea, and along every unheard-of shore; but by fishing up
ingots of gold, and bars of silver, from the wreck of a
Spanish hulk, which had been cast away on the coast of
La Plata, years and years before, and which he had
been told of by Mr. Paris, the minister of Salem,—a
worthy, studious, wayward man, who had met with some
account of the affair, while rummaging into a heap of
old newspapers and ragged books that fell in his way.

Another would have paid no attention, it is probable,
to the advice of the peacher—a man who had grown
old in poring over books that nobody else in that country had ever met with or heard of; but the hardy New-
Englander was too poor and too anxious for wealth to
throw a chance away; and having satisfied himself in
some degree about the truth of a newspaper-narrative
which related to the ship, he set sail for the mother
country, received the patronage of those, who if they
were not noblemen, would be called partners in every
such enterprise, with more than the privilege of partners—for they generally contrive to take the praise and
the profit, while their plebeian associates have to put up
with the loss and the reproach; found the wreck, and
after a while succeeded in weighing a prodigious quantity of gold and silver. He was knighted " in consequence," we are told; but in consequence of what, it
would be no easy matter to say: and after so short an ab-
sence that he was hardly missed, returned to his native
country with a new charter, great wealth, a great name,
the title of Sir, and the authority of a chief magistrate.

Such are a few of the many facts which every body
that knew him was acquainted with by report, and
which nobody thought of disbelieving in British-Ameri-
ca, till the fury about witches and witchcraft took possession of the people; after which they began to shake
their heads at the story, and getting more and more

courage as they grew more and more clear-sighted, they
went on doubting first one part of the tale, and then another, till at last they did not scruple to say of their
worthy Governor himself, and of the aged Mr. Paris,
that one of the two—they did not like to say which—had
got above their neighbors' heads, after all, in a very
strange way—a very strange way indeed—they did not
like to say how ; and that the sooner the other was done
with old books, the better it would be for him. He had
a Bible of his own to study, and what more would a
preacher of the Gospel have ?

Governor Phips and Matthew Paris were what are
called neighbors in America. Their habitations were
not more than five leagues apart. The Governor lived
at Boston, the chief town of Massachusetts-Bay, and the
preacher at Naumkeag, in a solitary log-house, completely surrounded by a thick wood, in which were
many graves ; and a rock held in great awe by the red
men of the north, and avoided with special care by the
whites, who had much reason to believe that in other
days, it had been a rock of sacrifice, and that human
creatures had been offered up there by the savages of
old, either to Hobbamocko, their evil deity, or to Raw-
tantoweet, otherwise Ritchtau, their great Invisible Father. Matthew Paris and Sir William Phips had each
a faith of his own therefore, in all that concerned
witches and witchcraft. Both were believers—but their
belief was modified, intimate as they were, by the circumstances and the society in which they lived. With
the aged, poor and solitary man—a widower in his old
age, it was a dreadful superstition, a faith mixed up
with a mortal fear. With the younger and richer man,
whose hope was not in the grave, and whose thoughts
were away from the death-bed ; who was never alone
perhaps for an hour of the day ; who lived in the very

whirl of society, surrounded by the cheerful faces of
them that he most loved on earth, it wore a less harrow-
ing shape—it was merely a faith to talk of, and to teach
on the Sabbath day, a curious faith suited to the bold
inquisitive temper of the age. Both were believers, and
fixed believers; and yet of the two, perhaps, the speculative man would have argued more powerfully—with
fire and sword—as a teacher of what he believed.

About a twelvemonth before the enterprise to La
Plata, whereby the "uneducated man of low birth"
came to be a ruler and a chief in the land of his nativi-
ty, Matthew Paris the preacher, to whom he was indebted for a knowledge of the circumstances which led
to the discovery, had lost a young wife—a poor girl who
had been brought up in his family, and whom he married not *because* of her youth, but in spite of her youth;
and every body knew as he stood by her grave, and saw
the fresh earth heaped upon her, that he would never
hold up his head again, his white venerable head, which
met with a blessing wherever it appeared. From that
day forth, he was a broken-hearted selfish man, weary
of life, and sick with insupportable sorrow. He began
to be afraid with a strange fear, to persuade himself that
his Father above had cast him off, and that for the rest
of his life he was to be a mark of the divine displeasure.
He avoided all that knew him, and chiefly those he had
been most intimate with while he was happy; for their
looks and their speech, and every change of their breath
reminded him of his poor Margaret, his meek beautiful
wife. He could not bear the very song of the birds—
nor the sight of the green trees; for she was buried in
the summer-time, while the trees were in flower, and
the birds singing in the branches that overshadowed her
grave; and so he withdrew from the world and shut
himself up in a dreary solitude, where neglecting his

duty as a preacher of the gospel, he gave up his whole
time to the education of his little daughter—the child of
his old age, and the live miniature of its mother—who
was *like* a child, from the day of her birth to the day of
her death.⌋ His grief would have been despair, but for
this one hope. It was the sorrow of old age—that insupportable sorrow—the sorrow of one who is ready to
cry out with every sob, and at every breath, in the des-
olation of a widowed heart, whenever he goes to the
fireside or the table, or sees the sun set, or the sky
change with the lustre of a new day, or wakes in the
dead of the night from a cheerful dream of his wife—
his dear, dear wife, to the frightful truth ; finding the
heavy solitude of the grave about him, his bridal chamber dark with the atmosphere of death, his marriage
bed—his home—his very heart, which had been occupied with a blessed and pure love a moment before, uninhabited forever.

His family consisted now of this one child, who was
in her tenth year, a niece in her twelfth year, and two
Indians who did the drudgery of the house, and were
treated as members of the family, eating at the same table and of the same food as the preacher.   One was a
female who bore the name of Tituba ; the other a praying warrior, who had become a by-word among the
tribes of the north, and a show in the houses of the
white men.

The preacher had always a belief in witchcraft, and
so had every body else that he knew ; but he had never
been afraid of witches till after the death of his wife.
He had been a little too ready perhaps to put faith in
every tale that he heard about apparition or shadow,
star-shooting or prophecy, unearthly musick, or spirits
going abroad through the very streets of Salem village,
and over the green fields, and along by the sea shore,

the wilderness, the rock and the hill-top, and always at noon-day, and always without a shadow—shapes of death, who never spoke but with a voice like that of the wind afar off, nor moved without making the air cold about them; creatures from the deep sea, who are known to the pious and the gifted by their slow smooth motion over the turf, and by their quiet, grave, unchangeable eyes. But though he had been too ready to believe in such things, from his youth up, he had never been much afraid of them, till after he found himself widowed forever, as he drew near, arm in arm with an angel, to the very threshold of eternity ; separated by death, in his old age, from a good and beautiful, and young wife, just when he had no other hope—no other joy—nothing but her and her sweet image, the babe, to care for underneath the sky. Are we to have no charity for such a man—weak though he appear—a man whose days were passed by the grave where his wife lay, and whose nights were passed literally in her death-bed ; a man living away and apart from all that he knew, on the very outskirts of the solitude, among those who had no fear *but* of shadows and spirits, and witch-craft and witches? We should remember that his faith after all, was the faith, not so much of the man, as of the age he lived in, the race he came of, and the life that he led. Hereafter, when posterity shall be occupied with our doings, they may wonder at our faith—perhaps at our credulity, as we now wonder at his.

But the babe grew, and a new hope flowered in his heart, for she was the very image of her mother ; and there was her little cousin too, Bridget Pope, a child of singular beauty and very tall of her age—how *could* he be unhappy, when he heard their sweet voices ringing together ?

—chapter → description of Paris

— author choosing to make Bridget "Pope" a child → "Bishop"
— daughter → Abby
subtle changes

CHAPTER IV.

Bridget Pope was of a thoughtful serious turn—the little Abby the veriest romp that ever breathed. Bridget was the elder, by about a year and a half, but she looked five years older than Abby, and was in every way a remarkable child. Her beauty was like her stature, and both were above her age ; and her aptitude for learning was the talk of all that knew her. She was a favorite every where and with every body—she had such a sweet way with her, and was so unlike the other children of her age—so that when she appeared to merit reproof, as who will not in the heyday of innocent youth, it was quite impossible to reprove her, except with a mild voice, or a kind look, or a very affectionate word or two. She would keep away from her slate and book for whole days together, and sit for half an hour at a time without moving her eyes off the page, or turning away her head from the little window of their school-house (a log-hut plastered with blue clay in stripes and patches, and lighted with horn, oiled-paper and isinglass) which commanded a view of Naumkeag, or Salem village, with a part of the original woods of North America—huge trees that were found there on the first arrival of the white man crowded together and covered with moss and dropping to pieces of old age ; a meeting-house with a short wooden spire, and the figure of death on the top for a weather-cock, a multitude of cottages that appeared to be lost in the landscape, and a broad beautiful approach from the sea.

Speak softly to Bridget Pope at such a time, or look at her with a look of love, and her quiet eyes would fill, and her childish heart would run over—it would be impossible to say why. But if you spoke sharply to her, when her head was at the little window, and her thoughts were away, nobody knew where, the poor little thing would grow pale and serious, and look at you with such a look of sorrow—and then go away and do what she was bid with a gravity that would go to your heart. And it would require a whole day after such a rebuke to restore the dye of her sweet lips, or to persuade her that you were not half so angry as you might have appeared. At every sound of your voice, at every step that came near, she would catch her breath, and start and look up, as if she expected something dreadful to happen.

But as for Abigail Paris, the pretty little blue-eyed cousin of Bridget Pope, there was no dealing with her in that way. If you shook your finger at her, she would laugh in your face ; and if you did it with a grave air, ten to one but she made you laugh too. If you scolded her, she would scold you in return. but always in such a way that you could not possibly be angry with her ; she would mimic your step with her little naked feet, or the toss of your head, or the very curb of your mouth perhaps, while you were trying to terrify her. The little wretch !—everybody was tired to death of her in half an hour, and yet everybody was glad to see her again. Such was Abigail Paris, before Bridget Pope came to live in the house with her, but in the course of about half a year after that, she was so altered that her very playfellows twitted her with being " afeard o' Bridgee Pope." She began to be tidy in her dress, to comb her bright hair, to speak low, to keep her shoes on her feet, and her stockings from about her heels, and before a twelve-

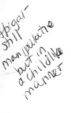

Abigal - still man/pulative but in a childlike manner

month was over, she left off wading in the snow, and
grew very fond of her book.

They were always together now, creeping about under the old beach-trees, or hunting for hazle-nuts, or
searching for sun-baked apples in the short thick grass,
or feeding the fish in the smooth clear sea—Bridget
poring over a story that she had picked up, nobody
knows where, and Abigail, whatever the story might be,
and although the water might stand in her eyes at the
time, always ready for a roll in the wet grass, a dip in
the salt wave, or a slide from the very top of the hay-
mow. They rambled about in the great woods together
on tip-toe, holding their breath and saying their prayers
at every step ; they lay down together and slept together on the very track of the wolf, or the she-bear ; and if
they heard a noise afar off, a howl or a war-whoop,
they crept in among the flowers of the solitary spot and
were safe, or hid themselves in the shadow of trees that
were spread out over the whole sky, or of shrubbery that
appeared to cover the whole earth—

> Where the wild grape hangs dropping in the shade,
> O'er unfledged minstrels that beneath are laid ;

Where the scarlet barberry glittered among the sharp
green leaves like threaded bunches of coral,—where at
every step the more brilliant ivory-plumbs or clustered
bunch-berries rattled among the withered herbage and
rolled about their feet like a handful of beads,—where
they delighted to go even while they were afraid to speak
above a whisper, and kept fast hold of each other's
hands, every step of the way. Such was their love,
such their companionship, such their behaviour while
oppressed with fear. They were never apart for a day,
till the time of our story ; they were together all day and
all night, going to sleep together and waking up togeth-

er, feeding out of the same cup, and sleeping in the same bed, year after year.

But just when the preacher was ready to believe that his Father above had not altogether deserted him—for he was ready to cry out with joy whenever he looked upon these dear children ; they were so good and so beautiful, and they loved each other so entirely ; just when there appeared to be no evil in his path, no shadow in his way to the grave, a most alarming change took place in their behavior to each other. He tried to find out the cause, but they avoided all inquiry. He talked with them together, he talked with them apart, he tried every means in his power to know the truth, but all to no purpose. They were afraid of each other, and that was all that either would say. Both were full of mischief and appeared to be possessed with a new temper. They were noisy and spiteful toward each other, and toward every body else. They were continually hiding away from each other in holes and corners, and if they were pursued and plucked forth to the light, they were always found occupied with mischief above their age. Instead of playing together as they were wont, or sitting together in peace, they would creep away under the tables and chairs and beds, and behave as if they were hunted by something which nobody else could see ; and they would lie there by the hour, snapping and snarling at each other, and at everybody that passed near. They had no longer the look of health, or of childhood, or of innocence. They were meagre and pale, and their eyes were fiery, and their fingers were skinny and sharp, and they delighted in devilish tricks and in outcries yet more devilish. They would play by themselves in the dead of the night, and shriek with a preternatural voice, and wake everybody with strange laughter—a sort of smothered giggle, which would appear to issue from the garret, or from the top of the house, while they were asleep, or pretending to be dead asleep in the great room below. They would break out all over in a fine sweat like the dew on a rose bush, and fall down as if they were struck to the heart with a knife, while they were on the way to meeting or school, or when the elders of the church were talking to them and every eye was fixed on their faces with pity or terror. They would grow pale as death in a moment, and seem to hear voices in the wind, and shake as with an ague while standing before a great fire, and look about on every side with such a piteous look for children, whenever it thundered or lightened, or whenever the sea roared, that the eyes of all who saw them would fill with tears. They would creep away backwards from each other on their hands and feet, or hide their faces in the lap of the female Indian Tituba, and if the preacher spoke to them, they would fall into a stupor, and awake with fearful cries and appear instantly covered all over with marks and spots like those which are left by pinching or bruising the flesh. They would be struck dumb while repeating the Lord's prayer, and all their features would be distorted with a savage and hateful expression.

The heads of the church were now called together, and a day of general fasting, humiliation and prayer was appointed, and after that, the best medical men of the whole country were consulted, the pious and the gifted, the interpreters of dreams, the soothsayers, and the prophets of the Lord, every man of power, and every woman of power,—but no relief was had, no cure, no hope of cure.

Matthew Paris now began to be afraid of his own child. She was no longer the hope of his heart, the joy of his old age, the live miniature of his buried wife. She

was an evil thing—she was what he had no courage to
think of, as he covered his old face and tore his white
hair with a grief that would not be rebuked nor appeased.
A new fear fell upon him, and his knees smote together,
and the hair of his flesh rose, and he saw a spirit, and
the spirit said to him look ! And he looked, and lo ! the
truth appeared to him ; for he saw neighbour after
neighbour flying from his path, and all the heads of the
church keeping aloof and whispering together in a low
voice. Then knew he that Bridget Pope and Abigail
Paris were bewitched.

A week passed over, a whole week, and every day and
every hour they grew worse and worse, and the solitude
in which he lived, more dreadful to him ; but just when
there appeared to be no hope left, no chance for escape,
just when he and the few that were still courageous
enough to speak with him, were beginning to despair,
and to wish for the speedy death of the little sufferers,
dear as they had been but a few weeks before to everybody that knew them, a discovery was made which threw
the whole country into a new paroxysm of terror. The
savages who had been for a great while in the habit of
going to the house of the preacher to eat and sleep " without money and without price," were now seen to keep
aloof and to be more than usually grave ; and yet when
they were told of the children's behaviour, they showed
no sort of surprise, but shook their heads with a smile,
and went their way, very much as if they were prepared
for it.

When the preacher heard this, he called up the two
Indians before him, and spoke to Tituba and prayed to
know why her people who for years had been in the habit
of lying before his hearth, and eating at his table, and
coming in and going out of his habitation at all hours of

the day and night, were no longer seen to approach his door.

"Tituppa no say—Tituppa no know," she replied.

But *as* she replied, the preacher saw her make a sign to Peter Wawpee, her Sagamore, who began to show his teeth as if he knew something more than he chose to tell ; but before the preacher could rebuke him as he deserved, or pursue the inquiry with Tituba, his daughter screamed out and fell upon her face and lay for a long while as if she were death-struck.

The preacher now bethought him of a new course, and after watching Tituba and Wawpee for several nights, became satisfied from what he saw, that she was a woman of diabolical power. A part of what he saw, he was afraid even to speak of ; but he declared on oath before the judges, that he had seen sights, and heard noises that took away his bodily strength, his hearing and his breath for a time; that for nearly five weeks no one of her tribe, nor of Wawpee's tribe had slept upon his hearth, or eaten of his bread, or lifted the latch of his door either by night or by day ; that notwithstanding this, the very night before, as he went by the grave-yard where his poor wife lay, he heard the whispering of a multitude ; that having no fear in such a place, he made a search ; and that after a long while he found his help Tituba concealed in the bushes, that he said nothing but went his way, satisfied in his own soul however that the voices he heard were the voices of her tribe ; and that after the moon rose he saw her employed with a great black Shadow on the rock of death, where as every body knew, sacrifices had been offered up in other days by another people to the god of the Pagan—the deity of the savage —employed in a way that made him shiver with fright where he stood ; for between her and the huge black shadow there lay what he knew to be the dead body of

his own dear child stretched out under the awful trees—
her image rather, for *she* was at home and abed and
asleep at the time. He would have spoken to it if he
could—for he saw what he believed to be the shape of
his wife ; he would have screamed for help if he could,
but he could not get his breath, and that was the last he
knew ; for when he came to himself he was lying in his
own bed, and Tituba was sitting by his side with a cup
of broth in her hand which he took care to throw away
the moment her back was turned ; for she was a creature of extraordinary art, and would have persuaded him
that he had never been out of his bed for the whole day.

The judges immediately issued a warrant for Tituba
and Wawpee, both of whom were hurried off to jail, and
after a few days of proper inquiry, by torture, she was
put upon trial for witchcraft. Being sorely pressed by
the word of the preacher and by the testimony of Bridget
Pope and Abigail Paris, who with two more afflicted
children (for the mischief had spread now in every quarter) charged her and Sarah Good with appearing to
them at all hours, and in all places, by day and by night,
when they were awake and when they were asleep, and
with tormenting their flesh. Tituba pleaded guilty and
confessed before the judges and the people that the poor
children spoke true, that she was indeed a witch, and
that, with several of her sister witches of great power—
among whom was mother Good, a miserable woman who
lived a great way off, nobody knew where—and passed the greater part of her time by the sea-side, nobody
knew how, she had been persuaded by the black man to
pursue and worry and vex them. But the words were
hardly out of her mouth before she herself was taken
with a fit, which lasted so long that the judges believed
her to be dead. She was lifted up and carried out into
the air ; but though she recovered her speech and her

strength in a little time, she was altered in her looks from that day to the day of her death.

But as to mother Good, when they brought her up for trial, she would neither confess to the charge nor pray the court for mercy ; but she stood up and mocked the jury and the people, and reproved the judges for hearkening to a body of accusers who were collected from all parts of the country, were of all ages, and swore to facts, which if they ever occurred at all, had occurred years and years before—facts which it would have been impossible for her to contradict, even though they had all been, as a large part of them obviously were, the growth of mistake or of superstitious dread. Her be- havior was full of courage during the trial ; and after the trial was over, and up to the last hour and last breath of her life, it was the same. *historically accurate*

You are a liar ! said she to a man who called her a witch to her teeth, and would have persuaded her to confess and live. You are a liar, as God is my judge, Mike ! I am no more a witch than you are a wizard, and you know it Mike, though you be so glib at prayer ; and if you take away my life, I tell you now that you and yours, and the people here, and the judges and the elders who are now thirsting for my blood shall rue the work of this day, forever and ever, in sackcloth and ash- es ; and I tell you further as Elizabeth Hutchinson told you, Ah ha ! . . . . . how do you like the sound of that name, Judges ? You begin to be afraid I see ; you are all quiet enough now ! . . . . But I say to you neverthe- less, and I say to you here, even here, with my last breath, as Mary Dyer said to you with her last breath, and as poor Elizabeth Hutchinson said to you with hers, if you take away my life, the wrath of God shall pursue you !—you and yours !—forever and ever ! Ye

individualism vs community *jeremiad*

Sarah Good—can't achieve this American dream—idealistic lifestyle

are wise men that I see, and mighty in faith, and ye
should be able with such faith to make the deep boil like
a pot, as they swore to you I did, to remove mountains,
yea to shake the whole earth by a word—mighty in faith
or how could you have swallowed the story of that
knife-blade, or the story of the sheet? Very wise are
you, and holy and fixed in your faith, or how could you
have borne with the speech of that bold man, who appeared to you in court, and stood face to face before
you, when you believed him to be afar off, or lying at
the bottom of the sea, and would not suffer you to take
away the life even of such a poor unhappy old creature
as I am, without reproving you as if he had authority
from the Judge of judges and the King of kings to stay
you in your faith!

Poor soul but I do pity thee! whispered a man
who stood near with a coiled rope in one hand and a
drawn sword in the other. It was the high-sheriff.

Her eyes filled and her voice faltered for the first
time, when she heard this, and she put forth her hand
with a smile, and assisted him in preparing the rope,
saying as the cart stopped under the large beam, Poor
soul indeed!—You are too soft-hearted for your office,
and of the two, you are more to be pitied than the poor
old woman you are a-going to choke.

Mighty in faith she continued, as the high-sheriff
drew forth a watch and held it up for her to see that she
had but a few moments to live. I address myself to
you, ye Judges of Israel! and to you ye teachers of
truth! Believe ye that a mortal woman of my age, with
a rope about her neck, hath power to prophesy? If ye
do, give ear to my speech and remember my words. For
death, ye shall have death! For blood, ye shall have
blood—blood on the earth! blood in the sky! blood in

the waters! Ye shall drink blood and breathe blood, you and yours, for the work of this day !

Woman, woman! we pray thee to forbear! cried a voice from afar off.

I shall not forbear, Cotton Mather—it is your voice that I hear. But for you and such as you, miserable men that ye are, we should now be happy and at peace one with another. I shall not forbear—why should I ? What have I done that I may not speak to the few that love me before we are parted by death ?

Be prepared woman—if you *will* die, for the clock is about to strike said another voice.

Be prepared, sayest thou ? William Phips, for I know the sound of thy voice too, thou hard-hearted miserable man ! Be prepared, sayest thou ? Behold—stretching forth her arms to the sky, and lifting herself up and speaking so that she was heard of the people on the house-tops afar off, Lo ! I am ready ! Be ye also ready, for now !—now !—even while I speak to you, he is preparing to reward both my accusers and my judges ——.

He !—who !

Who, brother Joseph ? said somebody in the crowd.

Why the Father of lies to be sure ! what a question for you to ask, after having been of the jury !

Thou scoffer !—

Paul ! Paul, beware !—

Hark—what's that ! Lord have mercy upon us !

The Lord have mercy upon us ! cried the people, giving way on every side, without knowing why, and looking toward the high-sea, and holding their breath.

Pho, pho, said the scoffer, a grey-haired man who stood leaning over his crutch with eyes full of pity and sorrow, pho, pho, the noise that you hear is only the noise of the tide.

Nay, nay, Elder Smith, nay, nay, said an associate or the speaker. If it is only the noise of the tide, why have we not heard it before ? and why do we not hear it now ? just now, when the witch is about to be—

True . . . true . . . , it may not be the Evil one, after all.

The Evil one, Joe Libby ! No, no ! it is God himself, our Father above ! cried the witch, with a loud voice, waving her arms upward, and fixing her eye upon a group of two or three individuals who stood aloof, decorated with the badges of authority.   Our Father above, I say ! The Governor of governors, and the Judge of judges ! . . . The cart began to move here . . . *He* will reward you for the work of this day ! He will refresh you with blood for it ! and you too Jerry Pope, and you too Micajah Noyes, and you too Job Smith, and you . . . . and you . . . . and you . . . .

Yea of a truth ! cried a woman who stood apart from the people with her hands locked and her eyes fixed upon the chief-judge. It was Rachel Dyer, the grandchild of Mary Dyer.   Yea of a truth ! for the Lord will not hold him guiltless that spilleth his brother's blood, or taketh his sister's life by the law—and her speech was followed by a shriek from every hill-top and every housetop, and from every tree and every rock within sight of the place, and the cart moved away, and the body of the poor old creature swung to and fro in the convulsions of death.

CHAPTER V.

It is not a little remarkable that within a few days after the death of Sarah Good, a part of her pretended prophecy, that which was directed by her to the man who called her a witch at the place of death, was verified upon him, letter by letter, as it were.

He was way-laid by a party of the Mohawks, and carried off to answer to the tribe for having reported of them that they ate the flesh of their captives.—It would appear that he had lived among them in his youth, and that he was perfectly acquainted with their habits and opinions and with their mode of warfare ; that he had been well treated by their chief, who let him go free at a time when he might lawfully have been put to death, according to the usages of the tribe, and that he could not possibly be mistaken about their eating the flesh of their prisoners. It would appear too, that he had been watched for, a long while before he was carried off; that his path had been beset hour after hour, and week after week, by three young warriors of the tribe, who might have shot him down, over and over again if they would, on the step of his own door, in the heart of a populous village, but they would not ; for they had sworn to trap their pray alive, and to bring it off with the hide and the hair on ; that after they had carried him to the territory of the Mohawks, they put him on trial for the charge face to face with a red accuser ; that they found him guilty, and that, with a bitter laugh, they ordered him to

eat of the flesh of a dead man that lay bleeding on the
earth before him ; that he looked up and saw the old
chief who had been his father when he belonged to the
tribe, and that hoping to appease the haughty savage,
he took some of the detestable food into his mouth, and
that instantly—instantly—before he could utter a prayer,
they fell upon him with clubs and beat him to death.

Her prophecy therefore did appear to the people to
be accomplished ; for had she not said to this very man,
that for the work of that day, " He should breathe blood
and eat blood ?"

Before a week had passed over, the story of death,
and the speech of the prophetess took a new shape, and
a variety of circumstances which occurred at the trial,
and which were disregarded at the time, were now
thought of by the very judges of the land with a secret
awe ; circumstances that are now to be detailed, for they
were the true cause of what will not be forgotten for
ages in that part of the world....the catastrophe of our
story.

At the trial of Sarah Good, while her face was turned
away from her accuser, one of the afflicted gave a loud
scream, and gasping for breath, fell upon the floor at
the feet of the judges, and lay there as if she had been
struck down by the weight of no mortal arm ; and being
lifted up, she swore that she had been stabbed with a
knife by the shape of Sarah Good, while Sarah Good
herself was pretending to be at prayer on the other side
of the house ; and for proof, she put her hand into her
bosom and drew forth the blade of a penknife which was
bloody, and which upon her oath, she declared to have
been left sticking in her flesh a moment before, by the
shape of Sarah Good.

The Judges were thunderstruck. The people were
mute with terror, and the wretched woman herself cov-

ered her face with her hands ; for she knew that if she
looked upon the sufferers, they would shriek out, and
foam at the mouth, and go into fits, and lie as if they
were dead for a while; and that she would be command-
ded by the judges to go up to them and lay her hands
upon their bodies without speaking or looking at them,
end that on her doing so, they would be sure to revive,
and start up, and speak of what they had seen or suffered while they were in what they called their agony.

The jury were already on their way out for consultation—they could not agree, it appeared ; but when they
saw this, they stopped at the door, and came back one
by one to the jury box, and stood looking at each other,
and at the judges, and at the poor old woman, as if they
no longer thought it necessary to withdraw even for
form sake, afraid as they all were of doing that, in a case
of life and death, for which they might one day or other
be sorry.   A shadow was upon every visage of the twelve
—the shadow of death ; a look in the eyes of everybody
there, a gravity and a paleness, which when the poor
prisoner saw, she started up with a low cry—a cry of
reproach—a cry of despair—and stood with her hands
locked, and her mouth quivering, and her lips apart before God—lips white with fear, though not with the
fear of death ; and looked about her on every side, as if
she had no longer a hope left—no hope from the jury, no
hope from the multitude ; nay as if while she had no
longer a hope, she had no longer a desire to live.

There was a dead preternatural quiet in the house—
not a breath could be heard now, not a breath nor a murmur ; and lo ! the aged foreman of the jury stood forth
and laid his hands upon the Book of the Law, and lifted
up his eyes and prepared to utter the verdict of death ;
but before he could speak so as to be heard, for his

heart was over-charged with sorrow, a tumult arose
afar off like the noise of the wind in the great woods of
America; or a heavy swell on the sea-shore, when a surge
after surge rolls booming in from the secret reservoir of
waters, like the tide of a new deluge.   Voices drew near
with a portentous hoof-clatter from every side—east,
west, north and south, so that the people were mute with
awe; and as the dread clamor approached and grew
louder and louder every moment, they crowded together
and held their breath, they and the judges and the
preachers and the magistrates, every man persuaded in
his own soul that a rescue was nigh.   At last a smoth-
ed war-whoop was heard, and then a sweet cheerful
noise like the laugh of a young child high up in the air—
and then a few words in the accent of authority, and a
bustle outside of the door, which gave way as if it were
spurned with a powerful foot; and a stranger appeared
in the shadow of the huge trees that over-hung the door-
way like a summer cloud—a low, square-built swarthy
man with a heavy tread, and a bright fierce look, tear-
ing his way through the crowd like a giant of old, and
leading a beautiful boy by the hand.

What, ho! cried he to the chief judge, walking up to
him, and standing before him, and speaking to him with
a loud clear voice.   What ho! captain Robert Sewall!
why do ye this thing? What ho, there! addressing himself to the foreman of the jury—why speed ye so to the
work of death? and you, master Bailey! and you governor Phips! and you doctor Mather, what business
have ye here? And you ye judges, who are about to become the judges of life and death, how dare ye! Who
gave you power to measure and weigh such mystery? Are
ye gifted men—all of you—every man of you—specially
gifted from above? Are you Thomas Fisk—with your

white hair blowing about your agitated mouth and your
dim eyes, are *you* able to see your way clear, that you
have the courage to pronounce a verdict of death on your
aged sister who stands there ! And you Josh Carter, se-
nior ! and you major Zach Trip ! and you Job Saltonstall ! Who are ye and what are ye, men of war, that ye
are able to see spirits, or that ye should become what ye
are—the judges of our afflicted people ! And who are we,
and what were our fathers, I beseech you, that we should
be base enough to abide upon earth but by your leave !

The judges looked at each other in consternation.

Who is it ! . . . . who is it ! cried the people as they
rushed forward and gathered about him and tried to get
a sight of his face. Who *can* it be !

Burroughs—Bur—Bur—Burroughs, I *do* believe !
whispered a man who stood at his elbow, but he spoke
as if he did not feel very sure of what he said.

Not George Burroughs, hey ?

I'd take my oath of it neighbour Joe, my Bible-oath
of it, leaning forward as far as he could reach with safety, and shading his eyes with his large bony hand—

Well, I *do* say ! whispered another.

I see the scar !—as I live, I do ! cried another, peering
over the heads of the multitude, as they rocked to the
heavy pressure of the intruder.

But how altered he is ! . . . . and how old he looks ! . . . .
—and shorter than ever ! muttered several more.

Silence there ! cried the chief judge—a militia-cap-
tain, it is to be observed, and of course not altogether so
lawyer-like as a judge of our day would be.

Silence there ! echoed the High Sheriff.

Never see nobody so altered afore, continued one of
the crowd, with his eye fixed on the judge—I *will* say
that much, afore I stop, Mr. Sheriff Berry, an' (dropping

his voice) if you dont like it, you may lump it . . . . who
cares for you ?

Well—an' who cares for you, if you come to that.

Officer of the court, how now ! cried the chief judge
in a very loud sharp voice.

Here I be mister judge—I ain't deef.

Take that man away.

I say . . . . you ! cried the High-Sheriff, getting up and
fetching the man a rap over the head with his white-oak
staff . . . . do you hear that.?

Hear what ?

What Mr. judge Sewall says.

I don't care for Mr. judge Sewall, nor you nyther.

Away with him Sir ! out with him ! are we to suffer
this outrage on the dignity of the court . . . . in the House
of the Lord—away with him, Sir.

Here's the devil to pay and no pitch hot—whispered
a sailor-looking fellow, in a red baize shirt.

An' there's thirteen-pence for you to pay, Mr. Outlandishman, said a little neighbour, whose duty it was
to watch for offenders in a small way, and fine them for
swearing, drinking, or kissing their wives on the sabbath
day.

What for ?

Why, for that air oath o'yourn.

What oath ?

Why, you said here's the devil to pay !

Ha—ha—ha—and there's thirteen-pence for *you* to
pay.

You be darned !

An' there's thirteen-pence more for you, my lad—ha
—ha—ha—

The officer now drew near the individual he was ordered to remove ; but he did so as if a little afraid of his

man—who stood up face to face with the judge, and planted his foot as if he knew of no power on earth able to move him, declaring he would'nt budge a peg, now they'd come to that; for the house they were in had been paid for out of the people's money, and he'd as much right there as they had ; but havin' said what he had to say on the subject, and bein' pooty considr'ble easy on that score now, if they'd mind their business he'd mind his ; and if *they'd* behave, he would.

Very well, said the chief judge, who knew the man to be a soldier of tried bravery. Very well! yon may stay where you are ; I thought we should bring you to your senses, neighbour Joe.

Here the stranger broke away from the crowd and leaped upon the platform, and setting his teeth and smiting the floor with a heavy iron-shod staff, he asked the judges why they did not enforce the order ? why with courage to take away life, they had no courage to defend their authority. How dare ye forgive this man ! said he ; how dare you bandy words with such a fellow ! What if you *have* been to the war with him ? Have ye not become the judges of the land ? With hardihood enough to undertake the awful representation of majesty, have ye not enough to secure that majesty from outrage ?

We know our own duty sir.

No such thing sir ! you do not—if you do, it shall be the worse for you. You are afraid of that man—

Afraid sir !—Who are you !

Yes—you are afraid of that man. If you are not, why allow him to disturb the gravity of such an hour as this ? Know your own power—Bid the High-sheriff take him into custody.

A laugh here from the sturdy yeoman, who having paid his quota for building the house, and fought his share of the fight with the Indians, felt as free as the best of them.

Speak but the word, Sirs, and I will do what I see your officer hath not valor enough to do. Speak but the word, Sirs! and I that know your power, will obey it, (uplifting the staff as he spoke, while the fire flashed from his eyes, and the crowd gave way on every side as if it were the tomahawk or the bow of a savage)—speak but the word I say! and I will strike him to the earth!

George Burroughs—I pray thee! said a female, who sat in a dark part of the house with her head so muffled up that nobody could see her face—I pray thee, George! do not strike thy brother in wrath.

Speak but the word I say, and lo! I will stretch him at your feet, if he refuse to obey me, whatever may be the peril to me or mine.

I should like to see you do it, said the man. I care as little for you, my boy,—throwing off his outer-garb as he spoke, and preparing for a trial of strength on the spot—as little for you, George Burroughs, if that *is* your name, as I do for your master.

Will you not speak! You see how afraid of him they all are, judges; you know how long he has braved your authority—being a soldier forsooth. Speak, if ye are wise; for if ye do not—

George! George!....No, no, George! said somebody at his elbow, with a timid voice, that appeared to belong to a child.

The uplifted staff dropped from his hand.

CHAPTER VI.

Here the venerable Increase Mather stood up, and after a short speech to the people and a few words to the court, he begged to know if the individual he saw before him was indeed the George Burroughs who had formerly been a servant of God.

Formerly, sir ! I am so now, I hope.

The other sat down, with a look of inquietude. You appear to be much perplexed about me. You appear even to doubt the truth of what I say. Surely....surely ....there are some here that know me. I know you, Doctor Mather, and you, Sir William Phips, and you.... and you....and you; addresssing himself to many that stood near—it is but the other day that we were associated together ; and some of us in the church, and others in the ministry; it is but the other day that—

Here the Judges began to whisper together.

—That you knew me as well as I knew you. Can I be so changed in a few short years ? They have been years of sorrow to be sure, of uninterrupted sorrow, of trial and suffering, warfare and wo ; but I did not suppose they had so changed me, as to make it over-hard for my very brothers in the church to know me—

It is Burroughs, I do believe, said another of the judges.—But who is that boy with you, and by what authority are you abroad again, or alive, I might say, if you are the George Burroughs that we knew ?

By what authority, Judges of Israel ! By authority

of the Strong Man who broke loose when the spirit of
the Lord was upon him ! By authority of one that hath
plucked me up out of the sea, by the hair of my head,
breathed into my nostrils the breath of new life, and endowed me with great power—

The people drew back.

You have betrayed me ; I will be a hostage for you
no longer.

Betrayed you !

Yes ! and ye would have betrayed me to death, if I
had not been prepared for your treachery—

The man is mad, brother Sewall.

You have broken the treaty I stood pledged for ; you
have not been at peace for a day. You do not keep
your faith. We do keep ours. You are churchmen...
we are savages ; we I say, for you made me ashamed
years and years ago of my relationship to the white
man ; years and years ago ! and you are now in a fair
way to make me the mortal and perpetual foe of the
white man. The brave Iroquois are now ready for battle with you. War they find to be better than peace
with such as you—

Who is that boy ?

Ask him. Behold his beauty. Set him face to face,
if you dare, with the girl that spoke to the knife just
now.

And wherefore ? said one of the jury.

Wherefore, Jacob Elliot—wherefore ! Stay you in
that box, and watch the boy, and hear what he has to
say, and you shall be satisfied of the wherefore.

Be quick Sir. We have no time to lose—

No time to lose—How dare ye ! Is there indeed
such power with you ; such mighty power....and you not
afraid in the exercise of it ! No time to lose ! Hereafter, when you are upon your death-bed, when every

moment of your life is numbered as every moment of
her life is now....the poor creature that stands there,
what will you say if the words of that very speech ring
in your ears ? Believe me—there is no such hurry. It
will be time enough to-morrow, judges, a week hence or
a whole year to shed the blood of a miserable woman
for witchcraft. For witchcraft ! alas for the credulity
of man ! alas for the very nature of man!

Master Burroughs ! murmured a compassionate-look-
ing old man, reaching over to lay his hand on his arm,
as if to stop him, and shaking his head as he spoke.

Oh but I do pity you ; sages though you are—continued Burroughs, without regarding the interposition.—
For witchcraft ! I wonder how you are able to keep
your countenances ! Do you not perceive that mother
Good, as they call her, cannot be a witch ?

How so ? asked the judge.

Would she abide your search, your trial, your judgment, if she had power to escape ?

Assuredly not brother, answered a man, who rose up
as he spoke as if ready to dispute before the people, if
permitted by the judges . . . . assuredly not, brother, if
she had power to escape. We agree with you there.
But we know that a period must arrive when the power
that is paid for with the soul, the power of witchcraft
and sorcery shall be withdrawn. We read of this and
we believe it ; and I might say that we see the proof
now before us—

Brother, I marvel at you—

—If the woman be unexpectedly deserted by the
Father of lies, and if we pursue our advantage now, we
may be able both to succeed with her and overthrow him,
and thereby (lowering his voice and stooping toward
Burroughs) and thereby deter a multitude more from
entering into the league of death.

Speak low .... lower—much lower, deacon Darby, or we shall be no match for the Father of lies : If he should happen to overhear you, the game is up, said another.

For shame, Elder Smith—

For shame ! cried Burroughs. Why rebuke his levity, when if we are to put faith in what you say, ye are preparing to over-reach the Evil One himself ? You must play a sure game, (for it *is* a game) if you hope to convict him of treachery in a case, where according to what you believe, his character is at stake.

Brother Burroughs !

Brother Willard !

Forbear, I beseech you.

I shall not forbear. If the woman is a witch, how do you hope to surprise her ? .... to entrap her ? .... to convict her ? And if she is not a witch, how can she hope to go free ? None but a witch could escape your toils.

Ah Sir .... Sir ! O, Mr. Burroughs ! cried the poor woman. There you have spoken the truth sir ; there you have said just what I wanted to say. I knew it .... I felt it .... I knew that if I was guilty it would be better for me, than to be what you know me to be, and what your dead wife knew me to be, and both of your dead wives, for I knew them both—a broken-hearted poor old woman. God forever bless you Sir ! whatever may become of me—however this may end, God forever bless you, Sir !

Be of good faith Sarah. He whom you serve will be nigh to you and deliver you.

Oh Sir—Sir—Do not talk so. They misunderstand you —they are whispering together—it will be the death of me ; and hereafter, it may perhaps be a trouble to you. Speak out, I beseech you ! Say to them whom it

is that you mean, whom it is that I serve, and who it is
that will be nigh to me and deliver me.

Who it is, poor heart! why whom should it be but
our Father above! our Lord and our God, Sarah?
Have thou courage, and be of good cheer, and put all
thy trust in him, for he hath power to deliver thee.

I have—I do—I am no longer afraid of death sir.
If they put me to death now—I do not wish to live—I
am tired and sick of life, and I have been so ever since
dear boy and his poor father—I told them how it would
be if they went away when the moon was at the full—
they were shipwrecked on the shore just underneath the
window of my chamber—if they put me to death
now, I shall die satisfied, for I shall not go to my grave
now, as I thought I should before you came, without a
word or a look of pity, nor any thing to make me com-
fortable.

Judges—may the boy speak?

Speak? speak? to be sure he may, muttered old Mr.
Wait Winthrop, addressing himself to a preacher who
sat near with a large Bible outspread upon his knees.
What say you? what say you Brother Willard, what
says the Book?—no harm there, I hope; what can he
have to say though, (wiping his eyes) what *can* such a
lad have to say? What say you major Gidney; what
say you—(half sobbing) dreadful affair this, dreadful
affair; what can he possibly have to say?

Not much, I am afraid, replied Burroughs, not very
much; but enough I hope and believe, to shake your
trust in the chief accuser. Robert Eveleth—here—this
way—shall the boy be sworn, Sir?

Sworn—sworn?—to be sure—why not? very odd
though—very—*very*—swear the boy—very odd, I confess—never saw a likelier boy of his age—how old is he?

Thirteen Sir—

Very—very—of his height, I should say—what can
he know of the matter though? what can such a boy
know of—of—however—we shall see—is the boy sworn?
—there, there—

The boy stepped forth as the kind-hearted old man—
too kind-hearted for a judge—concluded his perplexing
soliloquy, one part of which was given out with a very
decided air, while another was uttered with a look of
pitiable indecision—stepped forth and lifted up his right
hand according to the law of that people, with his large
grey eyes lighted up and his fine yellow hair blowing
about his head like a glory, and swore by the Everlasting
God, the Searcher of Hearts, to speak the truth.

Every eye was riveted upon him, for he stood high
upon a sort of stage, in full view of everybody, and face
to face to all who had sworn to the spectre-knife, and
his beauty was terrible.

Stand back, stand back . . . . what does that child do
there? said another of the judges, pointing to a poor
little creature with a pale anxious face and very black
hair, who had crept close up to the side of Robert Eveleth, and sat there with her eyes lifted to his, and her
sweet lips apart, as if she were holding her breath.

Why, what are you afeard of now, Bridgee Pope? said
another voice. Get away from the boy's feet, will you
. . . . why don't you move? . . . . do you hear me?

No . . . . I do not, she replied.

You do not! what did you answer me for, if you didn't
hear me?

Why . . . . why . . . . don't you see the poor little
thing's bewitched? whispered a bystander.

Very, true . . . . very true . . . . let her be, therefore, let
her stay where she is.

Poor babe! she don't hear a word you say.

O, but she dooze, though, said the boy, stooping down

and smoothing her thick hair with both hands ; I know
her of old, I know her better than you do ; she hears
every word you say .... don't you be afeard, Bridgee
Pope ; *I'm* not a goin' to be afeard of the Old Boy himself ....

Why Robert Eveleth ! was the reply.

Well, Robert Eveleth, what have you to say ? asked
the chief-judge.

The boy stood up in reply, and threw back his head
with a brave air, and set his foot, and fixed his eye on
the judge, and related what he knew of the knife. He
had broken it a few days before, he said, while he and
the witness were playing together ; he threw away a part
of the blade, which he saw her pick up, and when he
asked her what she wanted of it, she wouldn't say ....
but he knew her well, and being jest outside o' the door
when he heard her screech, and saw her pull a piece of
the broken blade out of her flesh and hold it up to the
jury, and say how the shape of old mother Good, who
was over tother side o' the house at the time, had stabbed her with it, he guessed how the judge would like to
see the tother part o' the knife, and hear what he had to
say for himself, but he couldn't get near enough to speak
to nobody, and so he thought he'd run off to the school-
house, where he had left the handle o' the knife, an' try
to get a mouthful o' fresh air ; and so .... and so ....
arter he'd got the handle, sure enough, who should he
see but that are man there (pointing to Burroughs)
stavin' away on a great black horse with a club—that
very club he had now.—" Whereupon," added the boy,
" here's tother part o' the knife, judge—I say .... you
.... Mr. judge .... here's tother part o' the knife ....
an' so he stopped me an' axed me where the plague I
was runnin to ; an' so I up an' tells him all I know about
the knife, an' so, an' so, an' so, that air feller, what

dooze he do, but he jounces me up on that air plaguy
crupper and fetches me back here full split, you see, and
rides over everything, and makes everybody get out o'
the way, an' *will* make me tell the story whether or no
.... and as for the knife now, if you put them are two
pieces together, you'll see how they match .... O, you
needn't be makin' mouths at me, Anne Putnam! nor you
nyther, Marey Lewis! you are no great shakes, nyther
on you, and I ain't afeard o' nyther on you, though the
grown people be ; you wont make *me* out a witch in a
hurry, I guess.

Boy .... boy .... how came you by that knife ?

How came I by that knife ? Ax Bridgy Pope ; she
knows the knife well enough, too—I guess—don't you,
Bridgy ?

I guess I do, Robert Eveleth, whispered the child, the
tears running down her cheeks, and every breath a sob.

You've seen it afore, may be ?

That I have, Robert Eveleth ; but I never expected to
see .... to see .... to see it again .... alive .... nor you
neither.

And why not, pray ? said one of the judges.

Why not, Mr. Major ! why, ye see 'tis a bit of a keep-
sake she gin me, jest afore we started off on that are
vyage arter the goold.

The voyage when they were all cast away, sir ....
after they'd fished up the gold, sir ....

Ah, but the goold was safe then, Bridgy—

But I knew how 'twould be Sir, said the poor girl
turning to the judge with a convulsive sob, and pushing
away the hair from her face and trying to get up, I never expected to see Robert Eveleth again Sir—I said so
too—nor the knife either—I said so before they went
away ——.

So she did Mr. Judge, that's a fact; she told me so down by the beach there, just by that big tree that grows over the top o'the new school-house there—You know the one I mean—that one what hangs over the edge o'the hill just as if 'twas a-goin' to fall into the water—she heard poor mother Good say as much when her Billy would go to sea whether or no, at the full o'the moon ——.

Ah!

That she did, long afore we got the ship off.

Possible!

Ay, to be sure an' why not?—She had a bit of a dream ye see—such a dream too! such a beautiful dream you never heard—about the lumps of goold, and the joes, and the jewels, and the women o'the sea, and about a—I say, Mr. Judge, what if you ax her to tell it over now—I dare say she would; would'n't you Bridgy? You know it all now, don't you Bridgy?

No, no Robert—no, no; it's all gone out o'my head now.

No matter for the dream, boy, said a judge who was comparing the parts of the blade together—no matter for the dream—these are undoubtedly—look here brother, look—look—most undoubtedly parts of the same blade.

Of a truth?

Of a truth, say you?

Yea verily, of a truth; pass the knife there—pass the knife. Be of good cheer woman of sorrow ——.

Brother! brother! ——.

Well brother, what's to pay now?

Perhaps it may be well brother—*perhaps* I say, to have the judgment of the whole court before we bid the prisoner be of good cheer.

How wonderful are thy ways, O Lord! whispered

Elder Smith, as they took the parts of the blade for him to look at.

Very true brother—very true—but who knows how the affair may turn out after all ?

Pooh—pooh !—if you talk in that way the affair is all up; for whatever should happen, you would believe it a trick of the father of lies—I dare say now —.

The knife speaks for itself, said a judge.

Very true brother—very true. But he who had power to strive with Aaron the High Priest, and power to raise the dead before Saul, and power to work prodigies of old, may not lack power to do this—and more, much more than this—for the help of them that serve him in our day, and for the overthrow of the righteous ——.

Pooh, pooh Nathan, pooh, pooh—there's no escape for any body now ; your devil-at-a-pinch were enough to hang the best of us.

Thirteen pence for you, said the little man at the desk.

Here a consultation was held by the judges and the elders which continued for half the day—the incredible issue may be told in few words. The boy, Robert Eveleth, was treated with favor ; the witness being a large girl was rebuked for the lie instead of being whipped ; the preacher Burroughs from that day forth was regarded with unspeakable terror, and the poor old woman—she was put to death in due course of law.

CHAPTER VII.

Meanwhile other charges grew up, and there was a dread everywhere throughout the whole country, a deep fear in the hearts and a heavy mysterious fear in the blood of men. The judges were in array against the people, and the people against each other; and the number of the afflicted increased every day and every hour, and they were sent for from all parts of the Colony. Fasting and prayer preceded their steps, and whithersoever they went, witches and wizards were sure to be discovered. A native theologian, a very pious and very learned writer of that day, was employed by the authorities of New England to draw up a detailed account of what he himself was an eye witness of ; and he says of the unhappy creatures who appeared to be bewitched, all of whom he knew, and most of whom he saw every day of his life, that when the fit was on, they were distorted and convulsed in every limb, that they were pinched black and blue by invisible fingers, that pins were stuck into their flesh by invisible hands, that they were scalded in their sleep as with boiling water and blistered as with fire, that one of the afflicted was beset by a spectre with a spindle that nobody else could see, till in her agony she snatched it away from the shape, when it became instantly visible to everybody in the room with a quick flash, that another was haunted by a shape clothed in a white sheet which none but the afflicted herself was able to see till she tore a piece of it away, whereupon it grew

visible to others about her, (it was of this particular story that Sarah Good spoke just before she was turned off)
that they were pursued night and day by withered hands
—little outstretched groping hands with no bodies nor
arms to them, that cups of blue fire and white smoke of
a grateful smell, were offered them to drink while they
were in bed, of which, if they tasted ever so little, as they
would sometimes in their fright and hurry, their bodies
would swell up and their flesh would grow livid, much
as if they had been bit by a rattle snake, that burning
rags were forced into their mouths or under their arm-
pits, leaving sores that no medicine would cure, that
some were branded as with a hot iron, so that very deep
marks were left upon their foreheads for life, that the
spectres generally personated such as were known to
the afflicted, and that whenever they did so, if the shape
or spectre was hurt by the afflicted, the person represented by the shape was sure to be hurt in the same way,
that, for example, one of the afflicted having charged a
woman of Beverly, Dorcas Hoare, with tormenting her,
and immediately afterwards, pointing to a far part of the
room, cried out, there !—there ! there she goes now !
a man who stood near, drew his rapier and struck at the
wall, whereupon the accuser told the court he had given
the shape a scratch over the right eye ; and that Dorcas
Hoare being apprehended a few days thereafter, it was
found that she had a mark over the right eye, which
after a while she confessed had been given her by the
rapier ; that if the accused threw a look at the witnesses,
the latter, though their eyes were turned another way,
would know it, and fall into a trance, out of which they
would recover only at the touch of the accused, that
oftentimes the flesh of the afflicted was bitten with a peculiar set of teeth corresponding precisely with the teeth
of the accused, whether few or many, large or small,

broken or regular, and that after a while, the afflicted were often able to see the shapes that tormented them, and among the rest a swarthy devil of a diminutive stature, with fierce bright eyes, who carried a book in which he kept urging them to write, whereby they would have submitted themselves to the power and authority of another Black Shape, with which, if they were to be believed on their oaths, two or three of their number had slept.

In reply to these reputed facts however, which appear in the grave elaborate chronicles of the church, and are fortified by other facts which were testified to about the same time, in the mother country, we have the word of George Burroughs, a minister of God, who met the accusers at the time, and stood up to them face to face, and denied the truth of their charges, and braved the whole power of them that others were so afraid of.

Man! man! away with her to the place of death! cried he to the chief judge, on hearing a beautiful woman with a babe at her breast, a wife and a mother acknowledge that she had lain with Beelzebub. Away with her! why do you let her live! why permit her to profane the House of the Lord, where the righteous are now gathered together, as ye believe? why do ye spare the few that confess—would ye bribe them to live? Would ye teach them to swear away the lives and characters of all whom they are afraid of? and thus to preserve their own? Look there!—that is her child—her only child—the babe that you see there in the lap of that aged woman—she has no other hope in this world, nothing to love, nothing to care for but that babe, the man-child of her beauty. Ye are fathers!—look at her streaming eyes, at her locked hands, at her pale quivering mouth, at her dishevelled hair—can you wonder now at anything she says to save her boy—for if she dies, he dies ? A wife and a mother ! a broken-hearted wife and a young mother accused of what, if she did not speak as you have now made her speak, would separate her and her baby forever and ever !

Would you have us put her to death? asked one of the judges. You appear to argue in a strange way. What is your motive ?—What your hope ?—What would you have us do ? suffer them to escape who will not confess, and put all to death who do ?

Even so.

Why—if you were in league with the Evil One yourself brother George, I do not well see how you could hit upon a method more advantageous for him.

Hear me—I would rather die myself, unfitted as I am for death, die by the rope, while striving to stay the mischief-makers in their headlong career, than be the cause of death to such a woman as that, pleading before you though she be, with perjury ; because of a truth she is pleading, not so much *against* life as *for* life, not so much against the poor old creature whom she accuses of leading her astray, as for the babe that you see there; for that boy and for its mother who is quite sure that if she die, the boy will die—I say that which is true, fathers! and yet I swear to you by the—

Thirteen-pence to you, brother B. for that !

—By the God of Abraham, that if her life—

Thirteen-pence more—faith !

The same to you—said the outlandishman. Sharp work, hey ?

Fool—fool—if it depended upon me I say, her life and that of her boy, I would order them both to the scaffold ! Ye are amazed at what you hear ; ye look at each other in dismay ; ye wonder how it is that a mortal man hath courage to speak as I speak. And yet—hear me ! Fathers of New-England, hear me ! beautiful as the boy is, and beautiful as the mother is, I would put the mark

of death upon her forehead, even though his death were
certain to follow, because if I did so, I should be sure
that a stop would be put forever to such horrible stories. —*lying to*
be free

I thought so, said major Gidney—I thought so, by my
troth, leaning over the seat and speaking in a whisper to
judge Saltanstall, who shook his head with a mysterious
air, and said—nothing.

Ye would save by her death, O, ye know not how much
of human life! — *Save her in afterlife by death*

Brother Burroughs!

Brother Willard!—what is there to shock you in what
I say? These poor people who are driven by you to
perjury, made to confess by your absurd law, will they
stop with confession? Their lives are at stake—will they
not be driven to accuse? Will they not endeavor to make
all sure?—to fortify their stories by charging the innocent, or those of whom they are afraid? Will they stop
where you would have them stop? Will they not rather
come to believe that which they hear, and that of which
they are afraid?—to believe each other, even while they
know that what they themselves do swear is untrue?—
May they not strive to anticipate each other, to show
their zeal or the sincerity of their faith?—And may they
not, by and by—I pray you to consider this—may they
not hereafter charge the living and the mighty as they
have hitherto charged the dead, and the poor, and the
weak?

Well—

Well!

Yes—well!—what more have you to say? → *witchcraft*
accusation

What more! why, if need be, much more! You drive
people to confession, I say—you drive them to it, step
by step, as with a scourge of iron. Their lives are at
stake, I *will* say—yet more—I mean to say much more now;
now that you will provoke me to it. I say now that

you—you—ye judges of the land !—*you* are the cause of
all that we suffer! The accused are obliged to accuse.
They have no other hope. They lie—and you know it,
or should know it—and you know, as well as I do, that
they have no other hope, no other chance of escape. All
that have hitherto confessed are alive now. All that
have denied your charges, all that have withstood your
mighty temptation—they are all in the grave—all—all—

Brother—we have read in the Scriptures of Truth,
or at least I have, that of old, a woman had power to
raise the dead. If she was upon her trial now, would
you not receive her confession? I wait your reply.

Receive it, governor Phips! no—no—not without
proof that she had such power.

Proof—how ?

How ! Ye should command her to raise the dead for
proof—to raise the dead in your presence. You are
consulting together ; I see that you pity me. Nevertheless, I say again, that if these people are what they say
they are, they should be made to prove it by such awful
and irresistible proof—ah !—what are ye afraid of,
judges?

We are not afraid.

Ye are afraid—ye are—and of that wretched old
woman there !

What if we call for the proof now—will you endure
it ?

Endure it! Yes—whatever it may be. Speak to
her. Bid her do her worst—I have no fear—you are
quaking with fear. I defy the Power of Darkness ;
you would appear to tremble before it. And here I set
my foot—and here I call for the proof! Are they indeed
witches ?—what can be easier than to overthrow such
an adversary as I am ? Why do ye look at me as if I were
mad—you are prepared to see me drop down perhaps,

or to cry out, or to give up the ghost? Why do ye shake your heads at me? What have I to fear? And why is it I beseech you, that *you* are not moved by the evil-eye of that poor woman? Why is it, I pray you, fathers and judges, that they alone who bear witness against her are troubled by her look?

Brother Sewall, said one of the judges who had been brought up to the law; Master Burroughs, I take it, is not of counsel for the prisoner at the bar?

Assuredly not, brother.

Nor is he himself under the charge?

The remark is proper, said Burroughs. I am aware of all you would say. I have no right perhaps to open my mouth—

No right, perhaps?—no *right* brother B., said Winthrop—no right, we believe?—but—if the prosecutors will suffer it?—why, why—we have no objection, I suppose—I am sure—have we brother G.?

None at all. What say you Mr. Attorney-general?

Say Sir! What do I say Sir! why Sir, I say Sir, that such a thing was never heard of before! and I say Sir, that it is against all rule Sir! If the accused require counsel, the court have power to assign her suitable counsel—such counsel to be of the law, Sir!—and being of the law Sir, he would have no right Sir, you understand Sir,—no right Sir—to address the jury, Sir —as you did the other day Sir—in Rex versus Good, Sir, —none at all Sir!

Indeed—what may such counsel do then?

Do Sir! do!—why Sir, he may cross-examine the witnesses.

Really!

To be sure he may Sir! and what is more, he may argue points of law to the court if need be.

Indeed!

Yes—but only points of law.

The court have power to grant such leave, hey ?

Yes, that we have, said a judge. You may speak us a speech now, if you will ; but I would have you confine yourself to the charge.—

Here the prosecutor stood up, and saying he had made out his case, prayed the direction of the court—

No, no, excuse me, said Burroughs ; no, no, you have taught me how to proceed Sir, and I shall undertake for the wretched woman, whatever may be thought or said by the man of the law.

Proceed Mr. Burroughs—you are at liberty to proceed.

Well Martha, said Burroughs—I am to be your counsel now. What have you to say for yourself ?

The lawyers interchanged a sneer with each other.

Me—nothin' at all, Sir.

Have you nobody here to speak for you ?

For me !—Lord bless you, no ! Nobody cares for poor Martha.

No witnesses ?

Witnesses !—no indeed, but if you want witnesses, there's a power of witnesses.

Where ?—

There—there by the box there—

Poor Martha ! You do not understand me ; the witnesses you see there belong to the other side.

Well, what if they do ?

Have you no witnesses of your own, pray ?

Of my own ! Lord you—there now—don't be cross with me. How should poor Martha know—they never told me ;—what are they good for ?

But is there nobody here acquainted with you ?

And if there was, what would that prove ? said a man of the law.

My stars, no ! them that know'd me know'd enough to keep away, when they lugged me off to jail.

And so there's nobody here to say a kind word for you, if your life depended on it ?

No Sir—nobody at all—nobody cares for Martha. Gracious God—what unspeakable simplicity !

O, I forgot Sir, I forgot ! cried Martha, leaning over the bar and clapping her hands with a cry of childish joy. I did see neighbor Joe Trip, t'other day, and I told him he ought to stick by me—

Well where is he—what did he say ?

Why he said he'd rather not, if 'twas all the same to me.

He'd rather not—where does he live ?

And I spoke to three more, said a bystander, but they wouldn't come so fur, some was afeared, and some wouldn't take the trouble.

Ah ! is that you, Jeremiah ?—how d'ye do, how d'ye do ?—all well I hope at your house ?—an' so they wouldn't come, would they ?—I wish they would though, for I'm tired o' stayin' here ; I'd do as much for them—

Hear you that judges ! They would not come to testify in a matter of life and death. What are their names ? —where do they live ?—they shall be made to come.

You'll excuse me, said the prosecutor. You are the day after the fair ; it's too late now.

Too late ! I appeal to the judges—too late !—would you persuade me Sir, that it is ever too late for mercy, while there is yet room for mercy ? I speak to the judges—I pray them to make use of their power, and to have these people who keep away at such a time brought hither by force.

The court have no such power, said the Attorney-General.

How Sir ! have they not power to compel a witness
to attend ?

To be sure they have—on the part of the crown.

On the part of the crown !

Yes.

And not on the part of a prisoner ?

No.

No ! can this be the law ?

Even so, said a judge.

Well, well—poor Martha !

What's the matter now ?—what ails you, Mr. Burroughs ?

Martha—

Sir !

There's no hope Martha.

Hope ?

No Martha, no ; there's no hope for you.   They *will*
have you die.

Die !—me !—

Yes, poor Martha—you.

Me !—what for ?—what have I done ?

O that your accusers were not rock, Martha !

Rock !

O that your judges could feel ! or any that anybody
who knows you would appear and speak to your piety
and your simplicity !

Law Sir—how you talk !

Why as for that now, said Jeremiah Smith, who stood
by her, wiping his eyes and breathing very hard ; here
am I, Sir, an' ready to say a good word for the poor
soul, if I die for it ; fact is, you see, Mr. Judge Sewall
I've know'd poor Martha Cory—hai'nt I Martha ?—

So you have Jerry Smith.

—Ever since our Jeptha warn't more'n so high,—

Stop Sir, if you please, you are not sworn yet, said one of the judges.

Very true—swear him, added another.

You'll excuse me, said the Attorney-general. I say, you—what's your name ?

Jerry Smith.

And you appear on the side of the prisoner at the bar, I take it ?

Well, what if I do ?

Why in that case, you see, you are not to be sworn, that's all.

Not sworn ! cried Burroughs. And why not Sir ?

Why we never allow the witnesses that appear against the crown, to take the oath.

Against the crown Sir ! what on earth has the crown to do here ?—what have we to do with such absurdity ?

Have a care, brother Burroughs !

Do you know Sir—do you know that, if this man be not allowed to say what he has to say on oath, less credit will be given to what he says ?

Can't help that Sir.—Such is the law.

Judges—judges—do ye hear that ?—*can* this be the law ? Will you give the sanction of oaths to whatever may be said here against life ?—and refuse their sanction to whatever may be said for life ? Can such be the law ?

The judges consulted together and agreed that such was the law, the law of the mother-country and therefore the law of colonies.

Of a truth, said Burroughs, in reply ; of a truth, I can perceive now why it is, if a man appear to testify in *favor* of human life that he is regarded as a witness *against* the crown.—God help such crowns, I say !

Brother !—dear brother !

God help such crowns, I say ! What an idea of king-

ship it gives! What a fearful commentary on the guardianship of monarchs! How much it says in a word or
two of their fatherly care! He who is *for* the subject,
even though a life be at stake, is therefore *against* the
king!

Beware of that Sir.—You are on the very threshold
of treason.

Be it so.—If there is no other way, I will step over
that threshold —.

If you do Sir, it will be into your grave. —

Sir!—

Dear brother, I beseech you!

Enough—enough–I have nothing more to do—nothing
more to say, Sir—not another word, Sir—forgive me
Sir—I—I—I—the tears of the aged I cannot bear ; the
sorrow of such as are about to go before God, I am not
able, I never was able to bear. I beseech you, however, to look with pity upon the poor soul there—poor
Martha!—let her gray hairs plead with you, as your gray
hairs plead with me—I—I—proceed, Mr. Attorney-
General.

I have nothing more to say ?

Nothing more to say!

With submission to the court—nothing.

Do you throw up the case then ? said a judge.

Throw up the case! no indeed—no!—But if Mr.
Counsellor Burroughs here, who has contrived in my
humble opinion, to make the procedure of this court
appear—that is to say—with all due submission—appear to be not much better than a laughing-stock to the
—to the—to my brethren of the bar—if Mr. Burroughs,
I say, if he has nothing more to say—I beg leave to say
—that is to say—that I have nothing more to say —.

Say—say—say—whispered one of his brethren of the
bar—what say you to that Mr. Burroughs ?

CHAPTER VIII.

What *should* I say? replied Burroughs. What would you have me say? standing up and growing very pale. What would you have me say, you that are of counsel for the prisoner, you! the judges of the court? You that appear to rejoice when you see the last hope of the prisoner about to be made of no value to her, by the trick and subterfuge of the law. Why do you not speak to her?—Why do you not advise me? You know that I depend upon the reply—You know that I have no other hope, and that she has no other hope, and yet you leave us both to be destroyed by the stratagem of an adversary. How shall I proceed? Speak to me, I entreat you! Speak to me judges! Do not leave me to grope out a path blind-folded over a precipice—a path which it would require great skill to tread—O, I beseech you! do not leave me thus under the awful, the tremendous accountability, which, in my ignorance of the law, I have been desperate enough to undertake!— Here by my side are two men of the law—yet have you assigned her, in· a matter of life and death, no counsel. They are afraid I see—afraid not only to rise up and speak for the wretched woman, but they are afraid even to whisper to me. And you, ye judges! are you also on the side of the prosecutor and the witnesses—are you all for the king?—all!—all!—not so much as one to say a word for the poor creature, who being pursued *for* the king, is treated as if she were pursued *by* the king—pursued by him for sacrifice! What! no answer—not a word! What am I to believe ?....that you take pride in the exercise of your terrible power ? that you look upon it as a privilege ?....that you regard me now with displeasure....that if you could have your own way, you would permit no interference with your frightful prerogative ?....O that I knew in what way to approach the hearts of men! O that I knew how to proceed in this affair! Will nobody advise me!

Sir—Sir!— allow me, said a man of the law who sat near, allow me Sir ; I can bear it no longer—it is a reproach to the very name of law—but—but (lowering his voice) if you will suffer me to suggest a step or two for your consideration—you have the courage and the power—I have not—my brethren here have not—you have —and you may perhaps be able to—hush, hush—to bring her off.

Speak out, Sir—speak out, I beseech you. What am I to do?

Lower if you please—lower—low——er—er—er— we must not be overheard—Brother Trap's got a quick ear. Now my notion is—allow me—(whispering) the jury are on the watch ; they have heard you with great anxiety—and great pleasure—if you can manage to keep the hold you have got for half an hour—hush—hush—no matter how—the poor soul may escape yet—

I'll address the jury—

By no manner of means! That will not be suffered— you cannot address the jury—

Good God! what shall I do!

Thirteen-pence more—carry five—paid to watchman.

I'll put you in the way (with a waggish leer.) Though you are not allowed to address the jury, you are allowed to address the court—hey ?—(chucking him with his

elbow)—the court you see—hey—sh!—sh!—you understand it—hey?

No—how cool you are!

Cool—you'd be cool too, if you understood the law.

Never—never—in a case of life and death.

Life and death? poh—everything is a case of life and
death, Sir—to a man o' the law—everything—all cases
are alike, Sir—hey—provided—a—a—

Provided what, Sir?

Where the quid is the same.

The quid?

The quid pro quo—

How can you, Sir?—your levity is a—I begin to be
afraid of your principles—what am I to do?

Do—just keep the court in play; keep the judges
at work, while I run over to the shop for an authority
or two I have there which may be of use.—You have the
jury with you now—lay it on thick—you understand the
play as well as I do now—

Stop—stop—am I to say to the judges what I would
say to the jury, if I had leave?

Pre—cisely! but—but—a word in your ear—so as
to be heard by the jury.—Tut—tut—

The head-prosecutor jumped up at these words, and
with a great show of zeal prayed the judges to put a
stop to the consultation, a part of which was of a character—of a character—that is to say, of a character—

Burroughs would have interrupted him, but he was
hindered by his crafty law-adviser, who told him to let
the worthy gentleman cut his own throat in his own
way, now he was in the humor for it.

Burroughs obeyed, and after his adversary had run
himself out of breath, arose in reply, and with a gravity
and a moderation that weighed prodigiously with the

court, called upon the chief-judge to put a stop to such
gladiatorial controversy—

What would you have us do ? said the judge.

I would have you do nothing more than your duty—

Here the coadjutor of Burroughs, after making a sign
to him to face the jury, slid away on tip-toe.

—I would have you rebuke this temper. Ye are the
judges of a great people. I would have you act, and I
would have you teach others to act, as if you and they
were playing together, in every such case—not for your
own lives—that were too much to ask of mortal man ;
but for another's life. I would have you and your officers behave here as if the game that you play were what
you all know it to be, a game of life and death—a trial,
not of attorney with attorney, nor of judge with judge,
in the warfare of skill, or wit, or trick, or stratagem,
for fee or character—but a trial whereby the life here,
and the life hereafter it may be, of a fellow-creature is
in issue. Yea—more—I would have you teach the king's
Attorney-general, the prosecutor himself, that representative though he be of majesty, it would be more digni-
fied and more worthy of majesty, if he could contrive to
keep his temper, when he is defeated or thwarted in his
attack on human life. We may deserve death all of us,
but we deserve not mockery ; and whether we deserve
death or not, I hope we deserve, under our gracious
Lord and Master, to be put to death according to law—

That'll do !—that'll do !—whispered the lawyer, who
had returned with his huge folios—that'll do my boy !
looking up over his spectacles and turning a leaf—that'll
do ! give it to 'em as hot as they can sup it—I shall be
ready for you in a crack —push on, push on—what a
capital figure you'd make at the bar—don't stop—don't
stop.

Why, what on earth can I say !

Talk—talk—talk—no matter what you say—don't give them time to breathe—pop a speech into 'em !

A speech !

Ay, or a sermon, or a whar-whoop, or a prayer—any thing—anything—if you do but keep the ball up—no matter what, if the jury can hear you—they are all agog now—they are pricking up their ears at you—now's your time !

Very well——Judges !

Proceed.

Judges. I am a traveller from my youth up. I have journied over Europe ; I have journied over America—I am acquainted with every people of both hemispheres, and yet, whithersoever I go, I am a stranger. I have studied much—thought much—and am already a show among those who watched over my youth. I am still young, though I appear old, much younger than you would suppose me to be, did you not know me—

Here he turned to the lawyer—I never shall be able to get through this ; I don't know what I am saying.—

Nor I—So much the better—don't give up—

——A youth—a lad in comparison with with you, ye judges, you that I now undertake to reprove——a spectacle and a show among men. They follow me every where, (I hope you'll soon be ready) they pursue me day after day—and week after week—and month after month—

—And year after year—by jings, that'll do !—

—And year after year ; they and their wives, and their little ones—

And their flocks and their herds, and their man-servants and their maid-servants, whispered the lawyer.

Do be quiet, will you.—They pursue me however, not because of their veneration or their love, but only that they may study the perpetual changes of my countenance and hear the language of one to whom all changes and all languages are alike, and all beneath regard. They follow me too, not because they are able to interpret the look of my eyes,or to understand the meaning of my voice, but chiefly because they hear that I have been abroad in the furthermost countries of all the earth, because they are told by grave men, who catch their breath when they speak of me,though it be in the House of the Lord, as you have seen this very day, that I have been familiar with mysterious trial and savage adventure, up from the hour of my birth, when I was dropped in the wilderness like the young of the wild-beast, by my own mother—

I say—Brother B.—I say though—whispered the lawyer, in much perplexity—I say though—what are you at now ? *You* are not on trial—are you ?

Yes—yes—let me alone, I beseech you....

Fire away....fire away....you've got possession of the jury, and that's half the battle....fire away.

Peace....peace, I pray you....Judges ! whenever I go abroad....wherever I go....the first place into which I set my foot, is the tribunal of death. Go where I may, I go first in search of the courts....the courts of *justice*, I should say, to distinguish them from all other courts—

Good !—

—And I go thither because I have an idea that nations are to be compared with nations, not in every thing—not altogether, but only in a few things ; and because after much thought, I have persuaded myself that matters of religion, politics and morals, are inadequate for the chief purposes of such comparison—the comparison of people with people, though not for the comparison of individual with individual perhaps; and that a variety of matters which regard the administration of law, in cases affecting either life or liberty, are in their very nature adequate, and may be conclusive. We may compare court with court and law with law ; but how shall we compare opinion with opinion, where there is no unchangeable record of either ? goodness with goodness—where goodness itself may be but a thing of opinion or hearsay, incapable of proof, and therefore incapable of comparison ?

Very fair—very fair—but what on earth has it to do with our case ?

Wait and you shall see ; I begin to see my way clear now—wherefore judges, I hold that the liberty of a people and therefore the greatness of a people may be safely estimated by the degree of seriousness with which a criminal is arraigned, or tried, or judged, or punished—.

—Very true—and very well spun out, brother B. . . . but a non sequitur nevertheless. That wherefore, with which you began the period was a bit of a ——

Pray—*pray*—don't interrupt me ; you will be overheard—you will put me out.—In a word, ye Judges of Israel ! I have had a notion that arbitrary power would betray itself in every case, and every-where on earth, by its mode of dealing with liberty and life—being, I persuade myself, more and more summary and careless, in proportion as it is more and more absolute of a truth, not as it is more and more absolute by character. You had for a time, while the northern savages were at your door, a downright military government.— You know therefore that my words are true. Your government was called free—to have called it arbitrary, would have offended you ; yet for a season you dealt with human life as the Turk would. You know, for you have seen the proof, that in proportion to the growth of power in those who bear sway among you, the forms and ceremonies which fortify and hedge in, as it were, the life and liberty of the subject, are either disregarded or trampled on.—

Oh ho!—I see what you are driving at now!

—For my own part, I love to see the foreheads of them who are appointed to sit in the high-places and give judgment forever upon the property or character, life or liberty of their fellow man.—

Property or character—life or liberty—of a fellow man! Very fair—very fair indeed.

—Expressive at least of decent sorrow, if not of profound awe. I would have them look as if they were afraid—as if they trembled under the weight of their tremendous authority; as if they were deeply and clearly and reverentially sensible of what they have undertaken to do—which is, to deal with the creatures of God, as God himself professes to deal with them—according to their transgressions—to do a part of his duty with his own Image—to shelter the oppressed and to stay the oppressor, not only now and for a time, but hereafter and forever—

Don't stop to breathe now; I shall be at your back in a jiffy—

I would that every man who has to do with the administration of law, wherever that law is to touch the life or liberty of another; and whoever he may be, from the highest judge in the highest court of all the earth, down to the humblest ministerial officer—I would that he should feel, or at least appear to feel, that for a time he is the delegate of Jehovah—I do not stop to say how, nor to ask why. That is for others to say.—I would have the judges remarkable for their gravity, not for their austerity; for their seriousness and for their severe simplicity, not for a theatrical carriage. I would have the bar, as you call it, above the trick and subterfuge of the law—incapable of doing what I see them do every day of my life; and I would have the bench as you call it, incapable of suffering what I see them not only suffer, but take pleasure in, every day of my life——are you ready?

Persevere—persevere—you may say what you please now, said the lawyer, shuffling his papers about with both hands, chuckling in his sleeve, and whispering without appearing to whisper.—Have your own way now.... they like to hear the lawyers and the judges, and the law cut up; it's a new thing to hear in such a place....fire away, fire away....you see how they enjoy it....you've got us on the hip now... fire away.

If a criminal be arraigned on a charge that may affect his life or character, limb or property, or if a witness be to be sworn, or the oath administered,...I care not how ....I care not why....if you will have oaths....ye should order silence to be proclaimed by the sound of trumpet.
—Pho! pho!

I would have a great bell, one so large that it might be heard far and wide over the whole town—I would have this tolled on the day of condemnation, if that condemnation were to death. And if it must be—if you will have it so—if you will that a man be put to death by the rope or the axe, on the scaffold or over an open grave—as the poor soldier dies—I would have him perish at night—in the dead of midnight—and all the town should wake up at the tolling of that heavy bell, or at the roar of cannon, with a knowledge that a fellow-creature had that instant passed away from the earth forever —just gone—that very instant—before the Everlasting Judge of the quick and the dead—that while they were holding their breath and before they could breathe again —he would receive the sentence from which there would be no appeal throughout all the countless ages of eternity.

Very fair—very fair—I see the foreman of the jury shudder—keep him to it—

I love theory, but I love practice better—

Zounds ! what a plunge !

—Bear with me, I beseech you. I had come to a conclusion years and years ago, before I went away into the far parts of the earth, Judges and Elders, that where human life is thought much of, there liberty is ; and that just in proportion to the value of human life are the number and variety, the greatness and the strength of the safe-guards forms and ceremonies, which go to make it secure, if not altogether inaccessible.

Very fair—stick to the foreman—keep your eye on his face—don't take it off, and you'll be sure of the jury.

I can hardly see his face now—

So much the better—we'll have candles for them yet ; and if we do, my boy, the game is our own....fire away ; my authorities are almost ready now—fire away.

—I journeyed the world over, but I found little to prove that human life was of much value anywhere—anywhere I should say, except among the barbarians and the savages. My heart was troubled with fear. I knew not whither to go, nor where to look. Should I pursue my way further into the cities of Europe, or go back into the wilderness of America ?—At last I heard of a nation—bear with me judges—where all men were supposed by the law to be innocent, until they were *proved* to be guilty, where the very judges were said to be of counsel for the accused, where the verdict of at least twelve, and in some cases of twenty-four men—their unanimous verdict too, was required for the condemnation of such accused ; where if a man where charged with a crime, he was not even permitted to accuse himself or to acknowledge the truth, till he had been put upon his guard by the judges—who would even allow him, nay press him to withdraw an avowal, though it were made by him with serious deliberation ; where the laws were so tender of human life to say all in a word, and so remarkable for humanity as to be a perpetual theme for declamation. I heard all this....I had much reason to believe it....for everybody that I knew believed it....I grew instantly weary of home....

Lights there ! lights....

—I could not sleep for the desire I had to see that country.

You'd better stop awhile, Mr. Burroughs, whispered the lawyer.

—And I lost no time in going to it.

Pull up where you are....but keep your face toward the jury.

CHAPTER IX.

Well, continued Burroughs, I departed for the shores of that other world, where human life was guarded with such care and jealousy. I inquired for the courts of justice and for the halls of legislation....I hurried thither; ....I elbowed my way up to the sources of their law, and I had the mortification to discover that in almost every case, their courts were contrived, not as I had hoped from the character of the people, so as to give the public an opportunity of seeing the operation of power at work in the high-places of our earth, for the detection of guilt and for the security of virtue, but so as to hinder that operation, whether evil or good, from being viewed by the public. Everywhere the courts of justice were paltry ...everywhere inconvenient. Seeing this I grew afraid for the people. I found but one large enough to accommodate its own officers, and but one which it was possible for a stranger to enter, even by the aid of money, without much delay, difficulty and hazard. Ye do not believe me—ye cannot believe that such things are, such courts or such men, or that ever a price hath been fixed in a proud free country, for which a few and but a few of a mighty and wise people may see, now and then, wherefore it is that some one of their number is to be swept away from the earth forever. What I say is true. To the Halls of Legislation I proceeded—to the place where that law is made of which I have had occasion to speak this day. I went without my dinner ; I paid my

last half-crown to see the makers of the law—and I
came away, after seeing—not the makers of the law, but
the door-keepers of their cage—it is true that while I
was there, I was happy enough to see a man, who was
looking at another man, which other man declared that
the wig of the Speaker was distinctly visible—

Are you mad ?

Be quiet Sir—

You have broken the spell—the jury are beginning
to laugh—

Leave the jury to me—what I have to say Sir, may
provoke a smile, but if I do not much mistake, a smile for
the advantage of poor Martha. We have been too serious....we may do better by showing that we have no fear
—if the lawgivers of that country *are* what I say they
are—if the judges are what I say they are, and what I
shall prove them to be—and if the people of that country are what I am afraid they are, under such law—why
should we bow to its authority ?

Pho—pho—pho....You are all at sea now.

Well Judges....I enquired when there would be a trial
to prove the truth of what I had been told, and whither
I should go in search of a Temple of Justice, where I
might see for myself how human life was regarded by the
brave and the free. I found such a temple, and for the
price of another dinner, was carried up into a gallery
and put behind a huge pile of masonry, which as it
stood for a pillar and happened to be neither perforated
nor transparent, gave me but a dreary prospect for my
money....Do not smile—do not, I beseech you—I never
was more serious in my life....At last I heard a man called up, heard I say, for I could not see him, called up
and charged with I know not what fearful crime—I
caught my breath—are you ready Sir ?....

Almost....almost....fire away—writing as fast as he

could make the pen fly over the paper....fire away for a few minutes more....

I caught my breath....I trembled with anxiety....Now said I to myself, (To the lawyer; I am afraid I shall drop.)

No no, don't drop yet....fire away!

Now, said I to myself, I shall see one of the most awful and affecting sights in the world. Now shall I see the great humanity of the law....the law of this proud nation illustrated.....the very judges becoming of counsel for the prisoner....and the whole affair carried through with unspeakable solemnity. I addressed myself to a man who stood near me with a badge of authority in his hand....the very key wherewith he admitted people at so much a head, to see the performance. Pray, Sir, said I, what is that poor fellow charged with? He didn't know, not he, some case of murder though, he thought, (offering me a pinch of snuff as he spoke) or of highway-robbery, or something of the sort....he would enquire with great pleasure and let me know. The case opened. A speech was made by a prosecutor for the crown, a ready and a powerful speaker. The charge a capital one. The accused....a poor emaciated miserable creature, was on trial for having had in possession, property which had been stolen out of a dwelling-house in the dead of night. Well, prisoner at the bar, what have you to say for yourself? said the judge with a stern look, after the case had been gone through with by the prosecutor. Now is your time....speak, said the judge. I have nothing to say for myself, said the poor prisoner; nothing more than what I have said four or five times already. Have you no witnesses? No my lord——

Soh soh, Mr. Burroughs! We understand your parable now, cried one of the judges with a look of dismay. We all know what country that is where a judge is a

lord....have a care Sir ; have a care.....Be wary....you
may rue this if you are not.

I shall endure the risk whatever it be....shall I proceed ?

We have no power to stop you....

No my lord, was the reply of the prisoner. I could
not oblige them to appear ; and they would not appear.
How came you by the property ? said his lordship. It
was left with me by a man who stopped at my house ;
he wanted a little money to carry him to see a sick wife
....and as I did not know him, he left this property in
pledge. Who was that man ? I do not know my lord,
I never saw him before....but one of my neighbors in the
same trade with me knew him, and if you had him here,
he would say so.

Judges, you have now heard my story. You know
what I was prepared to see ; you know what I expected.
Here was a man who, for aught we know, told the truth.
But he had no witnesses—he had no power to make
them testify—he had no refuge—no hope--the law was
a snare to him—the law of our mother-country.

How so pray ?

Property being found in his possession—property
which had been stolen, he was to suffer, because—mark
what I say, I beseech you—*because he could not prove his
innocence !*

Tut—tut—tut—rigmarole ! said the prosecutor.

Rigmarole Sir—what I say is the simple truth. Hear
me through. The moment that poor fellow was found
with the property in his possession, he was concluded
by the law and by the judges of the law to be guilty ;
and they called upon him to *prove* that he was *not guilty*—

Nature of things, my good brother—

Well—and if it is the nature of things, why deny the

existence of the fact? Why do you, as all men of the law have done for ages and still do—why say over and over again every day of your lives, that it is the characteristic of the law, that law of which you are the expounders, to regard every man as innocent, until he be *proved* to be guilty? Why not say the truth? Why quibble with rhetoric? Why not say that where a man is charged with a crime, you are, in the very nature of things, under the necessity of taking that for proof which is not proof? Look you Sir—how came you by the coat you wear? Suppose I were to challenge that cloth and put you to the proof, how could you prove that you purchased it fairly of a fair trader?

I would appeal to the trader—

Appeal to the trader! If he had not come honestly by it Sir, would he ever acknowledge that you had it of him? or that he had ever seen your face before?

Well then—I would prove it by somebody else.

By somebody else, would you! Are you so very cautious—do you never go abroad without having a witness at your heels? do you never pick up anything in the street Sir, without first assuring yourself that you are observed by somebody of good character, who will appear of his own accord in your behalf, should you be arraigned for having stolen property in your possession? What would you have to say for yourself?—your oath would not be received—and if it was, there would only be oath against oath—your oath against that of the trader of whom you purchased, or the individual of whom you received the property—and his oath against yours.—How would you behave with no witnesses to help you out?—or with witnesses who would not appear and could not be made to appear on your side, though your life were at stake?—nay, for that very reason, for if your property only were at stake, they might be made to appear—

Very well!

—Or with witnesses, who having appeared on your side, are not allowed to make oath to what they say—lest they may be believed—to the prejudice of our good king?

Really, cried one of the judges, really, gentlemen, you appear to be going very wide of the mark. What have we to do with your snip-snap and gossip? Are we to have nothing but speech after speech—about nobody knows what—now smacking of outrage—now of treason? Are we to stay here all night Sirs of the bar, while you are whispering together?

With submission to the court, said the Attorney-general—we have a case put here, which would seem to require a word of reply. We are asked what we should do if we were without witnesses—and the court will perceive that the sympathy of the jury is relied on—is relied on, I say!—on the authority of a case—of a case which!—of a case which I never heard of before! The court will please to observe—to observe I say!—that the prisoner at the bar—at the bar—has no witnesses—in which case, I would ask, where is the hardship—where we cannot prove our innocence—our innocence I say!—of a particular, charge—we have only to prove our character.

Here the Attorney-general sat down with a smile and a bow, and a magnificent shake of the head.

Only to prove our character, hey?

To be sure—

But how—if we have no witnesses—

Very fair—very fair, brother B.

What if you were a stranger?—what if you had no character?—or a bad one?

It would go hard with me, I dare say—and—and

(raising his voice and appealing to the bar with a triumphant look) and it *should* go hard with me.

Why then Sir—it would go hard with every stranger in a strange country, for he has no character ; and it would go hard with every man who might be unable to produce proof, though he had a good character ; and with every man who might be regarded as a profligate or a suspicious charater—as a cheat, or a jew, or a misbeliever.

And what have such men to complain of ?

Judges—Fathers—I appeal to you. I have not much more to say, and what I have to say shall be said with a view to the case before you. I have always understood that if a man be charged with a crime here, he is to be tried for that particular crime with which he is charged, and for no other till that be disposed of. I have always understood moreover, not only in your courts of law and by your books of law, but by the courts and by the books of which you are but a copy, that character is not to be put in issue as a crime before you ; and that nobody is to be put to death or punished merely because he may happen to have no character at all—nor because he may have a bad one—

You have understood no more than is true, said a judge.

If so....allow me to ask why you and other judges are in the habit of punishing people of a bad character.... nay of putting such people to death....for doing that which, if it were done by people of good character, you would overlook or forgive ?

How Sir....Do you pretend that we ever do such things ?

I do....Will you say that you do not ?....

Yes....and waive the authority of a judge, and the irregularity of your procedure that you may reply.

Then....if what I hear is true....if it is law I mean....
the judges before me will not regard character ?

Why as to *regarding* character....that's another affair
Mr. Burroughs....

I implore you.....take one side or the other ! Say
whether you do or do not regard character....I care not
for the degree, nor do I care which side you take. For if
you say that you do, then I say that you act in the teeth
of all your professions ; for you declare in every shape,
every man of you, every day of your lives, that nobody
shall be punished by law but for that which he has been
charged with in due course of law....technically charged
with and apprised of....and you never charge a man
with having a bad character....

Well, then....suppose we say that we do *not* regard
character ?

When character is not in issue, brother, added the
chief-judge ; for it may be put in issue by the traverser—
in which case we are bound to weigh the proof on both
sides along with the jury.

If you say that, in your character of judge....and if you
are all agreed in saying that....Lo, I am prepared for
you.

We are agreed—we perceive the truth now.

Lo, my answer!—You have heard the whole of our
case. You have heard all the witnesses for the crown ;
you have gathered all the proof. Now....bear with me,
judges....bear with me....what I say is a matter of life and
death....we have no witnesses....we have not put the character of Martha in issue....all that you know of her, you
know from your witnesses, and they have not said a syllable touching her character. Now.....fathers ! and
judges !....I ask you if that proof, take it altogether,
would be enough in your estimation, to prove....I beg
you to hear me....would it be enough to convict any one

of your number, if he had no witness to speak for him ?
..... Ye are astounded ! Ye know not how to reply, nor
how to escape ; for ye know in your own souls that such
proof....such proof and no more, would not be enough
to convict any one of you in the opinion of the other six.

Well Sir——what then ?

Why then Sir....then ye Judges—if that poor old woman before you—if she be not on trial for character—
on trial for that which has not been charged to her....
by what you have now said, she is free. Stand up,
on your feet Martha! stand up and rejoice ! By what
ye have now said, ye judges, that poor old woman hath
leave to go free!

The judges were mute with surprise, and the lawyer
started upon his feet and clapped Burroughs on the
back, and stood rubbing his hands at the Attorney-general and making mouths at the jury—Capital !....Capi-
tal !....never saw the like, faith—never, never....never
thought of such a view myself....but I say though (in a
whisper) you did begin to put her character in issue—
tut—tut—yes you did, you rogue you....say nothin'—
tut—tut—

Say nothing Sir !—excuse me. If I have said that
which is not true, I shall unsay it—

Pooh, pooh....your argument's all the same, and besides, you did not go far enough to make Jerry Smith
your witness....pooh, pooh—what a fool you are—

But the judges recovered their self-possession, and
laid their heads together and asked Burroughs if he had
anything more to say.

More to say—yes—much more—enough to keep you
employed for the rest of your lives, ye hard-hearted inaccessible men ! What—are ye so bent upon mischief!
Will ye not suffer that aged woman to escape the snare !
Ye carry me back all at once to the spot of which I

spoke. Ye drive me to the parable again. I saw the judges behave to their prisoner as I now see you behave to yours; and I would have cried out there as I do here, with a loud voice....Are ye indeed the counsel for the prisoner!—Why do ye not behave as other counsel do? But when I looked up and beheld their faces, and about me, and beheld the faces of the multitude, my courage was gone—I had no hope—my heart died away within me. They were as mute as you are—and their look was your look—a look of death. But where, said I, is the advocate for the prisoner? why does he not appear? He has none, was the reply. What, no advocate, no help—there is a provision of your law which enables the very pauper to sue....I have heard so, and surely he is not so very poor, the man I see at the bar; why do not the counsel that I see there unoccupied—why do they not offer to help him? They are not paid Sir. Do they require pay before they will put forth a hand to save a fellow-creature from death? Of course. But why do not the court assign counsel to him?—The reply there was the reply that you have heard here this day. The accused have no counsel in a matter of life and death....it is only by courtesy that counsel are permitted even to address the court on a point of law, when they are employed by a prisoner.

But why do I urge all this? Are not we, and were not they, living in a land of mercy, a land remarkable for the humanity of her laws? Do not mistake me, fathers! I would not that the guilty should escape....I have no such desire. But I would have the innocent safe, and I would have the guilty, yea the guiltiest in every case and everywhere, punished according to law. To know that a man has committed murder is not enough to justify you in taking his life—to see him do the deed with your own eyes, would not be enough to justify you in putting him to death—wherefore it is that however certain the guilt of the accused, and however great his crime, he should have counsel....

Absurd !—

Yea—counsel, judge—counsel !

You would allow the guilty every possible chance of escape.

Even so, judge ! every possible chance of escape. For the guilty have some rights to guard—rights the more precious for being so few, and for being in perpetual risk of outrage; the more to be guarded Sir, *because* they are the rights and the privileges of the wicked, who have nothing to hope from the public sympathy, no hope of pity, no hope of charity. Even so, Judge ! for the innocent are liable to appear otherwise. Even so—for till the trial be over, how do we know who is guilty and who not ? How do we know—how is it possible for us to know, till the accused have undergone their trial, whether they are, or are not unjustly charged ? For the innocent as well as for the guilty therefore, would I have counsel for the accused—yea, counsel, whatever were the charge, and however probable it might appear—nay the more, in proportion both to the probability and to the magnitude of the charge.

A fine theory that Sir. You have been abroad to much purpose, it would appear.

Even so judge—even so. Such *is* my theory, and I *have* been abroad, I believe, to much purpose; for if men are to die by the law, I would have them appear to die by the law. By the law, judge—not by popular caprice, popular indignation or arbitrary power. I would leave no ground for sorrow, none for self-reproach, none for misgiving, either to the public or to that portion of the public who have participated more immediately in the awful business of death. I would have no such case

on record as that of Mary Dyer....I would have no
Elizabeth Hutchinson offered up—no such trials, no
such graves, no such names for the people to be afraid
of and sorry for, ages and ages after the death of a miserable infatuated woman—a prophetess or a witch, forsooth—

George Burroughs!

—A prophetess or a witch I say!—after she has been
put to death no man is able to say wherefore.

George Burroughs!

Who speaks?

George Burroughs, beware! cried a female who stood
in a dark part of the house, with her head muffled up—
a deep shadow was about her and a stillness like death.

I know that voice—be of good cheer—I have nearly
done, though not being used to unprepared public-speak-
ing, I have said little that I meant to say, and much
that I did not mean to say; hardly a word however
even of that which I have said or meant to say, as I
would say it, or as I could say it, if I had a little more
experience—or as I could say it now on paper.   And if
I feel this—I—who have grown up to a habit if not of
speaking, at least of reading before a multitude; I, who
have been used from my youth up to arrange my
thoughts for the public eye, to argue and to persuade;
what must another, taken by surprise, wholly without
such practice and power, what must he—or she—or
that poor woman at the bar feel, were you to put her into
my place, and urge her to defend herself to a jury?
Pity her....I implore you....consider what I say and
have mercy upon her!—

Before you sit down, brother B....what if you give us
a word or two of the parallel you begun?—I see the drift
of it now—a word or two, you understand me—take a
mouthful o'water—and if you could manage to slip in a

remark or two about the nature of the proof required in witchcraft, I'll be after you in a crack, and we'll tire em out, if we can't do anything better.

I will—be prepared though—for I shall say *but* a word or two—I am weary; sick and weary of this—my throat is parched, and my very soul in a maze of perplexity.

So much the better—they can't follow you on t'other side.

Well, fathers! I pursued the inquiry. I found that even there, no prisoner could have a compulsory process to bring a witness *for* him into court, although such process could be had, backed by the whole power of the country, to bring a witness *against* him. And I discovered also, that if a witness for the accused were so obliging as to appear, they would not suffer him to speak on oath. I turned to the officer—I take it, Sir, said I, that in such a case, you have no punishment for untruth, and of course, that the witnesses for the wretched man at the bar are not so likely to be believed as the witnesses against him....the latter being on oath ?....Precisely. But is he a lawyer ? said I....Who! the prisoner at the bar....Yes....A lawyer—no. Is he accustomed to public speaking ? He....no, indeed !....Nor to close argument, perhaps ? nor to a habit of arranging his ideas on paper ?....I dare say not, was the reply. It would be no easy matter for a man to preserve his selfpossession... so at least I should suppose, however much he might be accustomed to public speaking....if he were on trial himself, and obliged to defend himself ?

There's an authority for you in the books, brother B. —The man who appeareth for himself, (in a loud voice) for himself, saith my lord.....Coke, hath a fool for his client....

Saith Lord Coke, hey ?

Pooh, pooh, (in a whisper) pooh, pooh ; never mind

who says it; give it for his, and let them show the contrary, if they are able.

But if it be a case of life and death—where great coolness and great precision were needed at every step, he would be yet more embarrassed? No doubt. And is not the prosecutor a very able man? Very, Sir—very. Chosen for that office, out of a multitude of superior men altogether on account of his ability? Very true, Sir—very true—on account of his ability and experience at the bar. And yet, Sir, said I—if I understand you, that poor fellow there, who is now in such grievious trepidation, so weak that he can hardly stand—his color coming and going with every breath, his throat and mouth and lips dry with excessive anxiety, his head inclined as if with a continual ringing in his ears—if I understand you, said I, he is now called up to defend himself, to make speech for speech before a jury, against one of your most able and eloquent speakers; a man whose reputation is at stake on the issue—a man who—if he be thawarted in his way, by a witness, or a fact, or a speech, or a point of law, will appear to regard the escape of the prisoner, whatever he may be charged with, and whether he be innocent or guilty, as nothing better than a reproach to the law, and high treason to the state—a man, to say all in a word, who dares to behave in a court of justice—in a matter of life and death too—as if the escape of a prisoner were disloyalty to the king—our father! and a disgrace to the king's Attorney-general—

Will you have done, Sir?

No....no....no!....*You have no power to stop me.* The jury could not agree. Two of their number were unwilling to find the accused guilty. They were sent back —it was in the dead of winter, and they were allowed neither food, nor fire—and so, after a while they were starved and frozen into unanimity—

Grant me patience ! what would you have, Sir ?—you appear to be satisfied with nothing—I believe in my soul, George Burroughs, that you are no better than a Reformer—

A shudder ran through the whole court.

Here was a pretty illustration of what I had been told by you, and by such as you, and of what I believed before I went abroad, about the humanity of the law—the humanity of British law ! of that very law that ye are now seeking to administer here, in this remote corner of the earth. Ye are amazed—ye do not believe me— and yet every word I have spoken is true ; and that which is law there, ye would make law here. The judges, we are told, are of counsel for the prisoner— God preserve me from such counsel, I say !.....

Five and one are six—six-and-sixpence, muttered a voice.

They never interfered while I was there, in favor of the prisoner ; but they did interfere two or three times, and with great acuteness too, for it was a trial of wit among three, to his disadvantage, even as ye have this day. The accused are held to be innocent there, even as they are here, till they are proved to be guilty—so say the lawyers there, and so say the judges, and so say all the writers on the law, and so they believe, I dare say. And yet....there as here, the man who happens to be suspected of a crime is held to be....not innocent of the charge. but guilty, and is called upon to *prove his innocence;* which if he fail to do, judgment follows, and after two or three days, it may be, death. He had no counsel permitted to him where his life was at stake, though he might have had the best in the whole empire in a civil case affecting property to the value of a few pounds. He had no power to bring witnesses....the law would not allow him witnesses therefore....and if they appeared in spite of the law, that law put a disqualification upon whatever they said in favor of the prisoner. And after all this....O the humanity of the law !....the jury, a part of whom believed him to be innocent were starved into finding him guilty. What was I to think of all this ? what of British law—that very law by authority whereof, ye are now trying that woman for her life—what of the—

Here Burroughs dropped into a chair completely out of breath.

Have you done Sir ? said the chief judge.

He signified by a motion of the head that he must give up.

Very well Sir—You cannot say that we have not heard you patiently ; nor that we have hurried the case of the prisoners at the bar, whatever else you may think proper to say. You have had such liberty as we never granted before, as we shall never grant again ; you have had full swing Sir—full swing, and would have been stopped a good hour ago but for the deplorable situation of the accused. To tell you the plain truth however—I did hope—I did hope I say, that we should hear something— *something* to the purpose, before you gave the matter up—

Something to the purpose, judge !—Have a care—you know me—

Silence !

Judge—judge—I have said more than you six will ever be able to answer, though you keep your heads together to all eternity—How can you answer what I say ?

How—in five words....

In five words !

I ask no more to satisfy all that hear me—my brethren of the bench, the bar, and the people—but five words, I tell you.

And what are they, I do beseech you ?....

The—wisdom—of—our—ancestors.

CHAPTER X.

Here the lawyer started up, and after prevailing upon Burroughs to forbear and be still, argued (with his face to the jury) five or six points of law, as he called them, every one of which had been argued over and over again at every trial of a serious charge that he had ever been occupied with in the whole course of a long life at the bar....four being about the propriety of capital punishments in general, and two about the propriety of capital punishments in the particular case of the prisoner at the bar—whom he protested before God (for which he had to pay thirteen-pence more) he believed to be innocent of the charge—and what was that charge?—nothing more nor less than the charge of sorcery and witchcraft! —a crime, the very possibility of which, he proceeded to deny, in the very language he had used about a twelve-month before, while arguing about the impossibility of marriage in a particular case.

Brother—brother—we do not sit here to try the possibility of such a thing as witchcraft—please to consider where you are, and what we are.

Speech after speech followed ; and it was near midnight, when the chief judge, after consulting with his brethren, proceeded to address the jury.

Ye have heard much that in our opinion does not need a reply, said he, after taking a general view of the case, with much that a brief reply may be sufficient for, and a very little, which, as it may serve to perplex you, if we pass it over without notice, we shall say a few words upon, though it has little or nothing to do with the case before you.

The law you have nothing to do with....right or wrong, wise or foolish, you have nothing to do with the law. So too....whatever may be the practice abroad or in this country, and whatever may be the hardship of that practice, you have nothing to do with it. One is the business of the legislature....of the law-makers; the other the business of the courts, and the judges....the law-expounders. You are to try a particular case by a particular law; to that, your whole attention is to be directed. If the law be a bad law, that is neither your business nor our business. We and you are to do our duty, and leave theirs to the sovereign legislature.

I propose now to recapitulate the evidence, which I have taken notes of—should I be wrong, you will correct me. After I have gone through with the evidence, I shall offer a few brief remarks in reply to the arguments which have been crowded into the case—I will not say for show—and which, idle as they are, would seem to have had weight with you.

The afflicted, you observe, do generally testify that the shape of the prisoner doth oftentimes pinch them, choke them, and otherwise afflict them, urging them always to write in a book she bears about with her. And you observe too, that the accusers were struck down with a fit before you, and could not rise up till she was ordered to touch them, and that several of their number have had fits whenever she looked upon them.

But we are to be more particular, and I shall now read my notes, and I pray you to follow me.

1. Deliverance Hobbs, who confessed herself a witch, testified that the prisoner tempted her to sign the book again, and to deny what she had confessed; and that

the shape of the prisoner whipped her with iron rods to
force her to do so, and that the prisoner was at a general meeting of witches at a field near Salem village, and
there partook of the sacrament with them.

2. John Cook testified that about five or six years ago,
he was assaulted with the shape of the prisoner in his
chamber, and so terrified that an apple he had in his
hand flew strangely from him into his mother's lap, six
or eight feet distance.

3. Samuel Gray testified that about fourteen years ago,
he waked one night and saw his room full of light and a
woman between the cradle and bed-side ; he got up but
found the doors fast, and the apparition vanished—however the child was so frighted, that it pined away and in
some time died. He confessed that he had never seen
the prisoner before, but was now satisfied that it was her
apparition.

4. John Bly and his wife testified that he bought a
sow of the prisoner's husband, but being to pay the
money to another, she was so angry that she quarrelled
with Bly, and soon after the sow was taken with strange
fits, jumping, leaping and knocking her head against
the fence which made the witnesses conclude the prisoner had bewitched it.

5. Richard Coman testified that eight years ago, he
was terrified with the spectre of the prisoner and others, who so oppressed him in his bed that he could not
stir hand nor foot, but calling up somebody to come to
his assistance, as soon as the people of the house spoke,
the spectre vanished and all was quiet.

6. Samuel Shattock testified that in 1680 (twelve
years before the trial) the prisoner often came to his
house on frivolous errands, soon after which his child
was taken with strange fits, and at last lost his understanding; the fits were manifestly epileptic, but the

witness verily believed it was bewitched by the prisoner.

7. John Londor testified that upon some little controversy with the prisoner about her fowls, going well to
bed, he awoke in the night and saw the likeness of this
woman greviously oppressing him. Another time he
was troubled with a black pig, but going to kick it, it
vanished. Another time as he was sitting in his room,
a black hobgobling jumped in the room, which spoke
to him these words—I understand you are troubled in
mind: Be ruled by me and you shall want nothing in
this world. But when he endeavored to strike it, there
was nothing. After this he ran out of his house and
saw the prisoner in her orchard, but had no power to
speak to her, but concluded his trouble was all owing
to her.

8. William Stacy testified that the spectre of the
prisoner had played him several pranks of the same
nature as the former; for example—having received
some money of the prisoner for work, he had not gone
above three rods from her when it was gone from him ;
some time after, discoursing with the prisoner about
grinding her grist, he had not gone above six rods from
her with a small load in his cart, before the off-wheel
sunk into a hole in plain ground, so that the deponent
was forced to get help for the recovery of it, but stepping back to look for the hole, there was none to be
found. Another time, as he was going home on a dark
night, he was lifted up from the ground and thrown
against the stone wall, and after that, he was hoisted up,
and thrown down a bank at the end of his house.

9. John and William Bly testified that being employed by the prisoner to take down her cellar-wall, they
found several poppets made of rags and hog's bristles,
with headless pins in them, the points being outwards.

In addition to all this, continued the chief-judge, you

have the testimony of Mr. Park, the magistrate, who
says that when her Paris's daughter and two other children accused the prisoner at the bar of afflicting them,
by biting, pricking, strangling, &c. saying that they
saw her likeness in their fits, coming toward them and
bringing them a book to sign, he asked her why she afflicted those poor children—to which she replied that
she did not; and that when he asked her who did then ?
she answered she did not know—

Burroughs groaned aloud.

—You will observe her answer, gentlemen of the jury....she did not know, but thought they were poor distracted creatures, whereupon the afflicted said that the
Black man was whispering in her ear and that a yel-
low-bird which used to suck between her fingers was
now there; and orders being given to see if there was
any sign, a girl said, it is now too late for she has removed a pin and put it on her head; and upon search
there was found a pin sticking upright there. He testifies too that when Mrs. Cory had any motion of her
body the afflicted would cry out, when she bit her lip
they would cry out of being bitten, and if she grasped
one hand with the other they would cry out of being
pinched.

You will observe too that a jury of women who were
empanelled to search her body, testify one and all
that they found a preternatural teat upon her body;
but upon a second search three or four hours after, there
was none to be found.

Thus much for the evidence, gentlemen of the jury;
I proceed now to remark on what has been urged for
the—officer—officer....look to your prisoner !

O, I am so tired and so sleepy ! said Martha a getting
up, and trying to pass the sheriff, who stood by her with
a drawn sword. Let me go, will you !—get out o' the

way and let me go—what's the use o' keeping me here ;
I've told you all 't I know o' the job. Do let poor Martha go !

Gracious God !—Father of Love ! cried Burroughs,
what an appeal to the executioners of the law ! Did
you not hear it, ye judges ? Do you not see her now,
tottering away....the poor bewildered creature.

Have done Sir.

Dear brother—if we are wise we shall not be strict
with him here—let us give the world nothing to complain
of, our duty require it, policy requires it—ah !

Prisoner at the bar—go back to your seat : Officer
—officer—

She don't hear a word you say, Mr. Judge.

Martha Cory—Martha !

Well, here I be, Mister Capun Sewall ; what d'ye
want o' me ?

Go back to your seat, Martha.

Back there ?—I shall not—

Officer !

The officer took her by the arm to lead her back.

Gently there—gently—gently.

There now ! cried Martha, in a peevish, querulous
tone—There now ; dropping into the seat with her arms
a-kimbo, and poking out her chin at the officer. There
now ; I hope that'll satisfy you—

Gentlemen of the jury, pursued the judge ; You have
now the evidence before you. You have gone through
the whole proof with me, step by step—it is for you to
say what is the value of that proof—

Proof, cried Burroughs—proof ! taking away his
hands from his pale face—and speaking through his
shut teeth. Call you that proof which proves nothing ?
that which relates to things that occured, if they ever
occurred at all, years and years ago ? that which is only

a sort of guess-work ? that which relates to transactions which the poor soul does not appear to have had either voice or part in ?

Bravely said, George Burroughs—bravely put, cried a female, who stood in the dark part of the house.

Such trivial matters too—so trivial that we should mock at them, but for the life we lead here, surrounded by savages, and by death in every shape, and by woods and waters that were never yet explored by man ; beset on every side by a foe that never sleeps ; afar and away from succor and liable to be surprised every hour of the day and every hour of the night, and butchered among our babes and our household-gods. Proof, say you ?— can that be proof, I appeal to you judges—that which, however false it may be, or however mistaken by the witnesses, cannot, in the very nature of things, be explained away nor contradicted ; that which calls upon a poor creature worn out with age and misery—an idiot —for of a truth she is little better—I pray you judges— I pray you—on me let your displeasure fall; not on her—I will abide your wrath—I see it in your eyes— but I pray you—I beseech you—can that be proof, *that* which calls upon a prisoner in such a case to go through the whole history of her life—hour by hour—step by step. Nay, speak to me !—By your oaths, answer me ! By your oath here, and by your hope hereafter, may you call upon her, in a matter of life and death, to do this ? And not only to do this, but to account for the epilepsy of a babe ? for the dreams, the diseases, the very night-mares of them that now accuse her ?——

If you do not stop Sir, we shall have to commit you.

Commit me if you dare ! You have made me counsel for the prisoner, and whatever may be the courtesy of the bar, whatever you may expect—and whatever may become of me—or of you—I shall not throw a chance away. He proceeded to review the whole of the evidence with a vigor and propriety which after a while rose up in judgment against him, as if it were supernatural ; he then argued upon the nature of the crime—saying it was a charge easily made but hard to disprove, and that it would require one to be a witch to prove that she was not guilty of witchcraft—

Beware of that man, said the chief judge, with a mysterious look. Beware, I tell you ; for whoever he may be, and whatever he may be, he will be sure to lead you astray, if you are not upon your guard.

Lo, the counsel for the prisoner ! Lo the humanity of the law ! cried Burroughs. Who could do more ?—I appeal to you, ye men of Massachusetts-Bay—could the prosecutor himself—could anybody on earth—in aid of the prisoner at the bar ?—Put upon your guard in that way, against the power and art of another—if you are not men of a marvellous courage indeed—of heroic probity—it would be impossible for him to convince you, however true were his argument, however conclusive his facts.

Very true, whispered the foreman of the jury, loud enough to be overheard by a judge, who rebuked him with great asperity.

Whatever I might say, therefore—however true it might be, and however wise, after that speech, you would not venture to heed me—you could not—such a thing were too much to hope for—unless you were indeed, every man of you, far, far superior to the race of men that are about and above you ———

Talk of art, said the chief judge, in dismay. Talk of address after that ! who ever heard of such art—who ever heard of such address before ?

What a compliment for your understandings !—But I do not give up in despair—I shall say the little that I now have to say, and leave you to decide between us—if I prevail, you may have courage enough perhaps to acquit the prisoner, though you *are* sneered at by the judges.

He proceeded with fresh vigor, and concluded the work of the day with a speech that appears to have been regarded by the court and the people as·above the ability of man. He spoke to the multitude, to the judges, to the bar, to the jury—man by man--saying to each with a voice and a power that are spoken of still by the posterity of them that were there.....You have heard the whole evidence.—You—you alone, Sir, that I speak too now, are to decide upon the life or death of the prisoner. You alone, Sir! and mark me.....if.....though you are but one of the twelve who are to decide....if you decide for death....observe what I say....if you so decide Sir, as one of the twelve....when. if you knew that her life depended upon you alone, you would have decided otherwise, mark me....her blood shall be upon your head....her death at your door!....at yours—and yours—and yours —though each of you be but one of the twelve.

Hear me. I address myself to you, John Peabody. Are you prepared to say—would you say—*guilty*, if her life depended upon you, and upon you alone ?—if you were her only judge ?—Think of your death-bed—of the Judge whom you are to meet hereafter, you that have so much need of mercy hereafter—ask yourselves what harm would follow her acquital, even though she were guilty. Then ask yourself what would be your feelings if you should ever come to know that you have put her to death wrongfully....So say I to you, Andrew Elliot.... Her life depends upon you—upon you alone ! You are in fact her only judge-—for you—or you—or you—or either of you may save her, and if you do not, her blood will be required hereafter at your hands—at the hands of each of you——I have done.

CHAPTER XI.

The chief judge would not reply—could not perhaps,
till after he and his brothers had prayed together ; and
when he did speak, he spoke with a subdued voice,
like one troubled with fear.

Gentlemen of the jury, said he ; I have but a few
words to urge in reply.

1. You have been told that one should be a witch to
prove that she is not guilty of witchcraft. I admire the
ingenuity of the speaker ; but my answer is, that by the
same rule, a man should be a wizard to prove that he is
not a manslayer—he being *proved* a manslayer. And
yet, *being* proved a manslayer, we put him to death. So
here—being proved a witch, if you are satisfied by the
proof, we put the prisoner to death, even though it would
require the exertion of diabolical power to overthrow the
proof.

2. You are told by one speaker that we are prone to
believe in the marvellous ; and that, therefore, when a
marvellous thing is related, we ought to be on our guard
against that proneness to belief, and require more
proof. Now it appears to me that if we are prone to
a belief in the marvellous, instead of requiring more
proof to witchcraft, we should require less. For why
require much, if less will do ?

3. But by another, it has been said that we are *not*
prone to belief in the marvellous ; that on the contrary,
so prone are we to disbelieve in what may appear mar-

vellous, that proof, which we would be satisfied with in
the ordinary affairs of life, we should pay no regard to,
if it were adduced in favor of what we consider preternatural ; and that therefore in the case you are now to
try, you should require more proof than you would in
support of a charge not marvellous.   To which we reply—that where you have the same number of witnesses, of the same character, in support of a marvellous
charge, you *actually have more proof*, than you would
have in the like testimony of the same witnesses, to a
charge not marvellous.   And why ?—Because by the
supposition of the speaker, as they are prone to a *dis-
belief* in the marvellous, *they* would have required much
proof, and would not have been persuaded to believe
what they testify to, but upon irresistable proof—more
proof than would have satisfied them in the ordinary
affairs of life.

4. It has been said moreover—that the greater the
crime charged, the more incredible it is ; that great
crimes are perpetrated less frequently than small ones ;
and that, therefore, more proof should be required of
parricide than of theft.   Our reply to which is, that if a
witness declare to a parricide on oath, *you have more
proof* than you would have to a theft sworn to by the
very same witness ; that, if the greater the crime, the
less credible it is, you are bound to attach more value to
his testimony where he testifies to parricide than where
he testifies to theft.   And why ?—Because, the greater
the crime charged, the greater the crime of the witness
if he charge falsely ; and therefore the less likely is it,
by the supposition, that he does charge falsely.

But here I would have you observe that proof is proof,
and that after all, the proof which at law or otherwise
would be enough to establish one charge, would be
enough to establish any other.   In every case you are to

be satisfied—you are to believe : and in the case now
before you, perhaps it may be well for you to look upon
the two improbabilities which I have now spoken of, as
neutralizing each other. If witchcraft is incredible
—it is incredible also that one should falsely charge
another with witchcraft.

5. It has been said too that the witnesses contradict
each other. Be it so. I confess that I see no such contradiction—but if I did, I might be called upon to say
that perjured witnesses are remarkable for the plausibility and straight-forwardness of their stories; and that
such plausibility and straight-forwardness are now regarded. like unanimity, as a sign of bad-faith by judges
of experience. You are to be told moreover, that where
slight contradictions appear in what may be said by
several witnesses to the same fact, such contradictions
are a sign of good-faith—showing that no preconcerted
story has been told. I might refer, and I may venture
to do so perhaps, in a matter of such awful moment, to
the gospels in proof. It is a mighty argument for their
truth my friends, that no two of them perfectly agree—
no two of the whole as they could have agreed, if, as
there have been people wicked enough to say (though
not to believe) they had been prepared for deception
by a body of conspirators——

Brother—brother—put off thy shoes....the ground is
holy—said Governor Phips.

I have....I have—

The people groaned aloud.

——If you were called upon, each of you, five years from
to-day, to give a particular account of what you now
see and hear, and if each of you depended upon himself,
your stories would be unlike ; but if you consulted together, your stories would be sure to approximate. So
much for this head.

6. I have gone so far as to say that proof is proof, whatever may be the case ; but I do not say that you are to
require at any time, in any case, more proof than the
nature of the case will admit of. In other words, you
are not to insist upon the same sort and degree of proof
in every case. You are to be satisfied with such proof
as you can get—if you suppose that none better is left
behind. So says the law—

Nonsense—for if that rule is good, you might prove
any-thing—*by* any thing, said Burroughs.

Be quiet Sir....few people see spectres ; and witches
will do their mischief, not in the light of day, and before a multitude, but afar and apart from all but their
associates. You are to be satisfied with less proof therefore in such a case, than it would be proper and rea-
sonable for you to require in a case of property—

And if so—why not in murder ?....murders being perpetrated afar and apart from the world—

Peace I bid you...Having—

How dare you !

—Having disposed of what has been urged respecting the proof, gentlemen of the jury, I should now leave
the case with you, but for a remark which fell from a
neighbour a few minutes ago. Doctor Mather will now
touch upon what I would gladly pass over—the growth
and origin of the evil wherewith we are afflicted.

Here a man of majestic presence of about fifty years
of age arose, and laying aside his hat, and smoothing
away a large quantity of thick glossy hair, which part-
ing on his forehead, fell in a rich heavy mass upon his
broad shoulders, prayed the jury and his brethren of
the church to bear with him for a few moments ; he
should try to be very brief. Brother George—he did
not question his motive he said, but brother George
Burroughs would have you believe that witches and wiz-

wonders of the invisible world ~ direct phrases?

ards are no longer permitted upon our earth ; and that sorcery, witchcraft, and spells are done with.

Whereto I reply....First—that there has been hitherto throughout all ages and among every people, and is now a general, if not a universal, belief in witchcraft and so forth. Now if such universality of belief respecting the appearance of departed souls after death, has been, as it certainly has, a great argument for the immortality of the soul with such as never heard of the Scriptures of Truth, I would ask why a like universality of belief respecting witchcraft and sorcery should be thought of no value, as an argument ? Every where the multitude believe in witchcraft or in that which is of a piece with it. Spirits and fairies, goblins and wizards, prophets and witches, astrologers and soothsayers are found mixed up with the traditionary love and the religious faith of every people on earth, savage and civilized—(so far as we know, I should say) ;—with that of people who inhabit the isles of the sea, afar and apart from each other and from all the rest of the world. I speak advisedly. They believe in spirits, and they believe in a future state—in sorcery and immortality. The wild Irish have what they call their banshees, and the Scotch their second-sight, and the French their loup-garoux, or men turned into wolves—and so also have the Irish ; and a part of our jocular superstition is the posterity of that which existed among the the terrible Goths. Maria—a word that we hear from the lips of the idle and profane, before they have got reconciled to the wholesome severity of our law, was in old Runic a goblin that seized upon the sleeper and took away all power of motion. Old Nicka too—he that we are in the habit of alluding to, in a grave way, as Old Nick, was a spright who used to strangle such as fell into the water. Bo—was a fierce Gothic captain, the warlike son of

Odin, whose name was made use of in battle to scare a surprised enemy. Every where indeed, and with every people, earth sea and air have been crowded with specters, and the overpeopled sky with mighty shadows—I do not know a——

Here the great black horse which Burroughs had left underneath a tree, trotted up to the very door, and stood still, with the reigns afloat upon his neck, and thrust his head in over the heads of the people, who gave way on every side, as he struck his iron hoofs on the step, and for a second or two there was a dead quiet over the whole house. The speaker stopped and appeared astonished, for the eyes of the animal in the strong light of the torches, were like two balls of fire, and his loose main was blowing forward in the draught of the door, so as actually to sound aloud.

Why do you stop—what are you afraid of, Doctor Mather? Not afraid of old Pompey are you?

Had n't you better tie him up? asked a judge.

No—I have something else to do, but I desire that somebody at the door will. But nobody would go near the creature.

—History abounds with proof, I say, respecting witchcraft and sorcery, witches and wizards, magic, spells and wicked power. If we put all trust in the records of history for one purpose, why not for another? If a witness is worthy of belief in one thing—why is he not another? If we find no treachery nor falsehood in a writer; if we meet with nothing but confirmation of what he says, when we refer to other writers of the same people and age, why disbelieve him when he speaks of that which, being new to our experience, we cannot be able to judge of? Able and pious men should be trusted, whatever they may say, so long as they are not contradicted by other able and pious men—

We are to believe not only in witches then, but in fairies and loups-garoux—

Be quiet Sir—

Softly judge....And we are to believe that he who in the course of a tale about the ordinary affairs of ordinary life—

Have done Sir.

—Testifies to a miracle, should be credited as much for what he says of the miracle as for the rest of the—

Be quiet Sir.

—As for the rest of the tale....You cannot escape me brother—

Will you be quiet Sir ?

No.

—The Bible is crowded with proof, continued the Doctor. Sooth-sayers and sorcerers, interpreters of dreams, false-prophets, and a witch with power to make the grave and the sea give up their dead ; men whose little rods became live serpents while they strove with Aaron the High-priest, multitudes who were clothed with a mischievous power....all these are spoken of in the Bible.

It has been said here that credulity is a sign of ignorance. It may be so, my dear friends—but you must know as well as I do, that incredulity is everywhere found among the ignorant. Able men believe much, *because* they are able men. The weak disbelieve much because they are weak. Who are they that laugh when they hear that our earth is a globe, and that once in every twenty-four hours, it turns completely round underneath our feet—

Much whispering here, and a look of surprise on every side of the speaker, encouraged him to a more emphatic delivery.

Who are they that refuse to believe much that the

learned and the wise, fortified in their wisdom by the
beauty of holiness, and the gravity of age, are steadfastly assured of? The truth is that extraordinary
minds have a courage that ordinary minds have not—
for they dare to believe what may expose them to ridicule. The longer we live and the more we know, the
more assured we are that impossible things are possible—

To be sure Doctor, said a judge.

—That nothing is impossible therefore....Now, my
friends of the jury—it appears to me that if witchcraft
had been a common thing with every people, and in all
ages, we could not possibly have had more evidence of
it, than we have now. We have the records of History,sacred as well as profane. We have a great body of
laws, made year after year, among the most enlightened people that ever inhabited the earth, about conjura-
tions, spells and witchraft, and this, in all parts of the
globe and especially in the land of our Fathers; judgment of death, day after day, and year after year, under that law; confessions without number by people
charged with sorcery and witchcraft, not only in various parts of England, but by our very fire-sides and at
our very doors. Added to all this,we have the universal
faith of which I spoke, and altogether, a body of proof,
which if it be false—would be more wonderful than
witchcraft is——

True....true....fearfully and wonderfully true, brother.

—But if such things *are* elsewhere why may they not
be here? If they have been heretofore, why may they
not be now, and forever? We do not know, worms that
we are, how the Lord God of Heaven and earth ope-
rates in His pavillion of thick darkness—we do not
know whether he will or will not work in a given way.
We only know that he may do whatever he will....that

for Him there is no such law as the law of nature. And if so, why may not witches be employed as the wicked are, as great warriors are, for scourging the nations of our earth, and for the glory of our Father above. —Let us pray.

Prayer followed, and after the prayer, the multitude sung a psalm together, and the jury withdrew.

They were not gone long, and when they came back there was but just light enough to see their faces. Not a breath could be heard....not a whisper—and the foreman stood up and was about to speak in the name of the twelve, when Burroughs, who could bear it no longer, leaped upon his feet, and turned to the jury with tenfold power, and gasping for breath, called upon each man by name, as he hoped for mercy hereafter, to speak for himself.

Brother Burroughs!

Brother Moody—

Be quiet Master Burroughs.

I will not be quiet, Master Judge—

Officer!

I will not be quiet I say! And hereafter you will remember my words, and if they prevail with you, men of Massachusetts-Bay, ye will be ready to cry out for joy that I was not brow-beaten by your looks; nor scared by your threats—

Have done Sir.—Do your duty Master High-Sheriff. —Begone Sir. Touch me if you dare.—You see this staff.—You know something of me and of my ways. —Touch me if you dare. What I have to say shall be said, though I die for it. By our Soverign Lord and Master and Mary his Queen, I charge you to hear me! You are shedding the blood of the innocent! You are driving away the good and the brave by scores from the land! You are saying to people of no courage, as to

that poor woman there—as I live she is fast asleep—
asleep !...while that grey-headed man who stoops over
her is about to pronounce the judgment of death upon
her—

Wake the prisoner....what, ho, there! cried the chief
judge.

The officer went up to poor Martha and shook her;
but she did not appear to know where she was, and fell
asleep again with her little withered hands crossed in
her lap.

You are saying to her and such as her....Confess and
you are safe. Deny, and you perish—

To the point Mr. Burroughs....We are tired of this;
we have put up with enough to-day—

I will. I demand of you judges that you call upon
every man there in that box to say, each man for himself, whether it be his opinion that Martha Cory should
suffer death. I *will* have it so....I *will* have it on record
—I will not permit a man of the twelve in such a case
to hide himself under the cloak of the majority—

It cannot be master Burroughs—it cannot be—such a
thing was never heard of....gentlemen of the jury, look
upon the prisoner.

Hear me but a word more! I see death in the very
eyes of the jury—I see that we have no hope. Hear
me nevertheless....hear me for a minute or two, and I
will go away from you forever—

Let us hear him, said another judge.

I proved to you the other day that an accuser had
perjured herself in this court, before your faces, ye
mighty and grave men. What was my reward? You
gave judgment of death on the accused—You let the
accuser go free—I see that accuser now. What will
be said of your justice at home, if you permit her to

escape? Will the judges of England forget you? or the majesty of England forgive you?—

The horse at the door began to grow impatient—snorting and striking with his feet.

—Ye know that the knife was a forgery; and the sheet which has made so much talk here, why even that was a——

He stopped short, and looking at a female who sat near him, appeared to lose himself entirely, and forget what he was going to say.

Well Sir——

Excuse me....I....I....excuse me....although I have no doubt of the fact, although as I hope to see the face of my Redeemer, I do believe the story of the sheet and the story of the spindle, to be of a piece with the story of the knife; a trick and a forgery, yet—yet—

Here he made a sign to the female, as if to encourage her.

—Yet I dare not say *now*, I dare not say *here*, on what my belief is founded. But hear me....they talk of teeth and of whole sets of teeth being discoverable by the prints which appear in their flesh. How does it happen I pray you that all these marks turn out to be on parts of the body which might be bitten by the afflicted themselves? And how does it happen, I pray you, that instead of corresponding teeth, or sets of teeth being found in the accused, ye have repeatedly found her as now, without a tooth in her head? Nay....how does it happen that Abigail Paris and Bridget Pope, who are indeed sufferers by a strange malady, babes that are innocent as the dove, I am sure....God forbid that I should lay the mischief at their door—

Seven and seven pence—muttered the man, who kept an account of the oaths.

——How does it happen I say, that of all the accusers

they and they alone have escaped the mark of the teeth?
How!....because they alone speak the truth; because
they are the deceived....we know not how, judges, but
in a fearful way. They are deceived....poor children,
but they do not seek to deceive others. Nor do they
lie in wait for a——

He was interrupted by a loud furious neigh, so loud
and so furious from the great black stallion at the door,
that Martha awoke and started up with a scream that
thrilled the very blood of the judges, and made the people hurry away from the bar.

Burroughs now saw that he had no hope, and that in a
moment the poor soul before him would hear the sentence of death. He caught up his iron-shod staff, and
breaking through the crowd which recoiled from his
path as if he were something whose touch would be fatal to life, sprang upon the back of the horse, and gal-
lopped away toward the sea-shore.

No language on earth, no power on earth can describe
the scene that followed his departure, the confusion, the
outcry, the terror of the people who saw the fire fly
from his rocky path, and heard leap after leap of the
charger bounding toward the precipice; nor the fright
of the judges; nor the pitiable distress and perplexity
of the poor childish woman, when she was made fully
to understand, after the tumult was over and the dread
clamor and fire-flashing had passed away, and everything was quiet as the grave—nothing to be heard but
a heavy trample afar off and the dull roar of the sea—
that she must be prepared for death

She could not believe it....she would not believe it—
she did not....such was her perfect simplicity, till the
chief judge came to her and assured her with tears in
his eyes, over and over again, that it must be so.

Ah me! said poor Martha, looking out toward the quarter of the sky where the horseman had so hastily disappeared, and where she had seen the last of the fire-light struck from his path ; Ah me, bending her head to listen, and holding up her finger as if she could hear him on his way back. Ah me!—ah me....and that was all she said in reply to her judges, and all she said when they drove her up to the place of her death, decked out in all her tattered finery, as if it were not so much for the grave, as for a bridal that she was prepared.

Ah me! said poor Martha when they put the rope about her neck....Ah me!—and she died while she was playing with her little withered fingers, and blowing the loose grey hair from about her mouth as it strayed away from her tawdry cap....saying over the words of a child in the voice of a child, Ah me—ah me—with her last breath—

God forgive her judges !

— gothic

— reverse of Martha Corey in trial transcripts

— why change her so dramatically?

— Strong → childish.

— Burroughs — hero ; he would not be needed

CHAPTER XII.

The work of that day was the death of George Burroughs. The unhappy allusion that he made to the knife, just before he stopped so suddenly and fixed his eyes upon a young female who sat near him with her back to the light, and her face muffled up so that nobody knew her till after she had gone away, was now in every body's mouth. She was the sister of Rachel Dyer, and her name was Mary Elizabeth; after Mary Dyer and Elizabeth Hutchinson. It was now concluded that what he knew of the perjury of the witnesses, of the sheet and of the knife, he had been told by Mary Elizabeth or by Rachel Dyer, who had been watching him all the livelong day, from a part of the house, where the shadow of a mighty tree fell so as to darken all the faces about her.

It was Rachel Dyer who spoke out with a voice of authority and reproved him for a part of his wild speech. And it was Rachel Dyer who came up to his very side, when he was in array against the judges and the elders and the people, and stood there and spoke to him without fear; while Mary Elizabeth sat by her side with her hands locked in her lap, and her blue eyes fixed in despair upon the earth.

Nor were the people mistaken; for what he knew of the forgery, he did know from Rachel Dyer, and from Mary Elizabeth Dyer, the two quaker women whose holy regard for truth, young as they were, made their

simple asseveration of more value than the oath of most
people.   To them was he indebted for the knowledge,
though he was not suffered to speak of it—for the times
were not ripe enough, that even as the knife-blade was,
the spindle and the sheet were, a wicked forgery ; and
the sign that he made to Elizabeth Dyer, when he stopped in the middle of his speech, and the look of sorrow and love which accompanied his endeavor to appease her frightful agitation, as she sat there gasping
for breath and clinging to Rachel's garb, were enough
to betray the truth to everybody that saw them.

It was fatal to him, that look of sorrow and love, and
ere long it was fatal to another, to one who loved him
with a love so pure and so high as to be without reproach,
even while it was without hope ; and it would have been
fatal to another in spite of her loveliness, but for the
wonderful courage of her....the heroine of our story,
whose behavior throughout a course of sore and bitter
trial which continued day after day, and month after
month, and year after year, deserves to be perpetuated
in marble. No hero ever endured so much—no man
ever yet suffered as that woman suffered, nor as a multitude of women do, that we pass by every hour, without so much as a look of pity or a word of kindness to
cheer them onward in their path of sorrow and suffering. If God ever made a heroine, Rachel Dyer was a
heroine—a heroine without youth or beauty, with no
shape to please, with no color to charm the eye, with
no voice to delight the ear.

But enough—let us go to our story.   Before the sun
rose again after the trial of poor Martha, the conspirators of death were on the track of new prey, and fear
and mischief were abroad with a new shape.   And before the sun rose again, the snare was laid for a preacher of the gospel, and before a month was over, they

dragged him away to the scaffold of death, scoffing at his piety and ridiculing his lofty composure, and offered him up a sacrifice to the terrible infatuation of the multitude. But before we take up the story of his death, a word or two of his life. It was full of wayward and strange adventure.

He appears to have been remarkable from his earliest youth for great moral courage, great bodily power, enthusiastic views, and a something which broke forth afterwards in what the writers of the day allude to, as an extraordinary gift of speech. He was evidently a man of superior genius, though of a distempered genius, fitful, haughty and rash. " He appeared on earth," says an old writer of America, " about a hundred years too soon. What he was put to death for in 1692, he may be renowned for (if it please the Lord) in 1792, should this globe (of which there is now small hope, on account of the wars and rumors of wars, and star-shooting that we see) hold together so long."

He was not a large man, but his activity and strength were said to be unequalled. He went about every where among the nations of the earth; he grew up in the midst of peril and savage warfare ; and at one period of his life, his daily adventures were so strange, so altogether beyond what other men are likely to meet with, even while they are abroad in search of adventure, that if they were told in the simple language of truth, and precisely as they occurred, they would appear unworthy of belief. The early part of his life, he spent among a people who made war night and day for their lives, and each man for himself—the men of Massachusetts-Bay, who did so, for about a hundred and fifty years after they went ashore on the rocks of New-Plymouth—putting swords upon the thighs of their preachers, and Bibles into the hands of their soldiers, whither-

soever they went, by day or by night, for sleep, for battle or for prayer.

On account of his birth, he was brought up to the
church, with a view to the conversion of a tribe to
which his father belonged : Constituted as he was, he
should have been a warrior. He made poetry ; and he
was a strong and beautiful writer : He should have made
war—he might have been a leader of armies—a legisla-
tor—a statesman—a deliverer. Had he appeared in the
great struggle for North-American liberty, fourscore
years later, he probably would have been all this.

He never knew his father ; and he was dropped by
his mother, as he said, in the heart of the wilderness,
like the young of the wild-beast ; but he escaped the
bear and the wolf, and the snake, and was bred a savage, among savages, who while he was yet a child, put
him upon the track of his unnatural mother, and bid him
pursue her. He did pursue her with the instinct of a
blood-pup, and found her, and fell upon her neck and
forgave her and kissed her, and wept with her, and
stood by her in the day of her trouble. On her death-
bed she told him her story. She had been carried away
captive by the Indians while she was yet a child. She
grew up to their customs and married a warrior who
was descended from a white man. Of that marriage
the boy about her neck was born. She had no other
child, but she was very happy until she saw the Rev.
Mr. Elliot of Plymouth, a man who seeing others of
the church occupied in warfare and cruel strife, turned
his back upon the white men that he loved, and struck
into the woods of the north, and went about every where
preaching the gospel to the savages and translating precious books for them, such as " Primers, catechisms,
the practice of piety, Baxter's Call to the Unconverted,
several of Mr. Shepard's composures, and at length the

Bible itself, which was printed the first time in their
language in 1664, and a second time, not long after,
with the corrections of Mr. Cotton, minister of Plymouth." After meeting with Mr. Elliot, who soon added
her to his Indian church, and filled her heart with fear
about original sin, faith, free grace and a future life, she
grew melancholy ; and being assured that her brave
wild husband, a chief who hated the white man with a
hatred passing that of the red men, would never permit
her to preach or pray if he knew it, she forsook him and
fled for refuge to New-Plymouth—her boy, whom she
could not bear to leave with his pagan father, strapped
to her back, and her soul supported by the prayers of
the true church. For a time she doated on the boy, for
a time she was all that a mother could be ; but before a
twelvemonth was over, perceiving that she was regarded by the whites, and by the women especially (her sis-
terhood of the church) as unworthy to associate with
them because of the babe, and because of the father,
whose lineage they said was that of Anti-Christ and the
scarlet-woman, she took to prayer anew, and bethought
herself anew of the wrath of God—her Father—and re-
solving to purify herself as with fire, because of what
she had been to the savages—a wife and a mother, she
strapped the boy on her back once more, and set off
a-foot and alone to seek the hut of his wild father;—and
having found it she kissed her boy, and laid him at his
father's door in the dead of night, and came away with
a joyous heart and a free step, as if now—*now*, that the
little heathen was in a fair way of being devoured by the
wolf or the wild hog, under the very tree which over-
hung the very spot of green earth where she had begun
to love his father, as he lay asleep in the shadow, after
a day of severe toil—she had nothing more to do to be
saved.

her died in battle before the boy had strength
o draw a child's arrow to the head. The boy
        pursuit of his mother at the age of twelve, and
by her he was taught the lessons of a new faith. She
persuaded him to leave the tribe of his father, to forsake
the wild men who were not of the true church, and to
come out from the shadow of the wilderness. The
whites aware of the value of such a youth and of the
use he might be in their bold scheme for the overthrow
of Indian power throughout all North America—the
spread of the Gospel of truth and peace and charity, as
they called it—added their solicitation to hers. But
no—no—the brave boy withstood them all, he would
neither be bribed nor flattered, nor trapped, nor scared ;
nor was he, till he saw his poor mother just ready to die.
But then he gave up—he threw aside the bow and the
arrow, he tore off the rich beaver dress that he wore,
buried the tomahawk, offered up the bright weapons of
death along with the bright wages of death, on the altar of a new faith—prayed his mother to look up and
live and be happy, and betook himself with such fervor
and security to the Bible, that he came to be regarded,
while yet a youth, as a new hope for the church that
had sprung up from the blood of the martyrs.

He married while he was yet a boy. At the age of
twenty, he was a widower. At the age of twenty-four
he was a widower again, with a new love at his heart
which he dared not avow—for how could he hope that
another would be found to overlook his impure lineage ;
now that two had died, he believed in his own soul, a
sacrifice to the bitter though mute persecution they had
to endure for marrying with one who was not altogether a white man ? a love which accelerated his death,
for till the name of Elizabeth Dyer came to be associated with his, after the trial of Martha Cory, the wretch-

ed women, who had acquired such power by their pretended sufferings, were able to forgive his reproof, his enquiry, and his ridicule of what they swore to, whenever they opened their lips to charge anybody with witchcraft. From the day of the trial it was not so. They forgave him for nothing, after they saw how much he loved Mary Elizabeth Dyer. And yet, he was no longer what he had been—he was neither handsome nor youthful now ; and they who reproached others for loving him when he was both, why should they pursue him as they did, when the day of his marvellous beauty and strength was over ? when his hair was already touched with snow, and his high forehead and haughty lip with care ? Merely because he appeared to love another.

He had been a preacher at Salem till after the death of his first wife, where he had a few praying Indians and a few score of white people under his charge. They were fond of him, and very proud of him (for he was the talk of the whole country) till, after her death, being seized with a desire to go away—to escape for a time, he cared not how nor whither, from the place where he had been so very happy and for so short a period, he left his flock; and went eastward, and married anew—and was a widower again—burying a second wife ; the second he had so loved, and so parted from, without a wish to outlive her—and then he crossed the sea, and traversed the whole of Europe, and after much trial and a series of strange vicissitude, came back—though not to the church he had left, but to the guardianship of another a great way off.

He could bear to live—and that was all ; he could not bear to stay, year after year, by the grave where the women that he so loved were both asleep in their youth and beauty—and he forbidden to go near them. But he prospered no more—so say the flock he deserted,

when he went away forever from the church he had
built up, and took refuge again among the people of
Casco Bay, at Falmouth—a sweet place, if one may
judge by what it is now, with its great green hill and
smooth blue water, and a scattered group of huge pine
trees on the north side. It was a time of war when he arrived at Falmouth, and the Indians were out, backed by
a large body of the French and commanded by a French
officer, the Sieur Hertel, a man of tried valor and great
experience in the warfare of the woods. At the village
of Casco Bay, there was a little fort, or block house,
into which about a hundred men with their wives and
little ones were gathered together, waiting the attack
of their formidable and crafty foe, when the preacher
appeared.

There was no time to throw away—they were but a
handful to the foe, afar from succor and beyond the
reach of sympathy. He saw this, and he told them there
was no hope, save that which pious men feel, however
they may be situated, and that nothing on earth could
save them but their own courage and a prayerful assidu-
ity.   They were amazed at his look, for he shewed no
sign of fear when he said this, and they gathered about
him and hailed him as their hope and refuge ; the servant of the Lord, their Joshua, and the captain of
their salvation, while he proceeded to speak as if he had
been familiar with war from his boyhood.

For weeks before the affair came to issue, he and they
slept upon their arms. They never had their clothes
off by night nor by day, nor did they move beyond the
reach of their loaded guns. If they prayed now, it was
not as it had been before his arrival in a large meeting-
house and all together, with their arms piled or stacked
at the door, and the bullet-pouch and powder-horn,
wherever it might please the Lord,—but they prayed

together, a few at a time, with sentries on the watch now, with every gun loaded and every knife sharpened, with every bullet-pouch and every powder-horn slung where it should be ; and they prayed now as they had never prayed before—as if they knew that when they rose up, it would be to grapple man to man with the savages.

At last on a very still night in the month of May, one of the two most beautiful months of the year in that country of rude weather, a horseman who was out on the watch, perceived a solitary canoe floating by in the deep shadow of the rocks, which overhung the sea beneath his feet. Before he had time to speak, or to recollect himself, he heard a slight whizzing in the air, and something which he took for a bird flew past him—it was immediately followed by another, at which his horse reared—and the next moment a large arrow struck in a tree just over his head. Perceiving the truth now, the horseman set off at full speed for the fort, firing into the canoe as he darted away, and wondering at his narrow escape after the flight of two such birds, and the twang of a bowstring at his very ear.

CHAPTER XIII.

He *had* a narrow escape—for the shore was lined with canoes that had come in one by one with the tide, stealing along in the shadow that lay upon the edge of the water, and the woods were alive with wild men preparing to lay an ambuscade. They were not quite ready for the attack however, and so they lay still on both sides of the narrow path he took, and suffered him to ride away in safety when he was within the reach, not only of their balls and arrows but of their knives. They knew with whom they had to deal, and the issue proved their sagacity, for when the poor fellow arrived at the fort and related what he had seen, there was nobody to believe the story but Burroughs, and he would not put much faith in it, although he had reason to think well of the man ; for how were the savages to get across the Bay in such a clear still night—with a sea like the sky, and a sky like the air that men breathe in their boyhood or when they are happy—without being discovered by the boats ? And how were they to approach from the woods, without coming over a wide smooth level of water, seldom deep enough to float a large canoe, nor ever shoal enough to be forded without much risk on account of the mud ?

No attack followed for three nights and for three days, and already the garrison were beginning to be weary of the watch, and to murmur at the restraint he had imposed. It grieved him to the soul to see their fright passing off and their vigilance with it. I beseech you said he, on the afternoon of the fourth day, toward night-fall, as he saw them lying about under the trees, and a full fourth of their number asleep in the rich warm grass, with hardly a knife or a gun where it should be, a pike or a powder-horn—I do beseech you to hear me. You are in jeopardy, in great jeopardy—I know it ; I am sure of it—

So you said a week ago, answered one of the men, stretching himself out, with a rude laugh, and resting his chin on both hands, with his elbows fixed in the turf.

Ah, you may laugh, Mark Smith, but I am satisfied of what I say—the woods are much too still for the time o' the year—

Fiddlestick, parson Burroughs ! what a queer fish you be, to be sure, added another. You are skeered when there's nothin' at all to be skeered at—

So he is Billy Pray, and yet he aint afeard o' the old One himself, when other folks air.

Skeered one day at a noise, and another day at no noise at all—haw, haw, haw !

Do you see how the birds fly ?

What birds ?

The birds that come up from the shore—they fly as if they were frightened—

Well, what if they do ?

An' so I say, Mark Smith—what if they do ? rolling over in the grass and preparing for another nap—Who cares how they fly ? if they're frightened, haw, haw, haw, that's their look out, I spose—haw, haw, haw.

I beseech you to be serious, men—we have heard no shot fired for several days in that quarter, and yet you see the birds fly as if they were hunted. Now, it is my opinion that they are struck with arrows, and arrows you know are made use of by people who are afraid to make a noise when they kill their food—

Ha, ha, ha ;—haw, haw, haw ! gi' me you yit, parson —haw, haw, haw !—what if they're under the shore—can't they kill fish without makin' a noise ? haw, haw, haw !

Fish—fish—but no, I will not be angry with you Taber ; I dare not, much as you deserve it, for every thing we have in the world is now at stake—everything. I entreat you therefore, my friends—I implore you, instead of laying by your arms, to double your guard this very night ; instead of sleeping, to watch more than ever—I feel afraid of this deep tranquility—

Nonsense—double the watch now, when every thing is quiet in the woods, and down by the beach, and not a breath o' noise to be heard anywhere ?

Yea—yea—for that very reason. Look you, David Fisher—I know well what the Indians are, better than you do now, and better than you ever will, I hope. I have now done *my* duty. Do you yours—I have nothing more to say ; but I shall be prepared as I would have you prepare, for the night which is now at hand. Our foes are not on the water, Smith, nor nigh the water now, or they might fish for their food without alarming us. But whether you believe me or no, I say again that they are not far from us, and that we shall find it so, to our sorrow, if you do not keep a better look out for the ——there—there—do you see how that partridge flies !—I tell you again and again, there's something alive in that very wood now.

I dare say there is—haw, haw, haw !

And so I say, Mark Smith, hee, hee, hee—

It may be one o' the dogs—ha, ha, ha !—And they all sprang up together with a jovial outcry, and began to caper about in the grass, and call to a group that were at work a little way off, to go with them and help scour the wood, where the new Joshua thought there was something alive.

You forget Mark Smith—dogs do not go into the woods—stay, stay, I beseech you—don't be so fool-hardy—try to make one of the dogs go to the top of that hill before you—nay, nay, Carver ; nay, nay, and you too, Clark—are you mad Sir ?—you a lieutenant of war, and the first of our men to play the fool.

Here you men, said Clark. Here you men, I say !— Whose afeard among the whole boodle of you ?

No answer.

Nobody's afeard—so I thought. Hourra then—hourra for the king !

Hourra !—hourra !—hourra for the king !

Pooty well, that—pooty fair too—now le'me see you hourra for the queen.

Hourra then—hourra !—hourra for the queen !

That's you, faith !

Hourra—hourra—hou——

No, no that's enough ; a belly full o' hurrah is as good's a feast now—hold up your heads.—How many is there of you, all told ?—Soh—soh—steady there, steady —turn out your heels—

Turn out your toes you mean—haw, haw, hee !

No I don't—hee, hee, haw—give that up long ago.— Now then ! hold still there, hol' still I say, while I count you off—one—two—three—darn your hide Matthew Joy, aint there no hold still to you ? Stan' still, I say ; —four, five—Out o' that snarl, there—one, two, three, four !—very well, very well indeed, never see the wrig-glars do't half so well—clean as a whistle—soh, soh— five an' five is ten, and five is fifteen—there now ; you've put me out—hold your gab, Sargeant Berry ;—how am I goin' to count off the men if you keep a jabberin' so ?

—twenty-five—eight—nine—thirty, and two is thirty-four—now look me right in the eye every one o' you. Heads up—heels out—heels out I say—that's you Jake Berry, you never stoop none, I see—heels out there, every man of you, what are you afeard on ?—You there with the striped jacket on, what's your under jaw out there for ? you want to tumble over it, hey ?—heads up there, heads up—have your ears buttoned back, head soaped and a bladder drawn over it hey ?—Soh, soh !—attention—very well—very well indeed—pooty fair—now I'm goin' to give the word for you—

Wåll....an' what's the word you're goin' to give....hey?

You be quiet our Jake, and you'll see....

How shall we know what to do, when you give the word, if you don't tell us aforehand—I should like to know that....

Shet your clam, Obadiah P. Joy—aint you ashamed o' yourself; nice feller you for a sojer—aint he boys ?

Well, fire away then.

Now you see, I'm goin' to say now or never, three times....behave there ! behave I say !...and when I've said now or never the third time, off I go, you see ! right bang, slap dash into that are wood there, a top or that air hill, and them that's good enough to carry guts to a bear, they'll go with me. Soh....all ready now !

Ay, ay....ay, ay, Sir....ruther guess we be....

Now....or....never ! said Clark, leaning forward with a preparatory step, setting the breach of his heavy musket in the turf, and driving home the ramrod, to prove the weight of the charge. Now-or-never ! cocking it, and shaking the powder into the pan, with his eye on the troop, all of whom stood with their left leg forward, ready for the race....now-or-never ! and off he started before the words were fairly out of his mouth on the heels of two or three who had started before.

Keep together, keep together ! shouted Burroughs. Whatever else you do, keep together !

But no, no....they would have their own way.

If the indians are there, added he....If they are !....as he saw the whole thirty stretching away all out of breath for a wood which crowned the top of the hill---If they are ! it is all up with us....and I am sorely afraid of that narrow green lane there, with a brush-fence on the upper side of it....Ha !----God forgive them for their folly ....Did you see that ?

See what....I saw nothing....

Look....look....there's a glitter and a confused motion there....can't you see it ?....just where the sun strikes on the verge of the hill among the high grass, where a ----my God....I thought so !

I can't see nothin'....the sun hurts my eyes ; but as for you, you can look right into the sun....Hullow.... where now ?

To arms ! to arms ! cried the preacher, in a voice that might have been heard a mile....away with you to your post.

Away with you all, cried Burroughs.

What for ?

To arms ! to arms, I say, continued the preacher.

What for ?

To legs more like....what for ?

Away to the fort I beseech you (lowering his voice) away with you, every man of you—you and your wives and your little ones—you haven't a breath to lose now ....away with you.

Nation sieze the feller ; what for ?

Rattlesnakes an' toddy....what for !

What for—God of our fathers ! O, ye men of little faith !

Hourra for you ! you're cracked I vow ; pooty representative o' Joshua.

Hear me....hear me....Have I not more experience than you ?   Do I not know what I say ?....can you not believe me ? what do you risk by doing as I desire ;....O, if you but knew as well as I do, what is nigh to us!

Wall what is nigh to us ?

Death.

Death !

Ay....death....death....death....

Boo !

My friends....my dear friends....do, *do* be ruled by me....there....there—did you see that ?

See what ?....you *air* cracked, I'll be darned if you aint.

My God ! my God! cried the preacher, looking about in despair, and speaking as if he saw the savages already at the work of death, hatchets and arrows on every side of his path, and every clump of willow-trees near breaking out with fire and smoke. Will you not be persuaded....will you not give up?....see....see....Clark is getting the foolish men together, and if we betake ourselves to the refuge, there may be some hope of a—

What are they stoppin' for now, I wonder —.

Wait half a minute more young man, said the preacher, and you will be satisfied—now—now !

As he spoke, the men halted and came together a few yards from the top of the hill.

Out o' breath I guess?

Out of courage I fear —.

Hourra !—hourra !—shouted the men afar off, and the shout came through the still air, and passed off to the high sea, like a shout of triumph.

Hourra !—hourra !—answered all that were nigh Burroughs, and all that were in the fort.

Hourra!—hourra!—hourra!—echoed the people, and the shores and the rocks rung with their delirious outcry, as the brave thirty dashed forward.

There they go—there they go—yelled a man from the top of a tree just over the head of the preacher. There they go—they are up to the fence now.

Are they indeed—are you sure—God be praised if they are.

Sure!—that I be—there they go—there they go—ha, ha, ha! —they're tumblin' over each other—ha, ha, ha—there they go—I knowed there wasn't any thing there—ha, ha—halloo!—hey—what—

Well Job, what's to pay now?—they're t'other side o'the fence now, arn't they?

T'other side o'the fence!—no, indeed, not within a—Lord God!—Mr. Burroughs!—Mr. Burroughs!

Well—what's the matter now?

Lord have mercy upon us! Lord have mercy upon us!

You'll break your neck Job Hardy, if you're not careful.

O Lord, O lord! what will become of my poor wife? Ah, ha—now do you believe me?

Out broke the tremendous war-whoop of the Pequods, with peal after peal of musketry, and before the preacher could make himself heard in the uproar, two or three white men appeared afar off, running for their lives, and pursued by a score of savages. By and by, another appeared—another and another—and after a while five more—and these were all that had survived the first discharge of the enemy.

You perceive now why the men tumbled about as they did, when they got near the fence; they were struck with a flight of level arrows that we couldn't see—ah! you appear to have a—

O Mr. Burroughs, Mr. Burroughs—what shall we do ?

He made no answer—

O Sir—Sir—take pity upon us !

He stood as if the fear that he felt a moment before was gone away forever, and with it all concern, all hope, all care, all pity for the wretched people about him.

O God of Jacob—what *shall* we do !

Promise to obey me—

We will—we will—we do.

So you did, when I first came here—now you have begun to scoff at your Joshua, as you call me.

O Sir—Sir—do not mock us, we entreat you !— Here they come Sir, here they come ! O speak to us —do speak to us—what are we to do—

Choose me to lead you—

We will—we will—we do !

And with power—mark me—do you see this gun— with leave to put a ball through the head of the first man that refuses to obey me ?

Yes—yes—any thing—any thing—

Very well—that's enough. And I swear to you before God I'll do it. Now—hear what I have to say— Silence !—not a word. Here Bradish—here—take you twelve men out of these, and away with you to the edge of the creek there, so as to cover the retreat of your friends. Away with you.

Hourra—hourra !

Silence—off with you as if you were going, every man to his own funeral—don't hurry—don't lose your breath ; you'll have occasion for it, I promise you, before the work of this day is over—away with you, now ; and every man to a tree ; when you hear the bell, make your way to the fort, and if it please God. we'll whip the enemy yet.

Off sprang the twelve without another word.

Here Fitch, here—I know you—you are a married man—a father and a good father—take these eight who are all fathers ; and you Hobby, you take these—they are all unmarried, and away with you to the willow-hedge yonder ; you to the right, Fitch ; and you to the left, Hobby—and let us see who are the braver men, the married or the unmarried.—Stop—stop—don't hurry ; if you are to make a fair job of it, you must go coolly to work—

Off they started—

Stand by each other !—stick to your trees !—and loa d and fire as fast as you can—that'll do—off with you—

You'll see to the women-folks, I hope—

Off with you, Sir.

Off we go—but I say !—(looking back over his shoulder and bawling as he ran)—what are we to do when we hear the bell ?

Dodge your way in—tree by tree—man by man—

Hourra for you—hourra for Josh—hourra for Joshua !—

Before five minutes were over, the savages were in check, the people reassured, the remnant of poor Clark's party safe, and the whole force of the settlement so judiciously distributed, that they were able to maintain the fight, until their powder and ball were exhausted, with more than treble their number ; and after it grew dark, to retire into the fort with all their women, their children, their aged and their sick. It was no such place of security however as they thought ; for the Indians after they had fired the village and burnt every house in it, finding the powder exhausted, laid siege to the fort by undermining the walls and shooting lighted arrows into the wood-work. From that moment there was nothing to hope for ; and the preacher who

knew that if the place were carried by assault, every living creature within the four walls would be put to
death, and that there would be no escape for the women
or the babes, the aged or the sick, if they did not immediately surrender, drew the principal man of the fort
aside (major Davis) and assuring him of what he foresaw would be the issue, advised a capitulation.

A capitulation Sir, after the work of this day? said
the Major. What will become of you? you have killed
a chief and two or three warriors, and how can you hope
to be forgiven, if they once get you in their power.

Leave that to me—I know their language—I will try
to pass for one of the tribe—

But how—how—impossible, Sir.

Let me have my own way, I beseech you—leave me
to take care of myself....

No, Sir....we know our duty better.

Then, Sir, as I hope to see my God, I will go forth
alone to meet the savages, and offer myself up for the
chief that I have slain. Perhaps they may receive me
into their tribe ...give me a blanket, will you....and perhaps not....for the Pequod warrior is a terrible foe.

Here he shook his black hair loose, and parted it on
his forehead and twisted it into a club, and bound it up
hastily after the fashion of the tribe.

—And the faith which a Huron owes to the dead is
never violated....I pray you therefore—

—Stooping down and searching for a bit of brick, and
grinding it to dust with his heel—

I pray you therefore to let me go forth—

—Bedaubing his whole visage with it, before he lifted
his head—

You cannot save me, nor help me—

Shouldering up his blanket and grasping a short rifle.
What say you!—

Leaping to the turf parapet as he spoke, and preparing to throw himself over.

God of our Fathers—cried the Major, Is it possible! who are you?

A Mohawk! a Mohawk! shouted all that saw him on the parapet; even those who beheld the transfiguration were aghast with awe; they could hardly believe their own eyes.

What say you!—one word is enough....will you give up?

For the love of God, Mr. Burroughs! cried the Major, putting forth his hand to catch at the blanket as it was blown out by a strong breeze....I do pray you——

He was too late; for Burroughs bounded over with a shout which appeared to be understood by the savages, who received him with a tremendous war-whoop. A shriek followed....a cry from the peple within the fort of—treachery!—treachery!—and after a moment or two every-thing was quiet as the grave outside.

The garrison were still with fear—still as death.... Were they deserted or betrayed? Whither should they fly?—What should they do? Their deliverer....where was he? Their Joshua....what had become of him?

The attack was renewed after a few minutes with tenfold fury, and the brave Major was driven to capitulate, which he did to the Sieur Hertel, under a promise that the survivors of the garrison should be safely conducted to Saco, the next English fort, and that they and their children, their aged and their sick should be treated with humanity.

Alas for the faith of the red men! alas for the faith of their white leaders! Before they saw the light of another day, the treaty was trampled under foot by the savages, and hardly a creature found within the four walls of the fort was left alive. The work of butchery

—but no—no—I dare not undertake to describe the horrible scene.

And Burroughs....What of Burroughs?—Did he escape or die ?....Neither. He was carried away captive to the great lakes, and after much vicissitude, trial and suffering which lasted for upwards of a year, came to be an adopted Iroquois, and a voluntary hostage for the faith of the white men of Massachusetts-Bay. From this period we lose sight of him for a long while. It would appear however that he grew fond of a savage life, that his early affection for it sprang up anew, as he approached the deep of the solitude, where all that he saw and all that he heard, above or about him, or underneath his feet, reminded him of his youth, of his parentage and his bravery ; that he began after a time to cherish a hope—a magnificent hope, for a future coalition of the red men of America ; that he grew to be a favorite with Big Bear, the great northern chief, who went so far as to offer him a daughter in marriage ; that he had already begun to reflect seriously on the offer, when the whites for whom he stood in pledge, were guilty of something which he regarded as a breach of trust—whereupon he bethought himself anew of a timid girl—a mere child when he left her, and beautiful as the day, who when the shadow of death was upon all that he cared for, when he was a broken-hearted miserable man without a hope on earth, pursued him with her look of pity and sorrow, till, turn which way he would, her eyes were forever before him, by night and by day. It was not with a look of love that she pursued him—it was rather a look of strange fear. And so, having thought of Mary Elizabeth Dyer, till he was ready to weep at the recollection of the days that were gone, the days he had passed in prayer, and the love he had met with among the white girls of the Bay, he arose, and walked up to the Great northern chief, who but for the treachery of the whites would have been his father, and stood in the circle of death, and offered himself up a sacrifice for the white countrymen of the child that he krew—the lovely and the pure. But no—the Big Bear would not have the blood of a brother.

You know the Big Bear, said he to the young men of the Iroquois that were gathered about him. Who is there alive to harm a cub of the Big Bear? I am your chief—who is there alive to harm the child of your chief? Behold my daughter!—who is there alive to strike her sagamore? Warriors—look at him—He is no longer a pale man—he is one of our tribe. He is no longer the scourge of the Iroquois. The beloved of our daughter—who is there alive to touch him in wrath?

Here all the warriors of the tribe and all the chief men of the tribe stood up; and but one of the whole drew his arrow to the head—the signal of warfare.

White man—brother, said the Big Bear. Behold these arrows! they are many and sharp, the arrows of him that would slay thee, but few—but few brother—and lo!—they are no more. Saying this, he struck down the arrow of death, and lifted the hatchet and shook it over the head of the stubborn warrior, who retreated backward step by step, till he was beyond the reach of the Big Bear.

Brother—would ye that we should have the boy stripped and scourged? said the Big Bear, with all the grave majesty for which he was remarkable. White man—behold these arrows—they are dripping with blood—they are sharp enough to cleave the beach tree. White man—whither would you go? Feel the edge of this knife. That blood is the blood of our brave, who would not obey the law—this knife is the weapon of death. Fear not—for the arrows and the knife are not for the pale man—fear not—beloved of her in whom we have put our hope. The arrows and the knife are not for him—but for the dogs that pursue him. Speak !

I will, said Burroughs, going up to the resolute young savage, who stood afar off, and setting his foot upon the bare earth before him with all his might—I will. Big Bear—father—I must go away. I found you in peace —Let me leave you in peace. Your people and my people are now at war. I cannot strike a brother in battle. The white men are my brothers.

Big Bear made no reply.

Farewell....I must go away. I cannot be on either side when Big Bear and Long-knife are at war.

Good.

I cannot have Pawteeda now. I have done.

Speak.

Wherefore ?

Speak. Why not have Pawteeda now?

Pawteeda should be wife to some warrior, who, when he goes forth to war, will strike every foe of his tribe, without asking, as I should, who is he—and what is he? As a white man, I will not war with white men. As the adopted of the red men....with the blood of a red man boiling in my heart, as the captive and nursling of the brave Iroquois, I will not be the foe of a red man.

Good—

Let Pawteeda be wife to Silver-heels. He hath deserved Pawteeda, and but for me, they would have been happy.

Good.

Here the youthful savage, whose arrow had been struck aside by the Big Bear, lifted his head in surprise, but he did not speak.

I beseech you father ! let my beloved be his wife.

Good.

The youthful savage dropped his bow, threw off his quiver, and plucking the ornamented hatchet from his war-belt, after a tremendous though brief struggle, offered the weapon of death to Burroughs, thereby acknowledging that in some way or other he had injured the pale man. Big Bear breathed fiercely and felt for his knife, but Burroughs went up to the bold youth and gave him his hand after the fashion of the whites, and called him brother.

It shall be so, said the Big Bear. And from that day the youth was indeed a brother to Burroughs, who being satisfied that Pawteeda, if she married one of her own people, would be happier than with a white man, left her and the savages and the Big Bear and the woods forever, and got back among the white people again, at a period of universal dismay, just in time to see a poor melancholy creature, whom his dear wife had loved years and years before, on trial for witchcraft. He could hardly believe his own ears. Nor could he persuade himself that the preachers and elders, and grave authorities of the land were serious, till he saw the wretched old woman put to death before their faces.

CHAPTER XIV.

From that hour he was another man. His heart was alive with a new hope. The dark desolate chambers thereof were lighted up with a new joy. And what if there was no love, nor beauty, nor music sounding in them all the day through, such as there had been a few brief years before, in the spring-tide of his youthful courage; they were no longer what they had been at another period, neither very dark, nor altogether uninhabited, nor perplexed with apparitions that were enough to drive him distracted—the apparition of a child—the apparition of a dead hope—for with him, after the death of a second wife, hope itself was no more. He was now a messenger of the Most High, with every faculty and every power of his mind at work to baffle and expose the treachery of those, who pretending to be afflicted by witchcraft, ware wasting the heritage of the white man as with fire and sword. He strove to entrap them; he set spies about their path. He prayed in the public highway, and preached in the market place, for they would not suffer him to appear in the House of the Lord. He besought his Maker, the Searcher of Hearts, day after day, when the people were about him, to stay the destroyer, to make plain the way of the judges, to speak in the dead of the night with a voice of thunder to the doers of iniquity; to comfort and support the souls of the accused however guilty they might appear, and (if consistant with his Almighty pleasure) to repeat as with the

noise of a multitude of trumpets in the sky, the terrible
words, THOU SHALT NOT BEAR FALSE WITNESS.

But the death of Martha Cory discouraged him.   His
heart was heavy with a dreadful fear when he saw her
die, and before anybody knew that he was among the
multitude, he started up in the midst of them, and broke
forth into loud prayer—a prayer which had well nigh
exposed him to the law for blasphemy; and having made
himself heard in spite of the rebuke of the preachers and
magistrates, who stood in his way at the foot of the gal-
lows, he uttered a prophecy and shook off the dust from
his feet in testimony against the rulers of the land, the
churches and the people, and departed for the habitation
of Mr. Paris, where the frightful malady first broke out
resolved in his own soul whatever should come of it—
life or death—to Bridget Pope, or to Abigail Paris—or
to the preacher himself, his old associate in grief,
straightway to look into every part of the fearful mystery,
to search into it as with fire, and to bring every accuser with whom there should be found guile, whether high
or low, or young or old, a flower of hope, or a blossom
of pride, before the ministers of the law,—every accuser
in whom he should be able to see a sign of bad faith or a
look of trepidation at his inquiry—though it were the
aged servant of the Lord himself ; and every visited and
afflicted one, whether male or female, in whose language
or behaviour he might see anything to justify his fear.

It was pitch dark when he arrived at the log-hut of
Matthew Paris, and his heart died within him, as he
walked up to the door and set his foot upon the broad
step, which rocked beneath his agitated and powerful
tread ; for the windows were all shut and secured with
new and heavy wooden bars—and what appeared very
surprising at such an early hour, there was neither light
nor life, neither sound nor motion, so far as he could

percieve in the whole house. He knocked however, and as he did so, the shadow of something—or the shape of something just visible in the deep darkness through which he was beginning to see his way, moved athwart his path and over the step, as if it had pursued him up to the very door. He was a brave man—but he caught his breath and stepped back, and felt happy when a light flashed over the wet smooth turf, and a voice like that of Mr. Paris bid him walk in, for he was expected and waited for, and had nothing to fear.

Nothing to fear, brother Paris....He stopped short and stood awhile in the door-way as if debating with himself whether to go forward or back.

Why—how pale and tired you are—said Mr. Paris, lifting up the candle and holding it so that he could see the face of Burroughs, while his own was in deep shadow. You appear to have a—the Lord have pity on us and help us, dear brother! what can be the matter with you?— why do you hold back in that way?—why do you stand as if you have n't the power to move? why do you look at me as if you no longer know me?—

True—true, said Burroughs—very true—talking to himself in a low voice and without appearing to observe that another was near. No, no....it is too late now.... there's no going back now, if I would....but of a truth, it is very wonderful, very.....very.....that I should not have recollected my rash vow....a vow like that of Jeptha....very....very....till I had passed over that rocky threshold which five years ago this very night, I took an oath never to pass again. What if the day that I spoke of be near?....What if I should be taken at my word! Our Father who art in ......

Sir—Mr. Burroughs—my dear friend—

Well.

What is the matter with you?

With me ?....nothing.......Oh....ah....I pray you, brother, do not regard my speech ; I am weary of this work, and the sooner we give it up now, the better. I have done very little good, I fear....two deaths to my charge, where I had hoped a....ah, forgive me, brother ; pray forgive me.....But how is this ?....What's the matter with *you ?*

With me !

Yes—with you. What have I done, that you should block up the door-way of your own house, when you see me approach ? And what have I done that you should try to hide your face from me, while you are searching mine with fire, and looking at me with half-averted eyes ?

With half-averted eyes—

Matthew, Matthew—we are losing time—we should know each other better. You are much less cordial to me than you were a few days ago, and you know it. Speak out like a man....like a preacher of truth—what have I done ?

What have you done, brother George—how do I know ?

Matthew Paris....are we never to meet again as we have met ? never while we two breathe the breath of life ?

I hope....I do hope... I am not less glad to see you than I should be ; I do not mean to give you up, whatever others may do, but—but these are ticklish times brother, and just now (in a whisper) situated as we are, we cannot be too cautious. To tell you the truth....I was not altogether prepared to see you, after the—

Not prepared to see me ! Why you told me before you lifted the latch that I was expected, and waited for—

So I did brother....so I did, I confess—

And yet, I told nobody of my intention ; how did you know I was to be with you ?—

One of the children said so above a week ago, in her sleep.

In—deed.

Ah, you may smile now, brother George; but you looked serious enough a moment ago, when I opened the door, and if what they say is true—

How did I look, pray ?

Why—to tell you the truth, you looked as if you saw something.

Well....what if I did see something?

The Lord help us brother—what did you see

I do not say—I am not sure....but I thought I saw something.

The Lord have mercy on you, brother—what was it ?

A shadow—a short black shadow that sped swiftly by me, but whether of man or beast, I do not know. All that I do know, is—

Lower....lower....speak lower, I beseech you, brother B.

No brother P. I shall not speak lower.

Do....do—

I shall not.   For I would have the shadow hear me, and the body to know, whether it be man or devil, that if either cross my path again, I will pursue the shadow till I discover the body, or the body till I have made a shadow of that—

Walk in brother....walk in, I beseech you.

I'll not be startled again for nothing.   Ah—-what are you afraid of ?

Afraid—I—

Brother Paris—-

There now !

Look you brother Paris.   You have something to say to me, and you have not the courage to say it.   You are sorry to see me here....you would have me go away....I

do not know wherefore....I do not ask ; but I know by
the tone of your voice, by your look, and by everything
I hear and see, that so it is. In a word therefore....let
us understand each other. I shall not go away....here I
am Sir, and here I shall abide Sir, until the mystery
which brought me hither is cleared up.

Indeed, indeed Mr. Burroughs, you are mistaken.

I do not believe you.

Sir!

I do not believe you, I say ; and I shall put you to the
proof.

George Burroughs—I will not be spoken to, thus.

Poh--poh—

I will not, Sir. Who am I, Sir—and who are you,
that I should suffer this of you ?—I, a preacher of the
gospel—you, an outcast and a fugitive—

Burroughs drew up with a smile. He knew the temper of the aged man, he foresaw that he should soon
have the whole truth out of him, and he was prepared
for whatever might be the issue.

—Yea, an outcast and a fugitive, pursued by the law
it may be, while I speak ; I, a man old enough to be
your father—By what authority am I waylaid here, underneath my own roof—a roof that would have been a
refuge for you, if you were not a—

A what Sir ?

I have done—

So I perceive Matthew. I am satisfied now—I see
the cause now of what I charged you with. I do not
blame you—grievous though it be to the hope I had
when I thought of you—my—my—brother. I feel for
you—I pity you—I am sorry now for what I said—I
pray you to forgive me—farewell--

Hey—what—

Farewell. You saw me, as you thought, pursued by

the law—flying to the shadow of your roof as to a refuge, and so, you stood at the door and rebuked me, Matthew.

You wrong me—I love you—I respect you—there is no treachery here, and what I have said, I said rashly, and I know not why. Forgive me brother George.... forgive the old man, whose fear hath made him overlook what is due to them, whoever they are, that fly to his habitation for shelter.

I do forgive you....my brother. Let me also be forgiven.

Be it so....there....there....be it so.

But before I take another step, assure me that if I enter the door, neither you nor yours will be put in jeopardy.

In jeopardy!

Am I pursued by the law?....am I, of a truth?

Not pursued by the law, George: I did not say you were; I do not know that you will be....but indeed, indeed, my poor unhappy friend, here is my roof, and here am I, ready to share the peril with you, whatever it may be, and whatever the judges and elders and the people may say.

You are.

Yes.

I am satisfied. You have done your duty....I shall now do mine. You are a true brother; let me prove that I know how to value such truth. I am not pursued by the law, so far as I know or have reason to believe, and if I was....I should not come hither you may be assured for safety....nay, nay, I do not mean a reproach.... I have absolute faith in your word now; I do believe that you would suffer with me and for me....but you shall not. If I *were* hunted for my life, why should I fly to you?....You could be of no use to me....you could

neither conceal me nor save me....and I might bring
trouble upon you and yours forever.   What would become of you, were I to be tracked by the blood-hounds
up to your very door?

I pray you, said the aged man, I do pray you....look-
ing about on every side, shadowing the light with his
meagre hand, the whole inward structure whereof was
thereby revealed, and speaking in a low subdued whisper—as if he knew that they were overheard by invisible creatures....I pray you brother....dear brother....let us
have done with such talk—

Why so....what are you afraid of?

Softly....softly....if they should overhear us—

They....who....what on earth are you shaking at?

No matter.....hush.....hush......you may have no such
fear brother B....you are a bold man brother B....a very
bold man....but as for me....hark!....

What's the matter with you?....What ails you?

Hush!....hush....do you not hear people whispering
outside the door?

No.

A noise like that of somebody breathing hard?—

Yes—

You do....the Lord help us.

I do man, I do—but it is yourself—you it is, that are
breathing hard—what folly Matthew—what impiety
at your age!

At my age....ah my dear brother, if you had seen
what I have seen, or heard what I have heard, or suffered as I have, young as you are, and stout and powerful
as you are, you would not speak as you do now, nor look
as you do now....

Seen....heard....suffered.   Have I not seen....have I
not suffered!....How little you know of me....

Here Matthew Paris, after securing the door with a

multitude of bars and bolts of oak, led the way with a cautious and fearful step toward a little room, through the gaping crevices of which, a dim unsteady light, like the light of a neglected fire could be seen.

Death Sir....death in every possible shape, I might say....but who cares for death ?....peril which, whatever you may suppose Matthew, at your age—old as you are ....why—what am I to understand by your behaviour !.... you don't hear a word I am saying to you.

There, there—not so loud I entreat you....not so loud —there's no knowing what may be near us.

Near us—are you mad ?—what can be near us ?

There again—there, there !

Stop—I go no further.

My dear friend—

Not another step—if *you* are crazy, I am not—I will be satisfied before I go any further. Were I to judge by what I now see and hear—did I not believe what you said a few moments ago ; and were I not persuaded of your integrity, Matthew, I should believe my foes were on the look out for me, and that you had been employed to entrap me, as the strong man of old was entrapped for the Philistines, with a show of great love—

Brother !

—Nay, nay, it is not so ; I know that very well. But were I to judge by your behavior now, I say, and by that alone, I should prepare my fingers for the fight, and this weapon for war.

And I—if I were to judge by your looks and behaviour at the door, I should believe that you were flying for your life, and that betaking yourself to my roof, without regard for me or mine, you were willing to betray us to the law.

Man—man—how could you believe such a thing of me ?

You were pale as death, George—

Speak louder—

Pale as death, and you did not answer me, nor even appear to see me, till after I had spoken to you two or three times.

Of a truth?—

You appeared unwilling to trust yourself beneath my roof, when you saw me—

Did I—

—So that I was driven to recall the transaction which drove us apart from each other—

Did I, Matthew?--I am sorry for it—

Yes—and your behavior altogether was very strange —is very strange now ; it is in fact, allow me to say so, just what I should look for in a man who knew that his life was in jeopardy. Take a chair—you are evidently much disturbed, you appear to have met with some—— surely—surely—my brother, something *has* happened to you.

—Did I—

You do not hear me—

True enough, Matthew—I am very tired—please to give me a drop of water and allow me to rest myself here a few minutes —I must be gone quickly—I have no time to lose now, I percieve.

You take a bed with me to night, of course.

No.

You must—indeed you must, my good brother—I have much to ask—much to advise with you about. We are in a dreadful way now, and if we—

Impossible Matthew—I cannot—I dare not. I have more to do than you have to say. Are the children a-bed yet ?

Ah brother, brother—you have not forgotten the dear child, I see.

Which dear child ?

Which dear child !—why—oh—ah—I thought you meant little Abby—the very image of my departed wife.

Is Bridget Pope with you now ?

—She often speaks of you, the dear little babe....she wears the keep-sake you gave her, and won't let any body sit in your place, and if we desire to punish her, we have only to say that uncle George won't love her....

The dear child ! I saw her with Bridget on the day of the trial, but I had no time to speak to either. I hope they are both well—Bridget has grown prodigiously, I hear—

And so has Abby —

Indeed !

Indeed—why—is it so very wonderful that Abby should grow ?

To be sure—certainly not—she was very fair when I saw her last—when I left this part of the world, I mean.

Very—

So upright, and so graceful and free in her carriage....

Free in her carriage ?

For a child, I mean—so modest, and so remarkable in every way—so attentive, so quiet—

Ah my dear friend—how happy you make me. You never said half so much about her, all the time you lived here ; and I, who know your sincerity and worth and soberness—to tell you the truth George—I have been a little sore....

....So attentive, so quiet and so assiduous....

Very true....very true....and to hear *you* say so, is enough to make her father's heart leap for joy.

What—in the grave ?....

In the grave ?....

And after all, I do not perceive that her eyes are too large....

Too large ?

Nor that her complexion is too pale....

Nor I....

Nor that her very black hair is either too....

Black hair.....black.....pray brother B. do you know
what you are saying just now ? black hair.....why the
child's hair is no more black than—large eyes too—
why it is Bridget Pope that has the large eyes—

Bridget Pope—to be sure it is—and who else should
it be ?

CHAPTER XV.

So then—It was Bridget Pope you were speaking of all the time, hey, continued the father.

To be sure it was—what's the matter now ?

Why——a——a——the fact is, brother—

You are displeased, I see.

Not at all—not in the least—no business of mine, brother George—none at all, if you like Bridget Pope as much as ever—child though she is—no business of mine brother Burroughs—I am sure of that.

So am I—

You may laugh brother B., you may laugh.

So I shall brother P.—so I shall. O, the sick and sore jealousy of a father ! Why—do you not know Matthew Paris—have I not given you the proof—that your Abigail is to me even as if she were my own child —the child of my own dear Sarah ? And is not my feeling toward poor Bridget Pope that of one who fore-sees that her life is to be a life, perhaps of uninterrupted trial and sorrow, because of her extraordinary charac-ter. I do acknowledge to you that my heart grows heavy when I think of what she will have to endure, with her sensibility—poor child—she is not of the race about her—

There now George—there it is again ! That poor child has never been out of your head, I do believe, since you saw her jump into the sea after little Robert Eve-leth ; and if she were but six or eight years older, I am persuaded from what I now see, and from what I have seen before——

Matthew Paris !

Forgive me George—forgive me—I have gone too far.

You *have* gone too far.

Will you not forgive me ?

I do—I do—I feel what you have said though ; I feel it sharply—it was like an arrow, or a knife—

Allow me to say—

No, no—excuse me—I know what you would say.

Her great resemblance to your wife, which everybody speaks of, and her beauty—

No, no, Matthew, no, no....I cannot bear such talk.

Ah George !

Both my wives were very dear to me ; but she of whom you speak, she whom you saw upon the bed of death in all her beauty—she who died before you, in all her beauty, her glorious beauty ! but the other day as it were.....

The other day, George ?

—Died with her hand in yours but the other day, while I was afar off—she whom neither piety nor truth could save, nor faith nor prayer—she of whom *you* are already able to speak with a steady voice, and with a look of terrible composure—to me it is terrible Matthew she is too dear to me still, and her death too near, what-ever you may suppose ; you, her adopted father !—you, the witness of her marriage vow—you, the witness of her death—for me to endure it—O my God, my God—that such a woman should be no more in so short a time !

Dear George——

—No more on the earth....no more in the hearts of them that knew her.

Have I not lost a wife too ?....a wife as beautiful as the day, George, and as good as beautiful ?

—No more in the very heart of him, her adopted father, who sat by her and supported her when she drew her last breath——

Dear George....would you break the old man's heart ? why should I not speak of them that are dead, as freely as of—

The children....the children, Matthew—how are they? The children ?

I have work to do before I sleep. It grows late....how are they ?

No longer what they were, when you saw them about my table five years ago....

I dare say not—five years are an age to them.

But they are better now than they were at the time of the trial ; we begin to have some hope now—

Have you, indeed ?

Yes, for they have begun to....she has begun, I should say....Bridget Pope....

I understand you—the father will out....

—She has begun to look cheerful and to go about the house in that quiet smooth way—

I know, I know....it was enough to bring the water into my eyes to look at her—

Robert Eveleth is to be with us to-night, and if we can persuade him to stay here a week or two, I have great hope in the issue....

What hope—how ?—

That both will be cured of their melancholy ways— Bridget Pope and my poor Abby—

Their melancholy ways—why, what have they to do with Robert Eveleth ?

Why—don't you see they are always together when he is here—

Who—Abigail and he ?

No—Bridget Pope—

Well, what if they are—what does that prove ?

Prove !

Yes—prove—prove—you know the meaning of the word, I hope ?

Don't be angry, George.

Angry—who's angry?—-poh, poh, Matthew, poh, poh, poh ; talk about love in a girl of that age for a boy of that age—

Love—who said anything about love ?

Poh, poh, poh—affection, or love—or—whatever you please, Matthew—it isn't the word I quarrel with—it is the idea—I wonder that you should put such things into their head—

I !

A man of your age, Matthew Paris—

Ah, brother, brother.

Sir.

There you go again!—But I see how it is, and I shall say no more about Bridgy Pope or the boy, Robert Eveleth, till you are a——

For shame—

Why so, George ? All I wanted to say was, that when Robert is here, the children are happy together and cheerful. They go romping about in the woods together, up all the mows in the neighbourhood, or along by the sea-shore, (between schools) and spend half their play-time in the blackberry-swamp—you look very serious....

I feel so....good by'e.

Good by'e—I thought you had come to see the children ?

To see the children ?—so I did—as I live, Matthew ! Lead me to them—

Follow me in here—they are just going to bed, I see.

So I did—I came for no other purpose—

Really ?

Really—

A tip-toe, brother, if you please—the sight of you may do them good—

I hope so, said Burroughs—beginning to feel what he had never till that hour had the slightest idea of—jealousy—downright jealousy, and of a nature too absurd for belief, except with such as have been afraid in a like way, of losing the chief regard of no matter what—anything for which they cared ever so little, or ever so much —a bird or a kitten, a dog or a horse, a child or a woman.

I hope so, he repeated, as he followed the preacher on tip-toe and peeped into the little room to survey their faces before he entered, that he might enjoy their surprise. But he started back at the first view, and caught by the arm of his aged brother—for there sat the poor children with their little naked feet buried half leg deep in the wood-ashes, their uncombed hair flying loose in the draught of the chimney, each with her wild eyes fixed upon the hearth, and each as far from the other as she could well get in the huge fire-place ; and so pale were they, and so meagre, and their innocent faces were so full of care and so unlike what they should have been at their age—the age of untroubled hope and pure joy—that he was quite overcome.

They heard his approach, either his step or his breathing, and started away from their settles with a cry that pierced his heart.

I pray you ! said he.—But Abigail ran off and hid herself in a far corner of the room, where a bed was turned up in a niche, and waited there, gasping for breath, as if she expected to be eaten alive ; and Bridget Pope, although she stood still and surveyed him with a steady look, made no reply to what he said, but grew very pale, and caught by a chair when he spoke to her.

Why how now, said Mr. Paris, how now, children ? what's the matter with you, now ?

Father—father ! cried Abigail, peeping out with eyes full of terror, and speaking with a voice which made her father look toward the door as if he expected Burroughs to assume another shape, or somebody else to appear from the darkness behind. O father—father—O *my !* —there, there !—there he goes !

Where—where—what is it, my poor child ?

Why—Burroughs—Burroughs—there, there! there now, there he goes again !—that's he—there, there— don't you see him now, father ?

See whom, dear ?—see what ?

Why, Burroughs, to be sure—Burroughs, the bad man —there—there—there—

God help us !

I never saw him afore in that shape, father, never in all my days, but I know him though, I know him wel enough by the scar on his forehead—there, there—there he goes !—can't you see him now, father ?

See him—to be sure I do.

Gracious God—Almighty Father—what can be the matter with the poor child ? I begin to perceive the truth now, said Burroughs, I do not wonder now at your faith, nor at your dreadful terror.

There—there—didn't you hear that, father ?—it spoke then—I heard it speak as plain as day—didn't you hear it, father ?

Why—Abigail Paris—don't you know me dear ? don't you know your uncle George ?

There again—that's jest the way he speaks—help, father, help !

What *is* the matter with you, child ?

Nothin' father ; nothin' at all now—it stops now—it

was a comin' this way when you spoke—my stars! anybody might know it, father.

Know what, Abby?

Make me believe that aint George Burroughs, if you
can, father.

Why, to be sure it is, cried Burroughs, going a step
nearer to the place where the little creature lay, cuddled
up in a heap, with a quantity of split-wood and pitch-knots
gathered about her. Why do you tremble so, dear?—
what's the matter with you?—what are you afraid of?

Father—father—shrieked the poor child, stop it,
father!

Why!—don't you know me Abigail?—nor you neither Bridget Pope—don't *you* know me dear?

O Sir—Sir—is it you?—is it you yourself, Mr. Burroughs? cried the latter, huddling up into the shadow,
and catching her breath, and standing on tip-toe, as if
to get as far out of his reach as possible. O Sir—is it
you?....

To be sure it is—look at me—speak to me—touch
me—

O Sir, Sir——no, no, Mr. Burroughs—no, no.

Why what on earth can possess you Bridget Pope?
—what on earth is the matter with you?—what are you
afraid of?

O Lord Sir—I hope it *is* you!

Who else can it be?—don't you see me?—don't you
hear me speak?—O I'm ashamed of you, such a great
girl, to be afraid of a———

Who else?—how should I know Sir? and if I knew,
I should be afraid to say; but I don't know Sir, I don't
indeed Sir—and how should I, pray, when I never saw
you before to night—

Never saw me before to night!

No Sir, never—never—

Are you out of your head Bridget Pope ?—never saw me before ?

No Sir—never, never—I wish I may die if I ever did, though others have—your shape I mean Sir—but I would never allow they told the truth about you when they—O, Abigail, Abigail !

Did you speak to *me*, Bridgy Pope ?

O my, O my !—it *is* your uncle George !—it is indeed—I see the ring he used to wear—that's the very ring !

You don't say so Bridgy !—mother's pretty ring ?

Speak to it now Abby—you aint afeard now—speak to it, will you ?

No, no, Bridgy, no, no—you speak to it yourself—what are you cryin' about father ?

I did speak to it Abby—it's your turn now—

But you're the nearest—

But you're the furthest off—

Ah—but you're the oldest !—

But you are the youngest....

Father—father—its lookin' at me now !

Well, what are you afeard on Abby—I don't believe he's one o' the crew—is he, uncle Matthew ?

The preacher was afraid to open his mouth—his heart was too full.   It was the first time they had called each other Abby and Bridgy, for months.

And so—and so—they may say what they like ; and I—I—as for me Abby, I'm not afeard now, one bit—

How you talk Bridgy.

No—and I'll never be afeard again—so there !

Why—Bridgy !

And so you'd better come out o' your cubby-house, and go up to it and speak to it ; I'm not afeard now, you see.

Nor I.

Yes you be, or you wouldn't stay there.

What if you speak to it agin Bridgy?

So I will. How d'ye do Sir, how d'ye do?

My!—if 'taint a laughin' at you!

I hope you're satisfied now—

Aint you railly afeard one bit though, cousin Bridgy?

No indeed, not I. See if I be now—look at me and see what I'm a goin' to do. There Sir!—there Mr. Burroughs, or whatever you be, there's my hand Sir—there——

Laying it on the table before him and turning away her head just as if she were going to have some hateful operation performed....

—You may touch it if you like—

God bless you dear.

I'm not afeard of you now—am I Sir?

No, no—my brave girl.

And you are not ashamed of me now I hope—are you Sir?

No—no —but I am proud of you—

He touched her hand as he spoke, but released it immediately, for he saw that he had a very cautious game to play.

By jingo Abby!

By jingo—what for?

Why the hand is warm after all; it is Mr. Burroughs himself—it is, it is!—I know him now as well as I know you——hourra!

O my!

As sure as you are alive Abby.

Why, Bridget Pope, said her uncle. What on earth are you made of?

Me—uncle Matthew?

Why.. it appears that you did not know him just now, when you spoke to him.

No Sir—I wasn't very sure—not so sure as I am now.

There's courage for you—true courage, Matthew Paris; a spirit worthy of all admiration.

Very true—very true—but she is two years older than Abby.

Not so much, Matthew, not so much—well dear ?

May I go now—please....

You are not afraid of me now, dear ?

No Sir—if you please—not much—

And you never will be so again, I hope ?

So do I Sir—so do I....I hope so too....for its an awful thing to be afeard of anybody.

Poor child.

To be afeard in the dark Sir—in the dead o' the night Sir—when you're all livin' alone Sir—O, it *is* dreadful.

So it is, our Bridgy.

But I never mean to be afeard again Sir.

There's a good girl.

Never, never (catching her breath)—if I can help it.

Nor I nyther, Bridgy—

Never....(lowering her voice and peeping under the bed) never without I see the wicked Shape as they do —right afore me in the path, when I go after the cows, or when I go to look for the pretty shells on the seashore—

What wicked Shape ?

Your own Sir—please.

Ah.

And so Sir—and so—and so uncle Matthew—and so you'd better come out o' your hole, Abby dear.

After a deal of persuasion, *Abby dear* began to creep out of her hiding-place, and by little and little to work her way along, now by the split-wood, now by the wall, and now with her back toward the place where the Shape sat holding his breath and afraid to move, lest he should scare away the new-born courage of the little thing.

After a while she got near enough to speak; and holding by her father's coat all the time, she sidled up to Burroughs, who would not appear to see what she was about, and lifting up her innocent face, articulated just loud enough to reach him—There now.

Well dear—

Off she started, the moment he spoke.

But finding she was not pursued, she stopped a yard or two from his chair, and peeping over the flap of her father's coat—and seeing that the shape was looking another way—she came a little nearer—stopped—a little nearer still—inch by inch—stopped once more, and looking up at him, as if she knew not whether to run off or stay, said—You be Mr. Burroughs—*I* know?

He was afraid to speak yet, and afraid to move.

Uncle George—ee.

God bless the babe!

There now—I told you so—you be uncle George, baint you?

Yes dear—but who are you—you little wayward imp, with such a smutty face and such ragged hair....poh, poh ....poh....what are you afraid of?

O father, father! he's got me! he's got me!

Well—there, there—if you don't like to stay with me, go to your father....

Why....what a funny Shape it is father—if it *is* a shape.

I don't believe your hair has been combed for a twelvemonth.

O but it has though....

It is no fault of ours, my friend, said her father, delighted to see her at the knee of Burroughs. We do all we can, but the more we scrub, the more we may ; the

more we wash, the dirtier and blacker she grows, and
the more we comb, the rougher looks her beautiful hair
....it was beautiful indeed a year ago—

It was like spun gold when I left you.

—But she is no longer the same Abigail Paris that you
knew—

Why....father !....

Be careful Sir ; metaphors and poetry are not for
babes and sucklings....

You be a good man after all....baint you Sir? continued she, getting more confidence at every breath, now
that she found the Shape willing to let her go whenever
she chose to go. You be a good man after all Sir...
baint you Sir?

I hope so dear.

You never torments the people, do you? Leaning
with her whole weight upon his knee, letting go her father's coat, and shaking her abundant hair loose.

I !....no indeed I hope not....I should be very sorry to
torment the people.

Would you though?

Yes dear....

Uncle Georgee ! said the child in a whisper that
sounded like a whisper of joy....dear uncle George....and
he drew her into his lap, and she put her mouth close to
his ear and repeated the words again, so that they went
into his heart—O, I do love you, uncle Georgee !

Having passed a whole hour in examing the two little
sufferers (whom he left asleep in each other's arms) he
went away utterly confounded by their behaviour, and
with little hope of reaching the truth; for if Abigail Paris
and Bridget Pope were what they seemed to be....what
they undoubtedly were indeed,—innocent as the dove—
how could he say after all, that they were *not* bewitched ? Still however there was one hope. That which

he saw might proceed from disease or from fear, the
natural growth in that age and among that people, of a
solitary situation. But if so, what was he to think of
others, who had a like faith, and yet lived in a populous
neighborhood and were cheerful and happy ? Anxious
to arrive at the truth, he set off immediately to see Ra_
chel and Elizabeth Dyer, knowing that under their quiet
roof, he should be at peace, though he failed to procure
what he needed....further information about her who had
abused the people and the judges with a tremendous
forgery.

CHAPTER XVI.

He was not altogether disappointed. Rachel Dyer knew much of the woman who had fabricated the story of the spindle and sheet, and was only waiting for proof to impeach her for it, face to face, before the people and the judges. Her name was Hubbard ; she was in the prime of life, with a good share of beauty ; bold, crafty and sly, and very much feared by those who believed her story ; and Rachel Dyer, though a woman of tried worth and remarkable courage, was unwilling to appear against her, till she could do so with a certainty of success, for it would be a fearful stake to play for, and she knew it—nothing less than life to life—her life against that of Judith Hubbard.

But though she knew this, having been very familiar with the aspect of peril from her youth, and being aware that she was looked up to with awe by the multitude— not so much with fear, as with a sort of religious awe— great love mingled with a secret, mysterious veneration, as the chief hope of her grandmother, Mary Dyer, the prophetess and the martyr—she determined to play for that stake.

She knew well what a wager of death was, and she knew well the worth of her own life. But she knew what was expected of her, and of what she was capable, in a period of general and sore perplexity and sorrow ; for twice already in her short life she had approved her high relationship to the martyr, and the sincerity of

her faith as one of that people, who, when they were
smitten of one cheek, turned the other, and who, when
they were reviled,reviled not again,—by going forth into
the great woods of North-America, while they were beset with exasperated savages and with untamed creatures of blood, forever on the track of their prey, to in-
tercede for those who had been carried off into captivity
by the red heathen....pursuing her fearful path by night
and by day....in winter and in summer....and always
alone....to prove her faith; and prevailing in each case
where there seemed to be no sort of hope, and thereby
preserving to the colony eight of her precious youth; and
among others, one who had despitefully used her a little
time before, and whose grandfather was reputed to have
been the real cause of her beloved grandmother's death.

When Burroughs arrived at the door, and laid his
hand upon the rude latch, he started, for the door flew
open of itself; there was no lock on it, no fastening,
neither bolt nor bar. He found the two sisters with a
large book open before them, and Rachel reading to
Elizabeth in a low voice, with her arm about her neck.
How now ? said he.

They gave him a hearty cheerful shake of the hand ;
but he observed, or thought he observed a slight change
of colour in the face of Rachel, as he turned his eye to
the book and saw a paragraph with her name in it.

You were reading, said he, as he drew up a chair to
the table. Go on, if you please.

Thank thee, George ; we had nearly finished....

What are you reading, pray ?

We were just reading the beautiful story of....why,
Rachel Dyer....if thee ain't a goin' to shet up the book
afore we are half done with the chapter! said Elizabeth,
jumping up with a look of surprise....well, I do think !

Rachel turned away her head with a somewhat hasty

motion, pushed the book toward Elizabeth, and sat back as far as she could possibly get into her grandmother's huge arm-chair ; but she made no reply, and Elizabeth saw that something was the matter.

Thee's not well, I'm afeard, sister....dear sister, said she, going up to her and throwing her arms about her neck, and kissing her as a child would kiss a mother.

Rachel burst into tears.

Why ! exclaimed Elizabeth....why !....what is the matter with thee, Rachel......thee turns away thy head.... thee will not look at me....what have I done, I beseech thee, dear sister....what have I done to grieve thee ? Speak to her, George....do speak to her.'...I never saw her in this way before.

Poor soul, said he, going up to her and speaking with visible emotion ; but as he drew near and would have put his hand upon hers, like a brother, she pulled it away ; and then as if suddenly recollecting herself, she rose up, and after a short struggle, turned to him with a smile that affected him even more than her tears, and spoke to him very kindly, and put her hand into his, and prepared to finish the chapter. It was the story of the patriarch, who, after cheating his father in his old age, and betraying his brother Esau, went away into the land of the people of the East, where in due course of time he was overreached and betrayed by his mother's brother ; and the voice of the reader was firm and clear, and her look steady, till she came to these words—

" And Laban had two daughters : the name of the elder was Lear, and the name of the younger was Rachel.

" Lear was tender-eyed, but Rachel....

Her voice quavered now, and she proceeded with visible effort and hurry.

——" But Rachel was *beautiful and well favored. And Jacob loved Rachel.*

A moment more—and she recovered her voice entirely, and finished the chapter without a sign of emotion, as if she knew in her own soul that Burroughs and Elizabeth were watching her as they had never watched her before.

Strange morality—said he, as they laid the Book aside. This patriarch, and others who happen to have been greatly favored in that age by the God of the patriarchs were guilty of more than we, with our shortsighted notions of propriety, should be very willing either to overlook or forgive—

George Burroughs—

My dear friend—what I say is very true, and to pass over David, the man after God's own heart, I would ask you whether he who cheated his father and his brother, by the help of his mother, while he was yet a youth, and as he grew up laid before the stronger cattle the rods which he had peeled—as we have it in the Book—and suffered the cattle that were weak—as we read there---to conceive in their own way, so that " the feebler were Laban's cattle and the stronger Jacob's.... whether he, I say....

I see no advantage in this....we have a faith of our own, said Rachel, interrupting him with a mild seriousness which he dared not contend with. I pray thee to spare us,—and thyself George....

Are we not to bear witness to the truth, Rachel?

It may be the truth George, but....glancing at Elizabeth who sat as if she expected the roof to fall in, or the earth to give way under their feet and swallow them up for their dreadful impiety....some truths we know are for the strong, and some for the weak.

Ah....what was that! cried Elizabeth catching at her sister's arm.

Poor child....there George there....thee sees the effect of thy truth....why, Lizzy!

O I did hear something....I did, I did! continued Elizabeth, clinging to her sister and fixing her eyes upon the roof. O I'm sure there's something up there.

Well, and what if there is, pray? What's thee afraid of?....Is the arm of our Father shortened or his power shrunk, that we are not safe?

Nay nay Rachel....no wonder she's afraid. You are lying asleep as it were, in the very path-way of the prowling savage and the beast of blood, with no lock on your outer-door, not so much as a wooden bolt, with no sort of security for you, by day or by night; and all this in a time of war, and you living on the outskirts of the wood....why it's no better than tempting Providence, Rachel Dyer.....

Just what I say....said Elizabeth....

And I am sorry to hear thee say so....

Nay nay Rachel....why so grave? I confess to you that I should not like to live as you do....

I dare say, George....

It would be impossible for me to sleep....

No no....not impossible.

And I should expect a savage or a bear to drop in, every hour of the day....

Thee wouldn't always be disappointed George.

And every hour of the night, Rachel, without ceremony.

We disregard ceremony, George.

Why, what are you made of Rachel Dyer....

Of earth, George.

Not of common earth....

George Burroughs!

But of a truth now, are you not afraid of a call some

one of these dark nights from a stray savage, a Pequod, or a Mohawk—or an Iroquois?

She smiled.

Are you not? We are at open war now with half the tribes of the North.

No....and why should I be? I know them all and they know that Elizabeth and I are what they call poo-ka-kee....

Poor quakers, hey?....

Yes, and thee may be very sure that we have not much to be in fear of when I tell thee....prepare thyself George....that hardly a day goes over without my seeing some one or two of thy tribe, or of the Iroquois.

What! cried the preacher, leaping out of the chair and looking up at the roof....there may be somebody there now.

Not up there George....

Where then?

It would be no easy matter for me to say : for who-ever it is, he will not appear till thee is gone...why, what's thee afraid of?....and then he will open the door as thee did, and walk in. Thee may put up thy knife George, and lay down thy staff...they'll never cross thy path, nor harm a hair of thy head....

How can I be sure of that?

By believing what I say to thee.

I know the savages better than you do, my dear friend.

I have my doubts, George. They never harmed a visiter of mine yet, neither going or coming ; and I have had not a few of their mortal foes under my roof while they were lying within bow-shot of the door. Be assured of what I say....thee has nothing to fear....

Would we let thee come, George, if it wasn't very safe? asked Elizabeth.

Forgive me, said he, forgive me ; and his eyes flash-

ed fire, and Elizabeth hid her face, and Rachel turned
away her head.

Why, how now? said he, looking at both in astonishment, you appear to have a ——

He stopped short....he had an idea that he knew the character of both sisters well; he had been acquainted with Mary Elizabeth from her childhood up, and with her grave sister from her youth up, and he had always perceived that there was a something in the nature of both, but especially in that of Rachel Dyer, unlike the nature of anybody else that he ever knew; but he had never been so puzzled by either as he was now——

I hope I have not offended you? said he, at last.

Do thee feel safe George?

Yes....but you are not safe....ah, you may smile and shake your head, but you are not safe. How do you think the authorities of the land will endure to be told that you are on such familiar terms with the foe? Have a care....you will get yourself into trouble, if you don't.

Make thyself easy George. We are quite safe; we belong to neither side in the war, and both sides know it. By abiding here, I am able to do much good....

As how, pray?

By showing that I am not afraid to trust to the good-faith of savages; by showing them that they are safe in trusting to my good-faith, and above all, that weapons of war, whatever thee may say, George, are not necessary to them who put their trust in the Lord....

What if we were to entrap some of your visiters without your knowledge?

It would be no easy matter. They guard every path I do believe, that leads to my door....

Every path....

Yes....and let me tell thee now, that if it should ever happen to thee to go astray in these woods, thee will have nothing to fear so long as thee pursues a path which leads to my door....if thee should miss thy way, inquire aloud, and thee will be safe....

How so ?

Thee will be overheard....

You astonish me.

And guarded, if it be necessary....

Guarded !....

Up to my very door....thee can hardly put faith in what I say. Do thee know George, that to be a poo-ka-kee, is to bear a charmed life, as thee would say, not only here, but in the great wilderness ? Do thee know too, that among the tribes of the north, it is a common thing to charge a captive with cruelty to the quakers.

I do....and I have heard every cry of a pale man at the stake answered by....Ah ha ! what for you farver 'im choke-a poo-ka-kee-ooman ?

Poor soul....

They alluded I suppose to your grandmother. How you like em dat ? said a Mohawk chief, putting his belt round the neck of another, and pulling it just hard enough to choke him a little. Ah ha !....what for you do so ?....You choke-a poo-ka-kee ooman, hey ?....you kill um 'gin ? ah ha....

No, no George....no, no....I can't bear to hear thee....it reminds me of the poor youth I saved. They frightened him almost to death before they would give him up, only because they had a tradition in their tribe that his grandfather was in some way, the cause of my grandmother's death ; and I am quite sure that he would not have been given up to anybody but me......well....

Hark....hark ! said Elizabeth, interrupting her sister.

Well, what now ?

I heard a voice....

A voice....where....when....what was it like ?

Like the voice of a woman, a great way off—

A female panther I dare say....it's high time to look to the door.

There....there....oh, it's close to the door now!

A low sweet voice could be distinctly heard now, but whether on the roof or up the chimney, or at the window or the door, it was quite impossible to say.

CHAPTER XVII.

The preacher drew forth a knife, and went up to the door.

Sir....sir....you are wanted Sir....right away Sir, said a low voice at his elbow....

Who are you?....where are you? cried he....but the blood curdled about his heart, and he recoiled from the sound as he spoke.

Here I be....here....here.

Elizabeth dropped on her knees and hid her face in the lap of her sister; and Rachel, who was not of a temper to be easily frightened, gathered her up and folded her arms about her, as if struck to the heart with a mortal fear. But Burroughs, after fetching a breath or two, went back to the door and stood waiting for the voice to be heard again.

What are you?—speak—*where* are you?

Here I be, said the invisible creature.

And who are you---what are you? cried Burroughs running up to the door, and then to the window, and then to the fire-place, and then back to the window, and preparing to push the slide away---

Here I be sir---here---here---

Well--if ever!---cried Rachel. Why don't thee go to the door George—starting up and leaving poor Elizabeth on her knees. Why! thee may be sure there's something the matter---going to the door a-tip-toe.

No no Rachel---no no; it may be a stratagem---

A stratagem for what pray?---what have we to fear?

The door flew open as she spoke, and a boy entered all out of breath, his neck open, his hat gone, his jacket off, and his hair flying loose---

Why, Robert Eveleth---

O Sir---sir! said he, as soon as he could speak---O sir I've come to tell you---didn't you never see a Belzebub?---

A what?---

If you never did, now's your time; just look out o'the door there, and you'll see a plenty on 'em.

Why, Robert---Robert---what ails the boy?

No matter now, aunt Rachel---you're wanted Sir---they're all on the look-out for you now---you're a goin' to be tried to-morrow for your life---I come here half an hour ago to tell you so---but I saw one o' the Shapes here right by the winder...

A what?---

—A Shape—an' so d'ye see, I cleared out....and so, and so—the sooner you're off, the better; they're a goin' to swear *your* life away, now—

His life, murmured Elizabeth.

My life—mine—how do you know this, boy?

How do I know it Sir?—well enough....they've been over and waked Bridgy Pope, and want her to say so too—and she and Abby—they sent me off here to tell you to get away as fast as ever you can, all three of you, if you don't want to swing for it, afore you know where you be——

Robert Eveleth!—

O, it's all very true Sir, an' you may look as black as a thunder-cloud, if you please, but if you don't get away, and you—and you—every chip of you, afore day-light, you'll never eat another huckleberry-puddin' in this

world, and you may swear to that, all hands of you, as
we say aboard ship....

Robert Eveleth, from what I saw of you the other
day——

Can't help that Sir....you've no time to lose now, either of you ; you do as I say now, an' I'll hear you preach
whenever you like, arter you're all safe—no, no, you
needn't trouble yourself to take a chair—if you stop to
set down, it's fifty to five an' a chaw o' tobacco, 't you
never git up agin....why!....there's Mary Wa'cote and
that air Judith Hubbard you see....(lowering his voice)
an' I don't know how many more o' the Shapes out there
in the wood waitin' for you....

Poh.

Lord, what a power o' faces I did see ! when the
moon came out, as I was crackin' away over the path by
the edge o' the wood....I've brought you father's grey
stallion, he that carried off old Ci Carter when the Mohawks were out....are you all ready ?

All ready ?

Yes, all—all—you're in for't too, Lizzy Dyer, and so
are you, aunt Rachel—an' so—and so—shall I bring up
the horse ?

No—

No—yes, but I will though, by faith !

Robert !

Why Robert, thee makes my blood run cold—

Never you mind for that, Lizzy Dyer.

Robert Eveleth, I am afraid thy going to sea a trip or
two, hath made thee a naughty boy, as I told thy mother
it would.

No no, aunt Rachel, no no, don't say so ; we never
swear a mouthful when we're out to sea, we never ketch
no fish if we do—but here am I ; all out o' breath now,

and you wont stir a peg, for all I can say or do and be——gulp to you!

Here Burroughs interrupted the boy, and after informing the sisters of what had occurred while he was with Mr. Paris and the poor children, he made the boy go over the whole story anew, and having done so, he became satisfied in his own soul, that if the conspirators were at work to destroy the poor girl before him, there would be no escape after she was once in their power.

Be of good cheer, Elizabeth, said he, and as he spoke, he stooped down to set his lips to her forehead.

George—George—we have no time to lose—what are we to do? said Rachel, putting forth her hand eagerly so as to stay him before he had reached the brow of Elizabeth; and then as quickly withdrawing it, and faltering out a word or two of self-reproach.

If you think as I do, dear Rachel, the sooner she is away the better.

I do think as thee does—I do, George....(in this matter.) Go for the black mare, as fast as thee can move, Robert Eveleth.

Where shall I find her....it's plaguy dark now, where there's no light.

On thy left hand as the door slips away; thee'll find a cloth and a side-saddle over the crib, with a—stop, stop—will the grey horse bear a pillion?

Yes—forty.

If he will not, however, the mare will....so be quick, Robert, be quick....

Away bounded the boy.

She has carried both of us before to-day, and safely too, when each had a heavier load upon her back than we both have now. Get thee ready sister—for my own part—I—well George, I have been looking for sorrow and am pretty well prepared for it, thee sees. I knew four months ago that I had wagered my life against Judith Hubbard's life—I am sorry for Judith—I should be sorry to bring her to such great shame, to say nothing of death, and were it not for others, and especially for that poor child, (pointing to Elizabeth) I would rather lay down my own life—much rather, if thee'll believe me George, than do her the great mischief that I now fear must be done to her, if our Elizabeth is to escape the snare.

I *do* believe you—are you ready ?—

Quite ready ; but why do thee stand there, as if thee was not going too ?—or as if thee had not made up thy mind ?

Ah—I thought I saw a face—

I dare say thee did ; but thee's not afraid of a face, I hope ?

I hear the sound of horses' feet—

How now ?—it is not for such as thee to be slow of resolve.

He drew a long breath—

George—thee is going with us ?

No, Rachel—I'd better stay here.

Here ! shrieked Elizabeth.

Here !—what do thee mean, George ? asked her sister.

I mean what I say—just what I say—it is for me to abide here.

For thee to abide here ? If it is the duty of one, it is the duty of another, said Elizabeth in a low, but very decided voice.

No, Elizabeth Dyer, no—I am able to bear that which ought never to be expected of you.

Do thee mean death, George ?—we are not very much afraid of death, said Rachel—are we Elizabeth ?

No—not very much—

Rachel & Elizabeth don't fear death

You know not what you say. I am a preacher of the
gospel—what may be very proper for me to do, may be
very improper for a young beautiful———

George Burroughs—

Forgive me Rachel—

I do....prepare thyself, my dear Elizabeth, gird up thy
loins ; for the day of travail and bitter sorrow is nigh to
thee.

Here am I sister ! And ready to obey thee at the risk
of my life.   What am I to do ?

I advise thee to fly, for if they seek thy death, it is for
my sake—I shall go too.

Dear sister—

Well ?—

Stoop thy head, I pray thee, continued Elizabeth—
I—I—(in a whisper)—I hope he'll go with thee.

With me ?—

With us, I mean—

Why not say so ?

How could I ?

Mary Elizabeth Dyer !

Nay nay—we should be safer with him—

Our safety is not in George Burroughs, maiden.

But we should find our way in the dark better.

Rachel made no reply, but she stood looking at her
sister, with her lips apart and her head up, as if she
were were going to speak, till her eyes ran over, and
then she fell upon her neck and wept aloud for a single
moment, and then arose and, with a violent effort, broke
away from Elizabeth, and hurried into their little bed-
room, where she staid so long that Elizabeth followed
her—and the preacher soon heard their voices and their
sobs die away, and saw the linked shadows of both in
prayer, projected along the white roof.

A moment more and they came out together, Rachel

with a steady look and a firm step, and her sister with a show of courage that awed him.

Thee will go with us now, I hope, said Rachel.

He shook his head.

I pray thee George—do not thou abide here—by going with us thee may have it in thy power to help a——in short, we have need of thee George, and thee had better go, even if thee should resolve to come back and outface whatever may be said of thee—

What if I see an angel in my path ?

Do that which to thee seemeth good—I have no more to say—the greater will be thy courage, the stronger the presumption of thy innocence, however, should thee come back, after they see thee in safety—what do thee say Elizabeth ?—

I didn't speak, Rachel—but—but—O I *do* wish he would go.

I shall come back if I live, said Burroughs.

Nay nay George—thee may not see thy way clear to do so—

Hourra there, hourra ! cried Robert Eveleth, popping his head in at the door. Here we be all three of us—what are you at now ?—why aint you ready ?—what are you waitin' for ?

George—it has just occurred to me that if I stay here, I may do Elizabeth more good than if I go with you—having it in my power to escape, it may be of weight in her favor—

Fiddle-de-dee for your proof cried Robert Eveleth—that, for all your proof ! snapping his fingers—that for all the good you can do Elizabeth—I say, Mr. Burroughs—a word with you—

Burroughs followed him to a far part of the room.

If you know when you are well off, said the boy—make her go—you may both stay, you and Elizabeth too,

without half the risk ; but as for aunt Rachel, why as
sure as you're a breathin' the breath o' life now, if you
don't get her away, they'll have her up with a short turn;
and if you know'd all, you'd say so—I said 'twas *you*
when I fuss come, for I didn't like to frighten her—but
the fact is you are only one out o' the three, and I'd
rather have your chance now, than either o' their'n—

Why ? Robert—

Hush—hush— you stoop down your head here, an'
I'll satisfy you o' the truth o' what I say....Barbara
Snow, and Judy Hubbard have been to make oath,
and they wanted Bridgy Pope to make oath too—they'd
do as much for her they said—how 't you come to
their bed-side about a week ago, along with a witch that
maybe you've heerd of—a freckled witch with red hair
and a big hump on her back—

No no—cried the preacher, clapping his hand over
the boy's mouth and hastily interchanging a look with
Elizabeth, whose eyes filled with a gush of sorrow,
when she thought of her bave good sister, and of what
she would feel at the remark of the boy....a remark, the
bitter truth of which was made fifty times more bitter
by his age, and by the very anxiety he showed to keep
it away from her quick sensitive ear.

But Rachel was not like Elizabeth; for though she
heard the remark, she did not even change color, but
went up to the boy, and put both arms about his neck
with a smile, and gave him a hearty kiss....and bid him
be a good boy, and a prop for his widowed mother.

A moment more and they were all on their way. It
was very dark for a time, and the great wilderness
through which their path lay, appeared to overshadow
the whole earth, and here and there to shoot up a multitude of branches—up—up—into the very sky—where

the stars and the moon appeared to be adrift, and wallowing on their way through a sea of shadow.

Me go too? said a voice, apparently a few feet off, as they were feeling for a path in the thickest part of the wood.

The preacher drew up as if an arrow had missed him. Who are you? said he—

No no, George....let me speak—

Do you know the voice?

No—but I'm sure 'tis one that I have heard before.

Me go too—high!

No.

Where you go?—high!

Rachel pointed with her hand.

Are you afraid to tell? asked the preacher, looking about in vain for somebody to appear.

I have told him—I pointed with my hand—

But how could he see thy hand such a dark night? said Elizabeth.

As *you* would see it in the light of day, said the preacher.

High—high—me better go too—poo-ka-kee.

No, no—I'd rather not, whoever thee is—we are quite safe—

No—no, said the voice, and here the conversation dropped, and they pursued their way for above an hour, at a brisk trot, and were already in sight of a path which led to the Providence Plantations, their city of refuge—

High—high—me hear um people, cried the same voice. You no safe much.

And so do I, cried Burroughs. I hear the tread of people afar off—no, no, 'tis a troop of horse—who are you—come out and speak to us—what are we to do?— the moon is out now.

High, poo-kakee, high!

Yes—come here if thee will, and say what we are to do.

Before the words were well out of her mouth, a young savage appeared in the path, a few feet from the head of her horse, and after explaining to her that she was pursued by a troop, and that he and six more of the tribe were waiting to know whether she wanted their help, he threw aside his blanket and showed her, that although he was in the garb of a swift-runner, he did not lack for weapons of war.

No, no, not for the world poor youth! cried the woman of peace, when her eye caught the glitter of the knife, the tomahawk and the short gun—I pray thee to leave us....do leave us—do, do!—speak to him George ....he does not appear to understand what I say—entreat him to leave us.

High—high! said the young warrior, and off he bounded for the sea-shore, leaving them to pursue their opposite path in quietness. Rachel and Elizabeth were upon a creature that knew, or appeared to know every step of the way; but the young high-spirited horse the preacher rode, had become quite unmanageable, now that the moon was up, the sky clear, and the shadows darting hither and thither about her path. At last they had come to the high road—their peril was over—and they were just beginning to speak above their breath, when Burroughs heard a shot fired afar off—

Hush—hush—don't move ; don't speak for your lives, cried he, as the animal reared and started away from the path.....soh, soh—I shall subdue him in a moment —hark—that is the tread of a horse—another—and another, by my life—woa !—woa !—

My heart misgives me, George—that youth—

Ah—another shot—we are pursued by a troop, and that boy is picking them off—

O Father of mercies ! I hope not.

Stay you here—I'll be back in a moment—woa—
woa !—

George——George—

Don't be alarmed—stay where you are—keep in the
shadow, and if I do not come back immediately, or it
you see me pursued, or if—woa, woa—or if you see
the mare prick up her ears, don't wait for me, but make
the best of your way over that hill yonder—woa!—
keep out o' the high road and you are safe.

Saying this, he rode off without waiting for a reply,
intending to follow in the rear of the troop, and to lead
them astray at the risk of his life, should they appear to
be in pursuit of the fugitives. He had not gone far,
when his horse, hearing the tread of other horses—a
heavy tramp, like that of a troop of cavalry on the
charge, sounding through the still midnight air, gave a
loud long neigh. It was immediately answered by four
or five horses afar off, and by that on which the poor
girls were mounted.

The preacher saw that there was but one hope now,
and he set off at full speed therefore, intending to cross
the head of the troop and provoke them to a chase ; the
manœuvre succeeded until they saw that he was alone,
after which they divided their number, and while one
party pursued him, another took its way to the very spot
where the poor girls were abiding the issue. He and
they both were captured—they were all three taken
alive—though man after man of the troop fell from his
horse, by shot after shot from a foe that no one of the
troop could see, as they galloped after the fugitives.
They were all three carried back to Salem, Burroughs
prepared for the worst, Rachel afraid only for Elizabeth,
and Elizabeth more dead than alive.

But why seek to delay the catastrophe ? Why pause
upon that, the result of which every body can foresee ?

They put him upon trial on the memorable fifth day of August (1692) in the midst of the great thunder-storm. Having no proper court of justice in the Plymouth-colony at this period, they made use of a Meeting-House for the procedure, which lasted all one day and a part of the following night—a night never to be for-gotten by the posterity of them that were alive at the time. He was pale and sick and weary, but his bearing was that of a good man—that of a brave man too, and yet he shook as with an ague, when he saw arrayed against him, no less than eight confessing witches, five or six distempered creatures who believed him to be the cause of their malady, Judith Hubbard, a woman whose character had been at his mercy for a long while (He knew that of her, which if he had revealed it before she accused him, would have been fatal to her) John Ruck his own brother-in-law, two or three of his early and very dear friends of the church, in whom he thought he could put all trust, and a score of neighbors on whom he would have called at any other time to speak in his favor. What was he to believe now ?—what *could* he believe ? These witnesses were not like Judith Hub-bard ; they had not wronged him, as she had—they were neither hostile to him, nor afraid of him in the way she was afraid of him. They were about to take away his life under a deep sense of duty to their Father above. His heart swelled with agony, and shook—and stop-ped, when he saw this—and a shadow fell, or appeared to fall on the very earth about him. It was the shadow of another world.

CHAPTER XVIII.

A brief and faithful account of the issue....a few words more, and the tale of sorrow is done. " The confessing witches testified," to give the language of a writer who was an eye-witness of the " trial that the prisoner had been at witch-meetings with them, and had seduced and compelled them to the snares of witchcraft; that he promised them fine clothes for obeying him ; that he brought poppets to them and thorns to stick into the poppets for afflicting other people, and that he exhorted them to bewitch all Salem-Village, but to do it gradually."

Among the bewitched, all of whom swore that Burroughs had pursued them for a long while under one shape or another, were three who swore that of him which they swore of no other individual against whom they appeared. Their story was that he had the power of becoming invisible, that he had appeared to them under a variety of shapes in a single day, that he would appear and disappear while they were talking together—actually vanish away while their eyes were upon him, so that sometimes they could hear his voice in the air, in the earth, or in the sea, long and long after he himself had gone out of their sight. They were evidently afraid of him, for they turned pale when he stood up, and covered their faces when he looked at them, and stopped their ears when he spoke to them. And when the judges and the elders of the land saw this, they were satisfied of his evil power, and grew mute with terror.

One of the three chief accusers, a girl, testified that in her *agony*, a little black man appeared to her, saying that his name was George Burroughs, and bid her set her name to a book which he had with him, bragging at the time that he was a conjuror high above the ordinary rank of witches.   Another swore that in *her* agony, he persuaded her to go to a sacrament, where they saw him blowing a trumpet and summoning other witches therewith from the four corners of the earth.   And a third swore, on recovering from a sort of trance before the people, that he had just carried her away into the top of a high mountain, where he showed her mighty and glorious kingdoms which he offered to give her, if she would write in the book.   But she refused.

Nor did they stop here.   They charged him with practices too terrible for language to describe.   And what were the rulers to say ?   Here was much to strengthen a part of the charge.   His abrupt appearance at the trial of Sarah Good, his behaviour, his look of premature age—that look whereof the people never spoke but with a whisper, as if they were afraid of being overheard—that extraordinary voice—that swarthy complexion—that bold haughty carriage—that wonderful power of words—what were they to believe ?   Where had he gathered so much wisdom ?   Where had he been to acquire that—whatever it was, with which he was able to overawe and outbrave and subdue everything and everybody?   All hearts were in fear—all tongues mute before him.   Death—even death he was not afraid of.   He mocked at death—he threw himself as it were, in the very chariot-way of the king of Terrors ; and what cared he for the law ?

His behavior to the boy, his critical reproduction of the knife-blade, whereby their faith in a tried accuser was actually shaken, his bright fierce look when the peo-

ple gave way at his approach....his undaunted smile
when the great black horse appeared looking in over the
heads of the people, who crowded together and hurried
away with a more than mortal fear....and his remarkable
words when the judge demanded to know by what authority he was abroad....all these were facts and circumstances within the knowledge of the court. By the authority of the Strong Man, said he ; who was that
Strong Man ? By authority of *one* who hath endowed
me with great power ; who was that one ?

Yet more. It was proved by a great number of re-
spectable and worthy witnesses, who appeared to pity
the prisoner, that he, though a small man, had lifted a
gun of seven feet barrel with one hand behind the lock
and held it forth, at arm's length ; nay, that with only
his fore-finger in the barrel he did so, and that in the
same party appeared a savage whom nobody knew, that
did the same.

This being proved, the court consulted together, and
for so much gave judgment before they proceeded any
further in the trial, that " George Burroughs had been
aided and assisted then and there by the Black Man,
who was near in a bodily shape."

And it being proved that he " made nothing" of other
facts, requiring a bodily strength such as they had never
seen nor heard of, it was adjudged further by the same
court, after a serious consultation, that " George Burroughs had a devil."

And after this, it being proved that one day when he
lived at Casco, he and his wife and his brother-in-law,
John Ruck, went after strawberries together to a place
about three miles off, on the way to Sacarappa—" Burroughs on foot and they on horseback, Burroughs left
them and stepped aside into the bushes; whereupon
they halted and hallowed for him, but he not making

them any reply, they went homeward with a quick pace,
not expecting to see him for a considerable time; but
when they had got near, whom should they see but
Burroughs himself with a basket of strawberries newly
gathered, waiting for his wife, whom he chid for what
she had been saying to her brother on the road; which
when they marvelled at, he told them he knew their very
thoughts; and Ruck saying that was more than the
devil himself could know, he answered with heat, saying Brother and wife, my God makes known your
thoughts to me : all this being proved to the court, they
consulted together as before and gave judgment that
" Burroughs had stepped aside only that by the assistance of the Black Man he might put on his invisibility
and in that fascinating mist, gratify his own jealous humor to hear what they said of him."

Well prisoner at the bar, said the chief judge, after the
witnesses for the crown had finished their testimony—
what have you to say for yourself ?

Nothing.

Have you no witnesses ?

Not one.

And why not ?

Of what use could they be ?

You needn't be so stiff though ; a lowlier carriage in
your awful situation might be more becoming. You
are at liberty to cross-examine the witness, if you are
so disposed—

I am not so disposed.

And you may address the jury now, it being your
own case.

I have nothing to say....it being my own case.

Ah! sighed the judge, looking about him with a portentous gravity—You see the end of your tether now....
you see now that He whom you serve is not to be trust-

ed. It is but the other day you were clad with power
as with a garment. You were able to make a speech
whereby, but for the mercy of God——

I was not on trial for *my* life when I made that
speech. I have something else to think of now....Let
me die in peace.

Ah, sighed the chief judge, and all his brethren
shook their heads with a look of pity and sorrow.

But as if this were not enough—as if they were afraid
he might escape after all (for it had begun to grow very
dark over-head) though the meshes of death were about
him on every side like a net of iron; as if the very
judges were screwed up to the expectation of a terrible
issue, and prepared to deal with a creature of tremendous power, whom it would be lawful to destroy any
how, no matter how, they introduced another troop of
witnesses, who swore that they had frequently heard the
two wives of the prisoner say that their house which
stood in a very cheerful path of the town was haunted
by evil spirits; and after they had finished their testi-
money Judith Hubbard swore that the two wives of the
prisoner had appeared to her, since their death, and
charged him with murder....

Repeat the story that you told brother Winthrop and
me, said Judge Sewall.

Whereupon she stood forth and repeated the story she
had sworn to before the committal of Burroughs—repeated it in the very presence of God, and of his angels
—repeated it while it thundered and lightened in her
face, and the big sweat rolled off the forehead of a man,
for whose love, but a few years before, she would have
laid down her life——-

That man was George Burroughs. He appeared as
if his heart were broken by her speech, though about his
mouth was a patient proud smile—for near him were

Mary Elizabeth Dyer and Rachel Dyer, with their eyes
fixed upon him and waiting to be called up in their turn
to abide the trial of death ; but so waiting before their
judges and their accusers that, women though they were,
he felt supported by their presence, trebly fortified by
their brave bearing—Elizabeth pale—very pale, and
watching his look as if she had no hope on earth but in
him, no fear but for him—Rachel standing up as it were
with a new stature—up, with her forehead flashing to
the sky and her coarse red hair shining and shivering
about her huge head with a frightful fixed gleam,—her
cap off, her cloak thrown aside and her distorted shape, for
the first time, in full view of the awe-struck multitude.
Every eye was upon her—every thought—her youthful
and exceedingly fair sister, the pride of the neighborhood was overlooked now, and so was the prisoner at
the bar, and so were the judges and the jury, and the
witnesses and the paraphernalia of death.   It was Rachel Dyer—the red-haired witch—the freckled witch—
the hump-backed witch they saw now—but they saw not
her ugliness, they saw not that she was either unshapely
or unfair.   They saw only that she was brave.   They
saw that although she was a woman upon the very
threshold of eternity, she was not afraid of the aspect of
death.

And the story that Judith Hubbard repeated under
such circumstances and at such a time was—that the
two wives of the prisoner at-the bar, who were buried
years and years before, with a show of unutterable sorrow, had appeared to her, face to face, and charged him
with having been the true cause of their death ; partly
promising if he denied the charge, to reappear in full
court.   Nor should I wonder if they did, whispered the
chief judge throwing a hurried look toward the graves

which lay in full view of the judgment seat, as if he almost expected to see the earth open.

The multitude who saw the look of the judge, and who were so eager but a few minutes before to get nigh the prisoner, though it were only to hear him breathe, now recoiled from the bar, and left a free path-way from the graveyard up to the witness-box, and a visible quick shudder ran throughout the assembly as they saw the judges consult together, and prepare to address the immoveable man, who stood up—whatever were the true cause, whether he felt assured of that protection which the good pray for night and day, or of that which the evil and the mighty among the evil have prepared for, when they enter into a league of death—up—as if he knew well that they had no power to harm either him or his.

What say you to that ? said major Saltonstall. You have heard the story of Judith Hubbard. What say you to a charge like that, Sir ?

Ay, ay—no evasion will serve you now, added the Lieutenant Governor.

Evasion !

You are afraid, I see—

Afraid of what ? Man—man—it is you and your fellows that are afraid. Ye are men of a terrible faith—I am not.

You have only to say yes or no, said Judge Sewall.

What mockery ! Ye that have buried them that were precious to you—very precious—

You are not obliged to answer that question, whispered the lawyer, who had been at his elbow during the trial of Martha Cory—nor any other—unless you like—

Ah—and are *you* of them that believe the story ? Are *you* afraid of their keeping their promise ?—you that have a—

What say you to the charge? I ask again!

How dare you!—ye that are husbands—you that are a widower like me, how dare you put such a question as that to a bereaved man, before the Everlasting God?

What say you to the charge? We ask you for the third time.

Father of love! cried Burroughs, and he tottered away and snatched at the bare wall, and shook as if he were in the agony of death, and all that saw him were aghast with fear. Men—men—what would ye have me say?—what would ye have me do?

Whatever the Lord prompteth, said a low voice near him.

Hark—hark—who was that? said a judge. I thought I heard somebody speak.

It was I—I, Rachel Dyer! answered the courageous woman. It was I. Ye are all in array there against a fellow-creature's life. Ye have beset him on every side by the snares of the law....Ye are pressing him to death—

Silence!—

No judge, no! I marvel that ye dare to rebuke me in such a cause, when ye know that ere long I shall be heard by the Son of Man, coming in clouds with great glory to judge the quick and the dead—

Peace....peace, woman of mischief—look to yourself.

Beware Peter! and thou too Elias! Ye know not how nigh we may all be to the great Bar—looking up to the sky, which was now so preternaturally dark with the heavy clouds of an approaching thunder-storm, that torches were ordered. Lo! the pavillion of the Judge of Judges! How know ye that these things are not the sign of his hot and sore displeasure?

Mark that, brother; mark that, said a judge. They

must know that help is nigh, or they could never brave it thus.

Whatever they may know brother, and whatever their help may be, our duty is plain.

Very true brother....ah....how now!

He was interrupted by the entrance of a haggard old man of a majestic stature, who made his way up to the witness-box, and stood there, as if waiting for the judge to speak.

Ah, Matthew Paris.....thou art come, hey? said Rachel. Where is Bridget Pope?

At the point of death.

And thy daughter, Abigail Paris?

Dead.

George....George....we have indeed little to hope now.....Where is Robert Eveleth?

Here....here I be, cried the boy, starting up at the sound of her voice, and hurrying forward with a feeble step.

Go up there to that box, Robert Eveleth, and say to the judges, my poor sick boy, what thee said to me of Judith Hubbard and of Mary Walcott, and of their wicked conspiracy to prevail with Bridget Pope and Abby Paris, to make oath.....

How now....how now....stop there! cried the chief-judge. What is the meaning of this?

Tell what thee heard them say, Robert—

Heard who say? asked the judge.....who....who?

Bridget Pope and Abigail Paris.

Bridget Pope and Abigail Parris—why what have we to do with Bridget Pope and Abigail Paris?

I pray thee judge....the maiden Bridget Pope is no more; the child of that aged man there is at the point of death. If the boy Robert Eveleth speak true, they told him before the charge was made———

They—who?

Bridget Pope and Abigail Paris told him—

No matter what they told him....that is but hearsay—

Well, and if it be hear say?—

We cannot receive it; we take no notice of what may occur in this way—

How!—If we can prove that the witnesses have conspired together to make this charge, is it contrary to law for you to receive our proof? asked Burroughs.

Pho, pho—you mistake the matter—

No judge no....will thee hear the father himself?—said Rachel.

Not in the way that you desire....there would be no end to this, if we did—

What are we to do then judge? We have it in our power to prove that Judith Hubbard and Mary Walcott proposed to the two children, Bridget Pope and Abigail Paris, to swear away the life—

Pho, pho, pho—pho, pho, pho—a very stale trick that. One of the witnesses dead, the other you are told at the point of death—

It is no trick judge; but if....if....supposing it to be true, that Judith Hubbard and her colleague did this, how should we prove it?

How should you prove it? Why, by producing the persons to whom, or before whom, the proposal you speak of was made.

But if they are at the point of death, judge?

In that case there would be no help for you—

Such is the humanity of the law.

No help for us! Not if we could prove that they who are dead, or at the point of death, acknowledged what we say to a dear father?—can this be the law?

Stop—stop—thou noble-hearted, brave woman! cried Burroughs. They do not speak true. They are afraid of thee Rachel Dyer. Matthew Paris—

Here am I, Lord!—

Why, Matthew—look at me....Do you not—know me?

No—no—who are you?

— Matthew denies knowing Burroughs

— BETRAYAL

— Peter from Biblical account of Jesus' death

CHAPTER XIX.

Enough—enough—cried Burroughs, on finding Matthew Paris so disturbed in his intellect—enough—there is no hope now, Rachel. The father himself would be no witness now, though he had been told by our witnesses upon their death-bed, while they expected to die, just what, if it could be shown here, would be a matter of life and death to us. But still, before I give up, I should like to know the meaning of that rule of evidence you spoke of the other day, which would appear to make it necessary for me to produce only the best evidence which the nature of the case admits of. We have done that here....a rule which being interpreted by the men of the law is said to be this....that we are to give such evidence only, as that none better may appear to be left behind—we have done that now—

We are weary of this—what have you to say to the charge made against you by the apparition of your wife? Before you reply however, it is our duty to apprise you, that whatever you may happen to say in your own favor will go for nothing—

Nevertheless I am ready to reply.

—We do not seek to entrap you—

So I perceive. Repeat the charge.

You are charged with having—what ho, there!— lights—lights—more lights—

Lights—more lights! cried the people, what, ho there! How dark it grows—

And how chill the air is—

Ay......and quiet as the grave.

—You are charged I say, with having caused the death of your two wives....who have partly promised, if you deny the charge, to confront you here.

The people began to press backward from each other, and to gasp for breath.

You have only to say yes or no, and abide the proof.

Indeed—is that all ?

Yes—all—

Then...behold me.   As he spoke, he threw up his arms, and walked forth into a broad clear space before the bench, where every body could hear and see him, and was about to address the jury, when he was interrupted by a crash of thunder that shook the whole house, and appeared to shake the whole earth.   A dreadful outcry ensued, with flash after flash of lightning and peal after peal of thunder, and the people dropped upon their knees half blinded with light and half crazy with terror ; and covered their faces and shrieked with consternation.

Why, what are ye afraid of judges ? And you, ye people—cried the prisoner, that ye cover your faces, and fall down with fear....so that if I would, I might escape.

Look to the prisoner there....look to the prisoner.

—Ye do all this, ye that have power to judge me, while I....I the accused man....I neither skulk nor cower. I stand up....I alone of all this great multitude who are gathered together to see me perish for my sins....the Jonah of this their day of trouble and heavy sorrow.

Not alone, said Rachel Dyer, moving up to the bar.

If not altogether alone, alone but for thee, thou most heroic woman....O, that they knew thy worth !....And yet these people who are quaking with terror on every side of us, bowed down with mortal fear at the voice of the Lord in the Sky, it is they that presume to deal with us, who are not afraid of our Father, nor scared by the flashing of his countenance, for life and for death—

Yea George—

Be it so—

Prisoner at the bar—you are trifling with the court... You have not answered the charge.

Have I not!—well then—I prepare to answer it now. I swear that I loved them that I have buried there— there!—loved them with a love passing all that I ever heard of, or read of. I swear too that I nourished and comforted and ministered to the dear creatures, who, ye are told, have come out of the earth to destroy me— even me—me, their husband, their lover, and the father of their children ! I swear too—but why continue the terrible outrage ? Let my accusers appear ! Let them walk up, if they will, out of their graves !—their graves are before me. I am not afraid—I shall not be afraid— so long as they wear the blessed shape, or the blessed features of them that have disappeared from their bridal chamber, with a——

He was interrupted by great noises and shrieks that were enough to raise the dead—noises from every part of the grave-yard—shrieks from people afar off in the wood, shrieks from the multitude on the outside of the house—and shrieks from the sea-shore; and immediately certain of the accusers fell down as if they saw something approach ; and several that were on the outside of the meeting-house came rushing in with a fearful outcry, saying that a shed which had been built up over a part of the burial-ground was crowded with strange faces, and with awful shapes, and that among them were the two dead wives of the prisoner.

There they go—there they go ! screamed other voices outside the door ; and immediately the cry was repeated by the accusers who were within the house—all shrieking together. "Here they come!—here they come!—here they come!"—And Judith Hubbard looking up and uncovering her face, about which her cloak had been gathered in the first hurry of her distraction, declared that the last wife of Burroughs, on whom her eyes were fixed at the time, was then actually standing before him and looking him in the face, " O, with such a look—so calm, so piteous and so terrible!"

After the uproar had abated in some degree, the judges who were huddled together, as far as they could possibly get from the crowd below, ordered up three more of the witnesses, and were about to speak to them, when Burroughs happening to turn that way also, they cried out as if they were stabbed with a knife, and fell upon the floor at their whole length and were speechless.

Whereupon the chief judge, turning toward him, asked him what hindered these poor people from giving their testimony.

I do not know said Burroughs, who began to give way himself now, with a convulsion of the heart, before the tremendous array of testimony and weight of delusion; to fear that of a truth preternatural shapes were about him, and that the witnesses were over-persuaded by irresistible power, though he knew himself to be no party in the exercise of such power. I do not know, said he: I am utterly confounded by their behaviour. It may be the devil.

Ah—and why is the devil so loath to have testimony borne against *you*?

" Which query," says a writer who was there at the time, and saw the look of triumph which appeared in the faces of the whole bench, " did cast Burroughs into very great confusion."

And well it might, for he was weighed to the earth,

and he knew that whatever he said, and whatever he did ; and whether he spoke with promptitude or with hesitation; whether he showed or did not show a sign of dismay, everything would be, and *was* regarded by the judges, and the jury, and the people, as further corroboration of his turpitude.

Here the trial ended. Here the minds of the jury were made up ; and although he grew collected at last, and arose and spoke in a way that made everybody about him weep and very bitterly too, for what they called the overthrow of a mind of great wisdom and beauty and power; and although he gave up to the judges a written argument of amazing ingenuity and vigor which is yet preserved in the records of that people, wherein he mocked at their faith in witchcraft, and foretold the grief and the shame, the trouble and the reproach that were to follow to them that were so busy in the work of death ; yet—yet—so impressed were the twelve, by the scene that had occurred before their faces, that they found him guilty ; and as if the judges were afraid of a rescue from the powers of the air, they gave judgment of death upon him before they left the bench, and contrary to their established practice, ordered him to be executed on the morrow.

On the morrow ? said he, with a firm steady eye and a clear tone, though his lip quivered as he spoke. Will ye afford me no time to prepare ?

We would not that the body and soul both perish ; and we therefore urge you to be diligent in the work brother, very diligent for the little time that is now left to make your calling and election sure. Be ready for the afternoon of the morrow.

Hitherto the prisoner at the bar had shown little or no emotion ; hitherto he had argued and looked as if he did not believe the jury nor the judges capable of doing

what they had now done, nor the multitude that knew
him, capable of enduring it.   Hitherto he had been as it
were a spectator of the terrible farce, with no concern
for the issue; but now....now....all eyes were rivetted
upon him with fear, all thoughts with alarm ; for though
he stood up as before, and made no sort of reply to the
judges, and bore the wracking of the heavy irons with
which they were preparing to load him, as if he neither
felt nor saw them ; yet was there a something in his
look which made the officers of the court unsheathe their
swords, and lift up their axes, and the people who were
occupied about him, keep as far out of his reach as they
possibly could.

Yet he neither moved nor spoke, till he saw the wom-
en crowding up to a part of the house where he had seen
Elizabeth Dyer, and stoop as if she that had been kneel-
ing there a few moments before, lay very low, and lift
her up as if she had no life in her, and carry her away,
guarded by men with pikes, and with swords and with
huge firelocks.   Then he *was* moved—and his chains
were felt for the first time, and he would have called out
for a breath of air—prayed for a drop of water to save a
life more precious by far than his—but before he could
open his mouth so as to make himself heard, he saw
Rachel Dyer pressing up to the bar of death, and heard
the judges call out to the high-sheriff and his man to
guard the door, and look to the prisoner.

He will get away if you turn your head, Mr. sheriff,
said one of the judges.

That he will, added a witness, that he will ! if you
don't look sharp, as sure as my name is Peter P.

Watch and pray—watch and pray—added another.

Burroughs looked up to the bench with surprise, then
at the people, who were watching every motion of his
body as if they expected him to tear away the ponderous

fetters and walk forth as free as the wind of the desert, and then at the blacksmith who stood near with his hammer uplifted in the air ; and then his chest heaved and his chains shook, and the people hurried away from his path, and tumbled over each other in their eagerness to escape, and the chief-judge cried out again to the officer to look to the door and be prepared for a rescue.

Let *me* be tried now ! I entreat thee, said Rachel Dyer, throwing up her locked-hands before Judge Winthrop, and speaking as if she was about to plead not for death but for life. Let me be tried now, I beseech thee. Now.—

Yea—now !—before the maiden is brought back to life. O let her be at peace, ye men of power, till I have a— have a—

She gathered herself up now with a strong effort, and spoke with deliberate firmness....

—— Till I have gone through the work which is appointed for me by the twelve that I see there—

Be it so.—I say, Mr. high-sheriff !

Well, Mr. judge Winthrop ?

This way, this way ; you'll be so good as to remove a—a—a—(Looking at Burroughs who stood leaning against the wall)—you are to be a—a—(in a whisper of authority)—you are to be careful of what you do—a very hard case, very—very—

Yes judge—

Well, well—well, well—why don't ye do as I bid you ?

What am I to do ?

What are you to do....remove the prisoner—poor soul.

Which prisoner ?

Why that are....poh poh, poh—(pointing to Burroughs.)

Where to ?

Where to Sir?—Take him away; away with him
—pretty chap you are to be sure, not to know where
to take a man to, after its all over with hm—poh, poh,
poh.

I say, Mr. Judge, none o' that now—

Take the man away Sir.   Do as you are bid.

Who—me—cried Burroughs, waking up from his
fit of apathy and looking about on every side.

Away with him.

Judges—judges—hear me.   Let me remain, I pray
you, cried he, setting his back to the wall and lifting his
loaded arms high up in the air—suffer me to stay here
till the jury have said whether or no this heroic woman
is worthy of death—I do beseech you!

Take him away, I tell you—what are ye afraid of?

Judges—men—I would that ye would have mercy,
not on me, but on the people about me.   I would that
ye would suffer me to tarry here—in fetters—till the jury have given their verdict on Rachel Dyer.   Suffer
me to do so, I beseech you, and I will go away then, I
swear to you, whithersoever it may please you, like a
lamb to the slaughter.   I swear this to you before God!
—but, so help me God, I will not be carried away alive
before.   I will not stir, nor be stirred while I have
power to lift my arms, or to do what you now see me
do———

As he spoke, he lifted up his arms in the air—up—up,
as high as he could reach, standing on tip-toe the while;
and brought them down with such force, loaded as they
were, that he doubled the iron guard which kept him in
the box, and shattered the heavy door from the top to
the bottom.

—Behold—shorn though I be of my youth, betrayed
though I have been, while I forgot where I was, I do
not lack power.   Now bid your people tear me away

if you have courage! For lo, my feet are upon the foundations of your strength....and by Jehovah—the God of the strong man of other days!—I'll not be dragged off till I know the fate of the giantess before you.

We shall see—cut him down officer—cut him down!

Very well. Come thou near enough to cut me down, officer, and I'll undertake for thee.

Judges—how little ye know of that man's power— why not suffer him to stay? cried Rachel Dyer. Why will ye provoke it? On your heads be the issue, if ye drive your ministers to the toil! on yours their blood, if they approach him!

The sheriff hung back—and the judges, after consulting together, told Burroughs he might stay, and ordered the trial of the women to proceed.

— trial transcript —like

CHAPTER XX.

Already were they about to give judgment of death upon Rachel Dyer, when two or three of her accusers, who began to fear that she might escape, had another fit.

Why are these poor women troubled ? asked a judge.

I do not know, was her unstudied reply.

But according to your belief ?

I do not desire to say what my belief is. It can do no good, and it may do harm; for who shall assure me that I do not err ?

Don't you think they are bewitched ?

No.

Give us your thoughts on their behavior.

No, Ichabod, no ; my thoughts can be of no worth to thee or such as thee. If I had more proof, proof that ye would receive in law, I might be willing to speak at large both of them and of their master——

Their master ! cried a little man, with a sharp inquisitive eye, who had not opened his mouth before. Who is their master ?

If they deal in witchcraft or in the black art, Joseph Piper, thee may know as well as I do.

Woman....are you not afraid of death ?

No...........not much, though I should like to be spared for a few days longer.

Not afraid of death !—

No—not much, I say. And why _should_ I be afraid of death ? why should I desire to live ?—what is there to attach a thing of my shape to life, a wretched, miserable, weary.......

Ah, ha—now we shall have it—she is going to confess now—she is beginning to weep, said a judge. But he was overheard by the woman herself, who turning to the jury with a look that awed them in spite of their prejudice, told them to proceed.

They'll proceed fast enough, by and by, said another judge. What have you done to disturb the faculties of that woman there ?

What woman ?

Judith Hubbard.

Much. For I know her, and she knows that I know her ; and we have both known for a great while that we cannot both live. This world is not large enough. What have I done to disturb her faculties ? Much. For that woman hath wronged me ; and she cannot forgive me. She hath pursued me and mine to death ; all that are very near and dear to me, my poor sister and my—and the beloved friend of my sister—to death ; and how would it be possible for Judith Hubbard to forgive us ?

But your apparition pursues her.

If so, I cannot help it.

But why is it your apparition ?

How do I know ? He that appeared in the shape of Samuel, why should he not appear in the shape of another ?

But enough—Rachel Dyer was ordered for execution also. And a part of the charge proved against her was, that she had been spirited away by the powers of the air, who communicated with her and guarded her at the cost of much human life, on the night when she fled into the deep of the wilderness in company with George Burroughs and Mary Elizabeth Dyer ; each of whom had a like body-guard of invisible creatures, who shot with arrows of certain death on the night of their escape.

And Mary Elizabeth Dyer was now brought up for trial; but being half dead with fear, and very ill, so that she was reported by a jury empannelled for the purpose, to be mute by the visitation of God, they adjourned the court for the morrow, and gave her permission to abide with her sister till the day after the morrow.

And so Mary Elizabeth Dyer and Rachel Dyer met again—met in the depth of a dungeon like the grave; and Elizabeth being near the brave Rachel once more, grew ashamed of her past weakness.

I pray thee dear sister, said Mary Elizabeth, after they had been together for a long while without speaking a word, Rachel with her arm about Elizabeth's neck, and Elizabeth leaning her face upon the shoulder of Rachel, I pray thee to forgive me.

Forgive thee....for what pray?

Do, *do* forgive me, Rachel.

Why, what on earth is the matter with thee, child? Here we sit for a whole hour in the deep darkness of the night-season, without so much as a sob or a tear, looking death in the face with a steady smile, and comforting our hearts, weary and sick as they are, with a pleasant hope—the hope of seeing our beloved brother Jacob, our dear good mother, and our pious grandmother; and now, all of a sudden thee breaks out in this way, as if thee would not be comforted, and as if thee had never thought of death before—

O, I'm not afraid of death sister, now—I'm prepared for death now—I'm very willingly to die now—it is'nt that I mean.

Why *now?*—why do thee say so much of *now?* Is it only *now* that thee is prepared for death?

No, no, dear sister, but some how or other I do not even desire to live now, and yet——

And yet what ?—why does thee turn away thy head ? why does thee behave so to me....why break out into such bitter—bitter lamentation ?—what *is* the matter I say ?—what ails thee ?—

Oh dear !

Why—Elizabeth !—what am I to believe ?—what has thee been doin' ? Why do thee cling to me so ?—why do thee hide thy face ?—

O Rachel, Rachel—do not go away,—do not abandon me—do not cast me off !

Child—why—

No, no !—

Look me in the face, I beseech thee.

No no—I dare not—I cannot.

Dare not—cannot—

No no.—

Dare not look thy sister in the face ?

Oh no—

Lift up thy head thy head this minute, Mary Elizabeth Dyer !—let go of my neck—let go of my neck, I say—leave clinging to me so, and let me see thy face.

No no dear Rachel, no no, I dare not—I am afraid of thee now, for now thee calls me Mary Elizabeth—

Afraid of me—of me—O Elizabeth, what has thee done ?

Oh dear !

And what have *I* done to deserve this ?

Thee—thee !—O nothing dear sister, nothing at all ; it is I—I that have been so very foolish and wicked after—

Wicked, say thee ?

O very—very—very wicked—

But how—in what way—thee'll frighten me to death.

Shall I—O I am very sorry—but—but—thee knows I
cannot help it—

Cannot help it, Mary Elizabeth Dyer—cannot help
what ? Speak....speak....whatever it is, I forgive thee....
we have no time to lose now ; we may never meet again.
Speak out, I beseech thee. Speak out, for the day is
near, the day of sorrow——

I will, I will—cried Elizabeth, sobbing as if her heart
would break, and falling upon her knees and burying
her head in the lap of her sister—I will—I will, but—
pushing aside a heap of hair from her face, and smother-
ing the low sweet whisper of a pure heart, as if she
knew that every throb had a voice—I will, I will, I say,
but I am so afraid of thee—putting both arms about her
sister's neck and pulling her face down that she might
whisper what she had to say—I will—I will—I'm a goin'
to tell thee now—as soon as ever I can get my breath—
nay, nay, don't look at me so—I cannot bear it——

Look at thee—my poor bewildered sister—how can
thee tell whether I am looking at thee or not, while thy
head is there ?—Get up—get up, I say—I do not like
that posture ; it betokens too much fear—the fear not
of death, but of shame—too much humility, too much
lowliness, a lowliness the cause whereof I tremble to ask
thee. Get up, Elizabeth, get up, if thee do not mean to
raise a grief and a trouble in my heart which I wouldn't
have there now for the whole world ; get up, I beseech
thee, Mary Elizabeth Dyer.

Elizabeth got up, and after standing for a moment
or two, without being able to utter a word, though her
lips moved, fell once more upon her sister's neck ; and
laying her mouth close to her ear, while her innocent
face glowed with shame and her whole body shook with
fear, whispered—I pray thee Rachel, dear Rachel....do...

do let me see him for a minute or two before they put him to death.

Rachel Dyer made no reply. She could not speak—she had no voice for speech, but gathering up the sweet girl into her bosom with a convulsive sob, she wept for a long while upon *her* neck.

They were interrupted by the jailor, who came to say that George Burroughs, the wizard, having desired much to see Rachel Dyer and Mary Elizabeth Dyer, the confederate witches, before his and their death, he had been permitted by the honorable and merciful judges to do so—on condition that he should be doubly-ironed at the wrist; wherefore he, the jailor had now come to fetch her the said Rachel to him the said George.

I am to go too, said Elizabeth, pressing up to the side of her sister, and clinging to her with a look of dismay.

No, no—said he, no, no, you are to stay here.

Nay, nay, sister—dear sister—do let me go with thee!

It is not for me to speak, dear, *dear* Elizabeth, or thee should go now instead of me. However——

Come, come—I pity you both, but there's no help for you now—never cry for spilt milk—you're not so bad as they say, I'm sure—so make yourself easy and stay where you be, if you know when you're well off.

Do let me go!

Nonsense—you're but a child however, and so I forgive you, and the more's the pity ; must obey orders if we break owners—poh, poh,—poh, poh, poh.

A separation like that of death followed. No hope had the two sisters of meeting again alive. They were afraid each for the other—and Elizabeth sat unable to speak, with her large clear eyes turned up to the eyes of Rachel as if to implore, with a last look, a devout consideration of a dying prayer.

If it may be, said Rachel turning her head at the

door if it may be dear maiden, it shall be. Have courage—

I have, I have!

Be prepared though; be prepared Elizabeth, my *beautiful* sister. We shall not see each other again.... that is....O I pray thee, I do pray thee, my dear sister to be comforted.

Elizabeth got up, and staggered away to the door and fell upon her sister's neck and prayed her not to leave her.

I must leave thee...I must, I must....would thee have me forsake George Burroughs at the point of death?

O no—no—no!

We never shall meet again I do fear—I do hope, I might say, for of what avail is it in the extremity of our sorrow; but others may—he and thee may Elizabeth—and who knows but after the first shock of this thy approaching bereavement is over, thee may come to regard this very trial with joy, though we are torn by it, as by the agony of death now—let us pray.

The sisters now prayed together for a little time, each with her arm about the other's neck, interchanged a farewell kiss and parted——parted forever.

And Rachel was then led to the dungeons below, where she saw him that her sister loved, and that a score of other women had loved as it were in spite of their very natures—for they were bred up in fear of the dark Savage. He sat with his hands locked in his lap, and chained and rivetted with iron, his brow gathered, his teeth set, and his keen eyes fixed upon the door.

There is yet one hope my dear friend, whispered he after they had been together a good while without speaking a word or daring to look at each other—one hope—laying his pinioned arm lightly upon her shoulder, and

pressing up to her side with all the affectionate seriousness of a brother—one hope, dear Rachel—

She shut her eyes and large drops ran down her cheeks.

—One hope—and but one—

Have a care George Burroughs. I would not have
thee betray thyself anew—there is no hope.

It is not for myself I speak. There is no hope for me.
I know that—I feel that—I am sure of it ; nor, to tell
you the truth, am I sorry—

Not sorry George—

No—for even as you are, so am I—weary of this world
—sick and weary of life.

Her head sunk upon his shoulder, and her breathing
was that of one who struggles with deep emotion.

No—no—it is not for myself that I speak. It is for
you—

For *me*—

For you and for Elizabeth—

For *me* and for Elizabeth ?—well—

And if I could bring you to do what I am persuaded
you both may do without reproach, there would be hope
still for—for Elizabeth—and for you—

For Elizabeth—and for me ?—O George, George !
what hope is there now for me ? What have I to do on
earth, now that we are a——she stopped with a shudder
—I too am tired of life. She withdrew the hand which
till now he had been holding to his heart with a strong
terrible pressure.

Hear me, thou high-hearted, glorious woman. I
have little or no hope for thee—I confess that. I
know thee too well to suppose that I could prevail with
thee ; but....but....whatever may become of us, why not
save Elizabeth, if we may—

If we may George—but how ?

Why....draw nearer to me I pray thee ; we have not

much time to be together now, and I would have thee
look upon me, as one having a right to comfort thee and
to be comforted by thee—

A right....how George ?

As thy brother—

As my brother....O, certainly——

Nay, nay....do not forbear to lean thy head upon thy
brother....do not, I beseech thee. What have we to do
here....what have we to do now with that reserve which
keeps the living apart....our ashes, are they to be hindered of communion hereafter by the unworthy law of
—ah....sobbing....Rachel Dyer!....can it be that I hear
you—*you*! the unperturbale, the steadfast and the brave
....can it be that I hear you sobbing at my side, as if
your very heart would break....

No no....

There is to be a great change here, after we are out
of the way....

Where how ?

Among the people. The accusers are going too far ;
they are beginning to overstep the mark—they are flying too high.

Speak plainly, if thee would have me understand thy
speech—why do thee cleave to me so ?—why so eager—
why do thee speak in parables ? My heart misgives me
when I hear a man like thee, at an hour like this,
weighing every word that is about to escape from his
mouth.

I deserve the rebuke. What I would say is, that the
prisons of our land are over-crowded with people of high
repute. Already they have begun to whisper the charge
against our chief men. This very day they have hinted
at two or three individuals, who, a week before they over-
threw me, would have been thought altogether beyond
the reach of their audacity.

Who are they?

They speak of Matthew Paris.

The poor bewildered man....how dare they?

And of the Governor, and of two or three more in authority; and of all that participated in the voyage whereby he and they were made wealthy and wise and powerful——

I thought so....I feared as much. Poor man....his riches are now indeed a snare to him, his liberal heart, a mark for the arrows of death....

Now hear me....the accusers being about to go up to the high places and to the seats of power, a change, there must and there will be, and so——

And so....why do thee stop?

Why do I stop....did I stop?

Yea....and thy visage too....why does it alter?

My visage!

Yea....thy look, thy tone of voice, the very color of thy lips.

Of a truth, Rachel?

Of a truth, George.

Why then it must be....it is, I am sure....on account of the....that is to say....I'm afraid I do not make myself understood—

Speak out.

Well then....may I not persuade you, my dear, *dear* sister....to....to....in a word, Rachel....

To what pray....persuade me to what?....Speak to me as I speak to thee; what would thee persuade me to, George?

To....to....to confess....there!

To confess what, pray?

That's all....

George....

Nay, nay....the fact is my dear friend, as I said before,

I....I....if there be a change here, it will be a speedy one.

Well—

And if—and if—a few weeks more, a few days more, it may be, and our accusers, they who are now dealing death to us, may be brought up in their turn to hear the words of death—in short Rachel, if you could be persuaded just to—not to acknowledge—but just to suffer them to believe you to be a....to be a......I forget what I was going to say————

George — change of heart

CHAPTER XXI.

A long silence followed—a silence like that of death
—at last Rachel Dyer spoke :

George Burroughs—I understand thee now, said she,
I understand it all. Thee would have me confess that I
deserve death—only that I may live. Thee would have
me acknowledge (for nothing else would do) that I am
a liar and a witch, and that I deserve to die—and all
this for what ?—only that I may escape death for a few
days. O George !

No, no—you mistake the matter. I would not have
you confess that you deserve death—I would only have
you speak to them—God of the faithful !—I cannot—I
cannot urge this woman to betray her faith.

I understand thee, George. But if I were to do so,
what should I gain by it ?

Gain by it, Rachel Dyer ?

Why do thee drop my hand ? why recoil at my touch
now ?

Gain by it ! siezing both her hands with all his might,
and speaking as if he began to fear—not to hope—no,
but to fear that she might be over-persuaded—

Yea—what have I to gain by it ?

Life. You escape death—a cruel ignominious death
—a death, which it is not for a woman to look at, but
with horror.

Well George—

By death, you lose the opportunity of doing much good,
of bringing the wicked to justice, of aiding them that

are now ready to die with terror, of shielding the oppressed—

Well—

Well—and what more would you have ? Is not this
enough ?

No, George.

Hear me out Rachel. Do not reprove me, do not
turn away, till you have heard me through. My duty is
before me, a duty which must and shall be done, though
it break my heart. I am commanded to argue with
you, and to persuade you to live.

Commanded ?—

What if you were to confess that you deserve deatn ?
What if you were to own yourself a witch ? I take your
own view of the case.—I put the query to you in a shape
the least favorable to my purpose. What if you were to
do this ; you would be guilty at the most but of a—of a—

Of untruth George.

And you would save your own life by such untruth,
and the lives, it may be, of a multitude more, and the
life you know, of one that is very dear to you. *by telling lies, you save lives*

Well——

No no—do not leave me in this way ! Do not go till I
—I beseech you to hear me through—

I will—it grieves me, but I will.

Which is the greater sin—to die when you have it in
your power to escape death, if you will, by a word ? or
to speak a word of untruth to save your life—

George Burroughs—I pray thee—suffer me to bid
thee farewell.

No no, not yet. Hear me through—hear all I have
to say. By this word of untruth, you save your own
life, and perhaps many other lives. You punish the
guilty. You have leisure to repent in this world of that
very untruth—if such untruth be sinful. You have an

opportunity of showing to the world and to them that
you love, that you were innocent of that wherewith you
were charged.   You may root up the error that prevails
now, and overthrow the destroyer, and hereafter obtain
praise for that very untruth, whereby you hinder the
shedding of more innocent blood ; praise from every
quarter of the earth, praise from every body; from the
people, the preachers, the jury, the elders—yea from
the very judges for having stayed them in their headlong
career of guilt—

O George—

But if you die, and your death be sinful—and would
it not be so, if you were to die, where you might escape
death ?—you would have no time to repent here, no opportunity, no leisure—you die in the very perpetration
of your guilt—

If it is guilt, I do—

And however innocent you may be of the crimes that
are charged to you, you have no opportunity of showing
on this earth to them that love you, that you are so. Yet
more—the guilt of your death, if it be not charged hereafter to you, will be charged, you may be sure, to the
wretched women that pursue you ; and all who might be
saved by you, will have reason to lay their death at your
door—

Well—

About life or death, you may not much care ; but after death to be regarded with scorn, or hatred or terror,
by all that go by your grave, my sister—how could you
bear the idea of that ? What say you—you shudder—and
yet if you die now, you must leave behind you a character which cannot be cleared up, or which is not likely to
be cleared up on earth, however innocent you may be (as
I have said before)—the character of one, who being
charged with witchcraft was convicted of witchcraft and

executed for a witchcraft. In a word—if you live, you may live to wipe away the aspersion. If you die, it may adhere to you and to yours—forever and ever. If you live, you may do much good on earth, much to yourself and much to others, much even to the few that are now thirsting for your life—you may make lighter the load of crime which otherwise will weigh them down—you may do this and all this, if you speak : But if you do not speak, you are guilty of your own death, and of the deaths it may be of a multitude, here and hereafter.

Now hear *me*. I do not know whether all this is done to try my truth or my courage, but this I know—I will not leave thee in doubt concerning either. Look at me There——

Thee would have mo confess ?

I would.

Thee would have Elizabeth confess ?

I would.

Do thee mean to confess.

I—I !—

Ah George—

I cannot Rachel—I dare not—I am a preacher of the word of truth. But you may—what is there to hinder you ?

Thee will not ?

No.

Nor will I.

Just what I expected—give me your hand—what I have said to you, I have been constrained to say, for it is a part of my faith Rachel, that as we believe, so are we to be judged : and that therefore, had you believed it to be right for you to confess and live, it would have been right, before the Lord.—But whether you do or do not, Elizabeth may.

True—if she can be persuaded to think as thee would

have her think, she may.   I shall not seek to dissuade
her—but as for me, I have put my life into the hands of
our Father.   I shall obey him, and trust to the inward
prompting of that which upholds me and cheers me now
—even now, George, when, but for His Holy Spirit, I
should feel as I never felt before, since I came into the
world—altogether alone.

Will you advise with her, and seek to persuade her ?

No.

Cruel woman !

Cruel—no no George, no no.   Would that be doing
as I would be done by ? Is it for me to urge a beloved
sister to do what I would not do—even to save my life ?

I feel the rebuke--

George, I must leave thee—I hear footsteps.   Farewell—

So soon—so very soon ! Say to her, I beseech you—
say to her as you have said to me, that she *may* confess
if she will ; that we have been together, and that we
have both agreed in the opinion that she had better confess and throw herself on the mercy of her judges, till the
fury of the storm hath passed over.—It will soon have
passed over, I am sure now—

No George, no ; but I will say this. I will say to
her—

Go on—go on, I beseech you—

—I will say to her—Elizabeth, my dear Sister ; go
down upon thy knees and pray to the Lord to be nigh to
thee, and give thee strength, and to lead thee in the path
which is best for his glory ; and after that, if thee should
feel free to preseve thy life by such means—being on
the guard against the love of life, and the fear of death—
the Tempter of souls, and the weapons of the flesh—it
will be thy duty so to preserve it.

Burroughs groaned aloud—but he could prevail no

further. Enough, said he, at last : write as much on this paper, and let me carry it with me.

Carry it with thee—what do thee mean ?

I hardly know what I mean ; I would see her and urge her to live, but when I consider what must follow, though I have permission to see her, my heart fails me.

Thee is to meet her with me, I suppose ?

No, I believe not—

How—alone ?—

No no—not alone, said the jailor, whom they supposed to be outside of the door, till he spoke.

More of the tender mercies of the law ! They would entrap thee George—

And you too Rachel, if it lay in their power—

Give me that book—it is the Bible that I gave thee, is it not ?

It is—

It belonged to my mother. I will write what I have to say in the blank leaf.

She did so ; and giving it into the hands of the Jailor she said to him—I would have her abide on earth—my dear, *dear* sister !—I would pray to her to live and be happy, *if she can ;* for she—O she will have much to make life dear to her, even though she be left alone by the way-side for a little time—what disturbs thee George ?——

I am afraid of this man. He will betray us—

No—no—we have nothing to fear—

Nothing to fear, when he must have been at our elbow and overheard everything we have whispered to each other.

Look at him George, and thee will be satisfied.

Burroughs looked up, and saw by the vacant gravity of his hard visage, that the man had not understood a syllable to their prejudice.

But Elizabeth—I would have her continue on earth, I
say—I would—if so it may please our Father above ; but
I am in great fear, and I would have thee tell her so,
after she has read what I have written there in that book.
She will have sympathy, whatever may occur to us—
true sympathy, unmixed with fear ; but as for me, I have
no such hope—and why should I wrestle with my duty
—I—who have no desire to see the light of another day ?
None Rachel ?

None—but for the sake of Mary Elizabeth Dyer—and
so—and so George, we are to part now—and there—
therefore—the sooner we part, the better.   Her voice
died away in a low deeply-drawn heavy breathing.

Even so dear—even so, my beloved sister—

George—

Nay, nay—why leave me at all ?—why not abide here ?
Why may we not die together ?

George, I say—

Well—what-say ?

Suffer me to kiss thee—my brother—before we part....

He made no reply, but he gasped for breath and shook
all over, and stretched out his arms with a giddy convulsive motion toward her.

—Before we part forever George—dear George, putting her hand affectionately upon his shoulder and looking him steadily in the face.   We are now very near to
the threshold of death, and I do believe—I do—though
I would not have said as much an hour ago, for the
wealth of all this world....nay, not even to save my life
....no....nor my sister's life....nor thy life....that I shall die
the happier and the better for having kissed thee....my
brother.

Still he spoke not....he had no tongue for speech.   The
dreadful truth broke upon him all at once now, a truth
which penetrated his heart like an arrow...and he strove to

throw his arms about her; to draw her up to his bosom—
but the chains that he wore prevented him, and so he
leaned his head upon her shoulder....and kissed her
cheek, and then lifted himself up, and held her with one
arm to his heart, and kissed her forehead and her eyes
and her mouth, in a holy transport of affection.

Dear George....I am happy now....very, very happy
now, said the poor girl, shutting her eyes and letting two
or three large tears fall upon his locked hands, which
were held by her as if....as if....while her mouth was
pressed to them with a dreadful earnestness, her power
to let them drop was no more. And then she appeared
to recollect herself, and her strength appeared to come
back to her, and she rose up and set her lips to his forehead with a smile, that was remembered by the rough
jailor to his dying day, so piteous and so death-like was
it, and said to Burroughs, in her mild quiet way—her
mouth trembling and her large tears dropping at every
word—very, very happy now, and all ready for death.
I would say more....much more if I might, for I have not
said the half I had to say. Thee will see her....I shall
not see her again....

How—

Not if thee should prevail with her to stay, George.
It would be of no use—it would only grieve her, and
it might unsettle us both—

What can I say to you?

Nothing—Thee will see her; and thee will take her
to thy heart as thee did me, and she will be happy—very
happy—even as I am now.

Father—Father! O, why was I not prepared for this!
Do thou stay me—do thou support me—it is more
than I can bear! cried Burroughs, turning away from
the admirable creature who stood before him trying to

bear up without his aid, though she shook from head to foot with uncontrollable emotion.

Thee's very near and very dear to Mary Elizabeth Dyer ; and she—she will be happy—she cannot be otherwise, alive or dead—for all that know her, pity her and love her———

And so do all that know you—

No, no, George, love and pity are not for such as I— such pity I mean, or such love as we need here—*need* I say, whatever we may pretend, whatever the multitude may suppose, and however ill we may be fitted for inspiring it—I—I—

Her voice faltered, she grew very pale, and caught by the frame of the door—

—There may be love, George, there may be pity, there may be some hope on earth for a beautiful witch....with golden hair....with large blue eyes....and a sweet mouth ....but for a....for a....for a freckled witch....with red hair and a hump on her back—what hope is there, what hope on this side of the grave ?

She tried to smile when she said this....but she could not, and the preacher saw and the jailor saw that her heart was broken,

Before the former could reply, and before the latter could stay her, she was gone.

The rest of the story is soon told. The preacher saw Elizabeth and tried to prevail with her, but he could not. She had all the courage of her sister, and would not live by untruth. And yet she escaped, for she was very ill, and before she recovered, the fearful infatuation was over, the people had waked up, the judges and the preachers of the Lord ; and the chief-judge, Sewall had publicly read a recantation for the part he had played in the terrible drama. But she saw her brave sister no more ; she saw Burrows no more—he was put to

death on the afternoon of the morrow, behaving with
high and steady courage to the last—praying for all and
forgiving all, and predicting in a voice like that of one
crying in the wilderness, a speedy overthrow to the belief in witchcraft—a prophecy that came to be fulfilled
before the season had gone by, and his last words were
—"Father forgive them, for they know not what they
do!"

Being dead, a messenger of the court was ordered
away to apprise Rachel Dyer that on the morrow at the
same hour, and at the same place, her life would be required of her.

She was reading the Bible when he appeared, and
when he delivered the message, the book fell out of her
lap and she sat as if stupified for a minute or more; but
she did not speak, and so he withdrew, saying to her as
he went away, that he should be with her early in the
morning.

So on the morrow, when the people had gathered together before the jail, and prepared for the coming forth
of Rachel Dyer, the High-Sheriff was called upon to
wake her, that she might be ready for death; she being
asleep the man said. So the High-Sheriff went up and
spoke to her as she lay upon the bed; with a smile
about her mouth and her arm over a large book....but
she made no reply. The bed was drawn forth to the
light—the book removed (it was the Bible) and she was
lifted up and carried out into the cool morning air. She
was dead.

HISTORICAL FACTS.

That the reader may not be led to suppose the book he has just gone through with, a sheer fabrication, the author has thought it adviseable to give a few of the many facts upon which the tale is founded, in the very language of history. *Parris*

The true name of Mr. Paris was Samuel, instead of Matthew, and he spelt it with two r's; that of his child was Elizabeth and that of her cousin, Abigail Williams. With these corrections to prepare the reader for what is to follow, we may now go to the historical records alluded to.

And first—*Of the manner in which the accused were treated on their examination, and of the methods employed to make them confess.*

John Proctor, who was executed for witchcraft, gives the following account of the procedure had with his family, in a letter to Mr. Cotton Mather, Mr. Moody, Mr. Willard, and others.

"*Reverend Gentlemen.*—The innocency of our case, with the enmity of our accusers and our judges and jury, whom nothing but our innocent blood will serve, having condemned us already before our trials, being so much incensed and enraged against us by the devil, makes us bold to beg and implore your favourable assistance of this our humble petition to his excellency, that if it be possible our innocent blood may be spared, which undoubtedly otherwise will be shed, if the Lord doth not mercifully step in ; the magistrates, ministers, juries, and all the people in general, being so much enraged and incensed against us by the delusion of the devil, which we can term no other, by reason we know in our own consciences we are all innocent persons. Here are five persons who have lately confessed themselves to be witches, and do accuse some of us of being along with them at a sacrament, since we were committed into close prison, which we know to be lies. Two of the five are (Carrier's sons) young men, who would not confess any thing till they tied them neck and heels, till the blood was ready to come out of their noses ; and it is credibly believed and reported this was the occasion of making them confess what they never did, by reason they said one had been a witch a month, and another five weeks, and that their mother had made them so, who has been confined here this nine weeks. *My son William Proctor, when he was examined, because he would not confess that he was guilty, when he was innocent, they tied him neck and heels till the blood gushed out at his nose, and would have kept him so twenty-four hours, if one, more merciful than the rest, had not taken pity on him, and caused him to be unbound.* These actions are very like the popish cruelties. They have already undone us in our estates, and that will not serve their turns without our innocent blood. If it cannot be granted that we have our trials at Boston, we humbly beg that you would endeavor to have these magistrates changed, and others in their rooms ; begging also and beseeching you would be pleased to be here, if not all, some of you, at our trials, hoping thereby you may be the means of saving the shedding of innocent blood. Desiring your prayers to the Lord in our behalf, we rest your poor afflicted servants,   JOHN PROCTOR, &c.

Jonathan Cary, whose wife was under the charge, but escaped, has left a very affecting narrative of her trial, and of the behavior of the judges.

"Being brought before the justices, her chief accusers were two girls. My wife declared to the justices, that she never had any knowledge of them before that day. She was forced to stand with her arms stretched out. I requested that I might hold one of her hands, but it was denied me ; then she desired me to wipe the tears from her eyes, and the sweat from her face, which I did ; then she desired that she might lean herself on me, saying she should faint.

Justice Hathorn replied, she had strength enough to torment those persons, and she should have strength enough to stand. I speaking something against their cruel proceedings, they commanded me to be silent, or else I should be turned out of the room The Indian before mentioned was also brought in, to be one of her accusers : being come in, he now (when before the justices) fell down and tumbled about like a hog, but said nothing. The justices asked the girls who afflicted the Indian; they answered she, (meaning my wife) and that she now lay upon him ; the justices ordered her to touch him, in order to his cure, but her head must be turned another way, lest, instead of curing, she should make him worse, by her looking on him, her hand being guided to take hold of his ; but the Indian took hold of her hand, and pulled her down on the floor, in a barbarous manner ; then his hand was taken off, and her hand put on his, and the cure was quickly wrought. I, being extremely troubled at their inhuman dealings, uttered a hasty speech, *That God would take vengeance on them, and desired that God would deliver us out of the hands of unmerciful men.* Then her mittimus was writ. I did with difficulty and chagrin obtain the liberty of a room, but no beds in it ; if there had been, could have taken but little rest that night. She was committed to Boston prison ; but I obtained a habeas corpus to remove her to Cambridge prison, which is in our county of Middlesex. Having been there one night, next morning the jailer put irons on her legs (having received such a command ;) the weight of them was about eight pounds ; these irons and her other afflictions soon brought her into convulsion fits, so that I thought she would have died that night. I sent to entreat that the irons might be taken off ; but all entreaties were in vain, if it would have saved her life, so that in this condition she must continue. The trials at Salem coming on, I went thither, to see how things were managed ; and finding that the spectre evidence was there received, together with idle, if not malicious stories, against people's lives, I did easily perceive which way the rest would go ; for the same evidence that served for one, would serve for all the rest. I acquainted her with her danger ; and that if she were carried to Salem to be tried, I feared she would never return. I did my utmost that she might have her trial in our own county, I with several others petitioning the judge for it, and were put in hopes for it ; but I soon saw so much, that I understood thereby it was not intended, which put me upon consulting the means of her escape ; which through the goodness of God was effected, and she got to Rhode-Island, but soon found herself not safe when there, by reason of the pursuit after her ; from thence she went to New-York, along with some others that had escaped their cruel hands.

Of the trial of " good-wife Proctor," the following interpretation was had.

" About this time, besides the experiment of the afflicted falling at the sight, &c. they put the accused upon saying the Lord's prayer, which one among them performed, except in that petition, *deliver us from evil*, she expressed it thus, *deliver us from* all *evil :* this was looked upon as if she prayed against what she was now justly under, and being put upon it again, and repeating those words, *hallowed be thy name*, she expressed it, *hollowed be thy name :* this was counted a depraving the words, as signifying to make void, and so a curse rather than a prayer : upon the whole it was concluded that she also could not say it, &c. Proceeding in this work of examination and commitment, many were sent to prison.

" In August, 1697, the superior court sat at Hartford, in the colony of Connecticut, where one mistress Benom was tried for witchcraft. She had been accused by some children that pretended to the spectral sight : they searched her several times for teats; they tried the experiment of casting her into the water, and after this she was excommunicated by the minister of Wallinsford. Upon her trial nothing material appeared against her, save spectre evidence. She was acquitted, as also her daughter, a girl of twelve or thirteen years old, who had been likewise accused ; but upon renewed complaints against them, they both flew into New-York government.

Second—*Of the Confessions.*—The following is a letter written by six of the confessing witches, by which it may be understood in some degree how they came to accuse themselves.

" We, whose names are under written, inhabitants of Andover, when as that horrible and tremendous judgment beginning at Salem Village, in the year 1692, (by some called witchcraft) first breaking forth at Mr. Parris's house, several young persons being seemingly afflicted, did accuse several persons for afflicting them, and many there believing it so to be ; we being informed that if a person were sick, the afflicted person could tell what or who was the cause of that sickness : Joseph Ballard of Andover (his wife being sick at the same time) he either from himself, or by the advice of others, fetched two of the persons, called the afflicted persons, from Salem Village to Andover : which was the beginning of that dreadful calamity that befel us in Andover. And the authority in Andover, believing the said accusations to be true, sent for the said persons to come together to the meeting-house in Andover (the afflicted persons being there.) After Mr. Barnard had been at prayer, we were blindfolded, and our hands were laid upon the afflicted persons, they being in their fits, and falling into their fits at our coming into their presence [as they said] and some led us and laid our hands upon them, and then they said they were well, and that we were guilty of afflicting of them whereupon we were all seized as prisoners, by a warrant from a justice of the peace, and forthwith carried to Salem. And by reason of that sudden surprisal, we knowing ourselves altogether innocent of that crime, we were all exceedingly astonished and amazed, and affrighted even out of our reason ; and our nearest and dearest relations, seeing us in that dreadful condition, and knowing our great danger, apprehending that there was no other way to save our lives, as the case was then circumstanced, but by our confessing ourselves to be such and such persons, as the afflicted represented us to be, they out of tender love and pity persuaded us to confess what we did confess. And indeed that confession, that it is said we made, was no other than what was suggested to us by some gentlemen ; they telling us, that we were witches, and they knew it, and we knew it, and they knew that we knew it, which made us think that it was so ; and our understanding, our reason and our faculties almost gone, we were not capable of judging our condition ; as also the hard measures they used with us rendered us uncapable of making our defence ; but said any thing which they desired : and most of what we said was but in effect a consenting to what they said. Sometime after, when we were better composed, they telling of us what we had confessed, we did profess that we were innocent, and ignorant of such things. And we hearing that Samuel Wardwell had renounced his confession, and quickly after was condemned and executed, some of us were told that we were going after Wardwell.

MARY OSGOOD,	ABIGAIL BARKER,
MARY TILER,	SARAH WILSON,
DELIV. DANE,	HANNAH TILER."

" It may here be further added, concerning those that did confess, that besides that powerful argument, of life (and freedom from hardships, not only promised, but also performed to all that owned their guilt) there are numerous instances, too many to be here inserted, of the tedious examinations before private persons, many hours together; they all that time urging them to confess (and taking turns to persuade them) till the accused were wearied out by being forced to stand so long or for want of sleep, &c. and so brought to give an assent to what they said ; they then asking them, Were you at such a witch-meeting ? or, Have you signed the devil's book ? &c. Upon their replying, Yes, the whole was drawn into form, as their confession.

" But that which did mightily further such confessions was, heir nearest relations urging them to it. These, seeing no other way of escape for them, thought it the best advice that could be given ; hence it was that the husbands of some, by counsel often urging, and utmost earnestness, and children upon their knees intreating, have at length prevailed with them to say they were guilty.

Third—*Of the character of Burroughs ;*—about which there has been from that day to this, a great difference of opinion. His readiness to forgive.

" Margaret Jacobs being one that had confessed her own guilt, and testified against her grandfather Jacobs, Mr. Burroughs and John Willard, she the day before execution came to Mr. Burroughs, acknowledging that she had belied them, and begged Mr. Burroughs's forgiveness ; who not only forgave her, but also prayed with and for her.

Apparitions at the trial.—

"Accordingly several of the bewitched had given in their testimony, that they had been troubled with the apparitions of two women, who said they were G. B's two wives; and that he had been the death of them ; and that the magistrates must be told of it, before whom, if B. upon his trial denied it, they did not know but that they should appear again in the court. Now G. B. had been infamous, for the barbarous usage of his two successive wives, all the country over. Moreover, it was testified the spectre of G. B. threatening the sufferers, told them he had killed [besides others] Mrs. Lawson and her daughter Ann. And it was noted, that these were the virtuous wife and daughter of one, at whom this G. B. might have a prejudice, for being serviceable at Salem Village, from whence himself had in ill terms removed some years before ; and that when they died, which was long since, there were some odd circumstances about them, which made some of the attendants there suspect something of witchcraft, though none imagined from what quarter it should come.

" Well, G. B. being now upon his trial, one of the bewitched persons was cast into horror at the ghosts of B's two deceased wives, then appearing before him, and crying for vengeance against him. Hereupon several of the bewitched persons were successively called in, who all, not knowing what the former had seen and said, concurred in their horror of the apparition, which they affirmed that he had before. But he, though much appalled, utterly denied that he discerned any thing of it, nor was it any part of his conviction.

His bodily strength.—

" A famous divine recites this among the convictions of a witch; the testimony of the party bewitched, whether pining or dying ; together with the joint oaths of sufficient persons, that have seen certain prodigious pranks, or feats, wrought by the party accused.   Now God had been pleased so to leave G. B. that he had ensnared himself, by several instances, which he had formerly given, of a preternatural strength ; and which were now produced against him.   He was a very puny man, yet he had often done things beyond the strength of a giant. A gun of about seven feet barrel, and so heavy that strong men could not steadily hold it out, with both hands ; there were several testimonies given in by persons of credit and honour, that he made nothing of taking up such a gun behind the lock with but one hand, and holding it out, like a pistol, at arm's end.   G. B. in his vindication was so foolish as to say, that an Indian was there, and held it out, at the same time ; whereas, none of the spectators ever saw any such Indian ; but they supposed the black man (as the witches call the devil, and they generally say he resembles an Indian) might give him that assistance.   There was evidence likewise brought in, that he made nothing of taking up whole barrels filled with molasses, or cider, in very disadvantageous postures, and carrying them off, through the most difficult places, out of a canoe to the shore.

"Yea, there were two testimonies, that G. B. with only putting the fore-finger of his right hand into the muzzle of a heavy gun, a fowling piece of about six or seven feet barrel, lifted up the gun, and held it out at arm's end ; a gun which the deponents, though strong men, could not with both hands lift up, and hold out at the butt-end, as is usual.   Indeed one of these witnesses was over-persuaded by some persons to be out of the way upon G. B.'s trial ; but he came afterwards, with sorrow for his withdrawing, and gave in his testimony.

His death.—

"Mr. Burroughs was carried in a cart with the others, through the streets of Salem to execution, When he was upon the ladder, he made a speech for the clearing of his innocency, with such solemn and serious expressions, as were to the admiration of all present : his prayer [which he concluded by repeating the Lord's prayer] was so well worded, and uttered with such composedness, and such [at least seeming] fervency of spirit, as was very affecting, and drew tears from many, so that it seemed to some that the spectators would hinder the execution. The accusers said the Black Man stood and dictated to him. As soon as he was turned off, Mr. Cotton Mather, being mounted upon a horse, addressed himself to the people, partly to declare that he [Burroughs] was no ordained minister, and partly to possess the people of his guilt, saying that the devil has often been transformed into an angel of light; and this somewhat appeased the people, and the executions went on.

Fourth—*A trial at length.* Indictment of Elizabeth How.

ESSEX ss.   *Anno Regni Regis & Reginæ Willielmi & Mariæ, nunc Angliæ, &c. quarto* ——

The jurors for our sovereign lord and lady the king and queen present, that Elizabeth How, wife of James How, of Ipswich, in the county of Essex, the thirty-first day of May, in the fourth year of the reign of our sovereign lord and lady William and Mary, by the grace of God, of England, Scotland, France and Ireland, king and queen, defenders of the faith, &c. and divers other days and times, as well before as after, certain destestable arts, called witchcrafts and sorceries, wickedly and feloniously hath used, practised and exercised, at and within the township of Salem, in, upon and against one Mary Wolcott, of Salem Village, in the county aforesaid, single woman ; by which said wicked arts the said Mary Wolcott, the said thirty-first day of May, in the fourth year abovesaid, and divers other days and times, as well before as after, was and is tortured, afflicted, pined, consumed, wasted and tormented ; and also for sundry other acts of witchcrafts, by said Elizabeth How committed and done before and since that time, against the peace of our sovereign lord and lady, the king and queen, and against the form of the statute in that case made and provided.

Witnesses—Mary Wolcott, Ann Putman, Abigail Williams, Samuel Pearly, and his wife Ruth, Joseph Andrews, and wife Sarah, John Sherrin, Joseph Safford, Francis Lane, Lydia Foster, Isaac Cummins, jr.

Fifth—*Recantation of the chief judge and the jurors.*—A general fast was appointed by the following proclamation, after the accusers had become so bold as to accuse even the wife of Gov. Phips.—

By the honourable the lieutenant governor, council and assembly of his majesty's province of the Masachusetts-Bay, in general court assembled.

Whereas the anger of God is not yet turned away, but his hand is still stretched out against his people in manifold judgments, particularly in drawing out to such a length the troubles of Europe, by a perplexing war; and more especially respecting ourselves in this province, in that God is pleased still to go on in diminishing our substance, cutting short our harvest, blasting our most promising undertakings more ways than one, unsettling us, and by his more immediate hand snatching away many out of our embraces by sudden and violent deaths, even at this time when the sword is devouring so many both at home and abroad, and that after many days of public and solemn addressing him: and although, considering the many sins prevailing in the midst of us, we cannot but wonder at the patience and mercy moderating these rebukes, yet we cannot but also fear that there is something still wanting to accompany our supplications; and doubtless there are some particular sins, which God is angry with our Israel for, that have not been duly seen and repented by us, about which God expects to be sought, if ever he turn again our captivity:

Wherefore it is commanded and appointed, that Thursday, he fourteenth of January next, be observed as a day of prayer, with fasting, throughout this province; strictly forbidding all servile labour thereon; that so all God's people may offer up fervent supplications unto him, for the preservation and prosperity of his majesty's royal person and government, and success to attend his affairs both at home and abroad; that all iniquity may be put away, which hath stirred God's holy jealousy against this land; that he would shew us what we know not, and help us wherein we have done amiss to do so no more; and especially that whatever mistakes on either hand have been fallen into, either by the body of this people, or any orders of men, refering to the late tragedy, raised among us by Satan and his instruments, through the awful judgment of God, he would humble us therefor, and pardon all the errors of his servants and people, that desire to love his name; that he would remove the rod of the wicked from off the lot of the righteous; that he would bring in the American heathen, and cause them to hear and obey his voice.

Given at Boston, December 12, 1696, in the eighth year of his Majesty's reign.

ISAAC ADDINGTON, *Secretary.*

"Upon the day of the fast, in the full assembly at the south meeting-house in Boston, one of the honorable judges, [the chief justice Sewall] who had sat in judicature in Salem, delivered in a paper, and while it was in reading stood up ; but the copy being not to be obtained at present, it can only be reported by memory to this effect, viz. It was to desire the prayers of God's people for him and his ; and that God having visited his family, &c, he was apprehensive that he might have fallen into some errors in the matters at Salem, and pray that the guilt of such miscarriages may not be imputed either to the country in general, or to him or his family in particular.

" Some, that had been of several juries, have given forth a paper, signed with their own hands, in these words :

" We, whose names are under written, being in the year 1692 called to serve as jurors in court at Salem on trial of many, who were by some suspected guilty of doing acts of witchcraft upon the bodies of sundry persons :

" We confess that we ourselves were not capable to understand, nor able to withstand, the mysterious delusions of the powers of darkness, and prince of the air; but were, for want of knowledge in ourselves, and better information from others, prevailed with to take up with such evidence against the accused, as, on further consideration and better information, we justly fear was insufficient for the touching the lives of any, (*Deut.* xvii. 8) whereby we fear we have been instrumental with others, though ignorantly and unwittingly, to bring upon ourselves and this people of the Lord the guilt of innocent blood; which sin the Lord saith, in scripture, he would not pardon, (2 *Kings*, xxiv. 4) that is, we suppose, in regard of his temporal judgments. We do therefore hereby signify to all in general (and to the surviving sufferers in special) our deep sense of, and sorrow for, our errors, in acting on such evidence to the condemning of any person; and do hereby declare, that we justly fear that we were sadly deluded and mistaken; for which we are much disquieted and distressed in our minds; and do therefore humbly beg forgiveness, first of God for Christ's sake, for this our error ; and pray that God would not impute the guilt of it to ourselves, nor others ;

and we also pray that we may be considered candidly and a-right, by the living sufferers, as being then under the power of a strong and general delusion, utterly unacquainted with, and not experienced in matters of that nature.

"We do heartily ask forgiveness of you all, whom we have justly offended; and do declare, according to our present minds, we would none of us do such things again on such grounds for the whole world; praying you to accept of this in way of satisfaction for our offence, and that you would bles the inheritance of the Lord, that he may be entreated for the land.

Foreman,   Thomas Fisk,   Th. Pearly, sen.
                William Fisk,   John Peabody,
                John Bacheler,   Thomas Perkins,
                Thomas Fisk, jr.   Samuel Sayer,
                John Dane.   Andrew Eliot,
                Joseph Evelith,   H. Herrick, sen."